BALLS

OF LEATHER AND STEEL

BALLS

OF LEATHER AND STEEL

A NOVEL

GUY BUTLER

POLKAJIG
PRESS

PolkaJig Press
www.polkajigpress.com

ISBN 978-0-9848726-0-2

Flying Pig Media
www.flyingpigmedia.com

Book design by VMC Art & Design LLC
www.vmc-artdesign.com

ACKNOWLEDGEMENTS

This novel is dedicated to Malcolm and Margery Butler along with Chester and Jadwiga Wojciechowski and all their combined children and grandchildren—Most especially my wonderfully tolerant and understanding wife, Teri—and our children, Jadzia and Remy.

Several friends and acquaintances are most gratefully acknowledged for their diligent comments after reading countless earlier drafts: Mike Beale, Diana Buckley, Garth Buckner, Todd Demetriades, John Drake, Mark Estrin, Bill Fagan, Andrew Hungerford, Michael Johnston, Catherine Reeves, Bob Scott, Bryan Thomas, Jerry Wojciechowski and John Wojciechowski.

Very special thanks to the great Brian Callison who patiently believed in the story, Victoria Colotta for an amazing cover and Kristin Lindstrom, a lady who understands the nuances of today's publishing industry better than any person I know.

BALLS

OF LEATHER AND STEEL

PROLOGUE

The Protégé

No one would ever forget the moment. Spectators who had gathered around the Trotters Park soccer field suddenly leaned forward in their folding chairs as if choreographed. They could see what was about to happen and wished they had the power to stop the inevitable. This kind of horrified anticipation focuses concentration, similar to when a racecar loses control, crashes and then spins into the air. The actual incident spans only milliseconds but such fierce intensity expands time into slow motion.

Some parents jumped up, hands over their mouths to stifle gasps as the sleight blond kid everyone knew as Remy spiraled into the air like a helicopter as he was completely blindsided by a brutal tackle from behind. Apparently, the poor kid was the only person at the tournament who hadn't seen it coming.

It seemed like an eternity before a piercing, angry screel from the referee's whistle snapped the crowd back to reality. Several parents started to reach for their cell phones, ready to punch in 911. People frantically tried to remember if anyone in the shaken audience was a doctor.

Two elderly gentlemen had their chairs positioned no more than twenty feet from the collision but their contrary reaction went unnoticed. Remy's grandfathers had chosen to sit away from the other family members. Then, when a young lad named Neil Buckley lofted a perfectly weighted ball over the defense and their grandson sprinted through to collect it, both men noticed Remy deliberately slow down. While the crowd leaned forward, the two old men merely sank back in their ringside chairs as they watched the ensuing collision. They both shook their heads with disapproval, still oblivious to the shock running through the other spectators.

The players on both teams were 'taking a knee' to let the referee and both coaches assess the seriousness of the injuries when, quite unexpectedly, Remy got to his feet, apparently unhurt. This prompted the crowd to erupt into a spontaneous cheer of pent-up relief. His aggressive opponent, a man-child almost six feet tall, was bent over, hands on his knees as he struggled for oxygen and to hide his shame. The unusually talented youngster had been tormenting him since the kick off, turning him inside out with his ball skills. The final violent tackle resulted from his increasing humiliation at a smaller boy's refusal to submit to his aggressive efforts to intimidate him. The outcome was predictable; Paul Smith got a straight red card and was ejected, whereas Remy was awarded a penalty kick. Without any signs of being the worse for wear, the youngster confidently powered the ball off the spot and into the goal. It then cannoned off the right rear stanchion and back to the youngster who flicked it up, caught it and jogged back to the center circle. His team had seen this trick so often that not one of them would have bet a dollar on Remy missing.

The coach, Gary Russell, simply tagged the incident as dumb luck. In his view, it had been a miracle that his star player hadn't left the field on a stretcher.

"Okay boys, nobody got hurt. That nonsense down the right is over and, as a bonus, Remy was able to put us ahead." He was calling loudly to nobody in particular...but then, even Russell had not realized what had gone on out there. In truth, only three people at Trotters Park knew and they would be talking after the game ended.

When the final whistle blew, Remy was the last boy to leave the field. He figured that he had fooled everyone except perhaps his own grandfathers. They stood apart from everyone else and waited for their protégé who, despite the magnificent victory, had the slow skulking walk of a kid in loads of trouble.

The old men knew that their genes had manifested themselves in this 12-year-old. They began to notice something when Remy was only eighteen months. They were pretty sure he had it at three years old, but were absolutely positive by his fifth birthday. Their genes had filtered together into a highly potent mix from many prior generations gifted with balance, strength, speed and agility from both sides of the family. They and the world were well aware of their own athletic heritage because it had been well documented during their lifetimes but regardless, they were still surprised and grateful when this grandson came along with the potential to bring it all together in one young, coachable body.

With the full support of Remy's parents, both grandfathers visited Orlando frequently. They devoted their senior years to passing along knowledge they had gleaned from their own rough passages through life and professional careers. They'd been prepared for disappointment but received none.

Remy had soaked up their support like a sponge. His extraordinary balance and agility were exhibited when the youngster turned out for any sport, be it soccer, flag football, baseball, tennis or golf. Nevertheless, as the two old men were both from Europe, soccer became the chosen path and he was steered down that path with the colossal advantage of receiving private instruction from two legends who loved him more than life itself.

"Sorry, Poppa; sorry, Poppy," Remy called uneasily, a full ten paces before he reached his grandfathers. He tried to seize the initiative by raising both hands palms upwards as he pleaded his case. "He was trying to take me out the entire game and if I hadn't conned him when I got the chance, he might have broken my leg!"

"Oh, I'm certain about that," the elder of the two men began, his voice replete with the street idioms of Belfast. "Slowin' down enough to encourage that desperate lunge was really, really dumb. It could've easily backfired and we'd all be writin' jokes on your wee plaster cast!"

"But Poppa," Remy countered excitedly, now on a roll. "You always told me you can't swat a fly in the air, so I got both my feet up soon as I sensed him closing in on me. I was already four feet off the ground when he brushed under me. It must've looked a lot worse than it was. And you, Poppy, you taught me to land like a cat on all fours. My biggest problem was not hurting him as I came back down."

Remy's younger grandfather still looked every inch a gymnast and used his heavy Polish accent to effect. "The problem is twofold, Remington. You had a young man kicked out of the game. Not good!" He smiled wryly, though almost imperceptibly. "In truth, that boy should take up wrestling or football instead of soccer. You might've even done him or his next victim a big favor. But, your biggest mistake was jumping up and taking the penalty kick when all the parents thought you needed the ambulance. Most people are too smart to be fooled by those shenanigans. Please don't try that again. You've embarrassed both your grandfathers."

Sensing forgiveness, Remy spun around in elation and ran back to his team.

"It was still a dumb thing for him to do," the older man murmured whimsically as they watched Remy go.

"The time you saved my life in that Yugoslavian barn wasn't so smart either, but you've never heard me complain."

They said little more, both consumed by memories while staring into space, each dreaming variations of the same thought.

"I don't remember being that good when I was twelve!" One of them finally muttered with enormous satisfaction.

CHAPTER ONE

1912 – Turbulent Times in Belfast

The typical cold spring evening had near horizontal sleet whipping into Belfast from the east. This same wind had bitten through the animal skins of the first residents when the Celtic settlement had been known as Beal Feirste, or Mouth of the Sandy Ford. For the next 6,700 years Celtic traders continued to wade through this conveniently shallow, marshy crossing until in the late 17th century, a bridge was built to span the River Lagan before it flowed into the Irish Sea. This bridge helped catapult Belfast towards becoming the most important industrial city in Ireland.

The river's outlet, Belfast Lough, forms a natural, east-to-west wind funnel by using the Antrim Plateau to the north and County Down's Mountains of Mourne to the south. By the time cold water picked up from the Irish Sea reaches Belfast, this geographic anomaly has amplified it into a brutally cold, icy soaking for any soul unfortunate enough to be caught in the open. So this night was nothing special weather-wise; the early spring months in Belfast had been this way for the past millennia.

Undaunted by what was to him the norm, Billy McClain was smiling as he walked briskly on his way home from Harland & Wolff. This evening, he was a tired but proud man. The collar of his jacket was turned up and his tweed duncher—the flat hat that everyone in this part of the world seemed to wear— was pulled tight over his ears, helping him to hear his own voice as he sang to himself.

"Oh it's six miles from Bangor to Donaghadee…"

Billy had good reason to feel elated. As the foreman joiner in charge of furnishing the first class cabins on the new *RMS Titanic*, he and his team had successfully met the near-impossible deadlines for the launch and sea trials.

In 1912 the largest shipyard in the world, Harland & Wolff employed over 35,000 men, women and boys and the spanking new *RMS Titanic* was, along with her sisters, *RMS Olympic* and *RMS Britannic*, one of the three most luxurious ships ever built for the White Star Line. Billy, for his part, nursed the enormous pleasure of knowing he had played a major part in her construction. To be sure, there were a few fittings yet to be built and installed but White Star had established a firm publicity deadline for picking up VIPs and celebrities in Southampton before the maiden voyage to New York.

"*Those tardy cabinets can wait until the ship returns,*" Billy thought to himself as he continued to sing.

"*Tra-la-la, Tra-la-lee, Oh it's six miles from Bangor to Donaghadee…*"

He was comfortable with the shipyard's decision to postpone completion because no craftsman likes to rush the creation of fine furniture and none of the few pieces that were going to miss the maiden voyage were considered critical. In fact, he had a nice piece of mahogany left over from an armoire that he planned on making into an oval picture frame for the family studio photograph they'd posed for only last week. John Lizars, a photographic studio in Wellington Place, had been promoting a new development in photography called a cabinet card. Quite the rage throughout Europe, it required a long exposure and demanded the subjects hold perfectly still without smiling.

"Little wonder Lizars' motto is *'challenge.'* That cabinet card photograph isn't something I want to do again for a long while," Billy muttered to himself as he turned left at the baker's shop, leaving the Springfield Road for the final few hundred yards down his street.

"We must've held our breath for twenty minutes so the damn thing wouldn't blur. I don't know how young Ellen managed, God bless her."

Then he was home, gratefully climbing the three stone steps to his front door at number 27 Elswick Street.

Home for the McClains was in a staunchly Protestant area. In Belfast, Protestants lived in Protestant areas and Catholics in Catholic areas; it had been this way for as long as anyone could remember. It had certainly been so since the original branch of the McClain family had been driven out of Kilkenny in the 17th century by angry Roman Catholics seeking retribution against Cromwellian Puritan zealots. In those far-off days, Belfast had been a remote but growing settlement made up of about 2,500 displaced Protestants from Scotland and the south of Ireland.

Lead by patriarch George McClain, it had taken the transient family over two years to reach Belfast. But buoyed by the atmosphere of freedom offered by the expanding city, they had immediately turned to farming the land. They sold their produce in the regional market that had been established in the shadow of Belfast Castle.

Back in the 1650s, two of George's sons, Malcolm and Samuel, made a little side money by challenging all-comers to wrestle them in the market square. They were both tremendous athletes and neither man was ever beaten, always adamantly refusing the populist demand that they fight each other. Later, when married with families of their own, both men had decided to put their roots down in the center of town rather than around the family farm. The two brothers started a construction company, McClain & McClain, and later contributed their enormous physical strength to help build that first real bridge over the Lagan River in 1682.

Four generations later, the McClain family still lived on the west side of Belfast, now a city of over 350,000 but dangerously split, with Protestants clinging to a sixty-per-cent majority. Trouble was constantly fermenting just under the surface. The two religious communities had the 1798 rebellion in the South as a stark reminder of their philosophical differences.

Nevertheless, despite such brewing tensions, Belfast continued evolving into one of the great industrial cities of the world.

Billy McClain tried to maintain a low profile during his walk home, albeit he couldn't resist patting his chest occasionally to ensure the brown, manila envelope remained safely tucked in his inside jacket pocket. He had picked up a handsome bonus today. His wife, Annie, and their two-year old daughter, Ellen, would be able to enjoy a decent meal tonight to celebrate.

Elswick Street itself was a terrace of brick houses that cascaded from the Springfield Road for two hundred yards to the millpond owned by the Blackstaff Spinning and Weaving Company. Every morning from four o'clock, the ovens of the baker's shop on the corner wafted irresistible aromas through the casement windows of the dark red houses below. Most of these houses were on the north side of the street as the mill had demolished a large portion of the south side into a vacant site for planned expansion.

Happily for the McClains, the Blackstaff Company primarily spun flax into fine Irish Linen and during that period of Belfast's surge to prominence, their product was in high demand around the world. Annie was able to pick up as much part-time work as she wanted. With the birth of her first child, Ellen, then fifteen months later her son Malcolm, she could earn money without being too far away from her children, the youngest of whom was now a very loud baby. If nothing else, Malky McClain reminded neighbors for several houses on either side of number 27 that there was nothing wrong with his lungs.

However, everything changes. The shattering loss of *The Titanic* on her maiden voyage the previous April shocked the entire world. The ripple effect was slow in coming but when it did arrive, Harland & Wolff suffered badly from the adverse publicity. It was an unfair body blow and the popular slogan throughout Belfast responded with, *"She was alright when she left here!"*

Nevertheless, even that disaster paled under the imminent prospect of a World War looming on the horizon. Ten short months after Malcolm Partridge McClain had been born, Archduke Ferdinand's assassination threw the world into turmoil. The stories covering the unfortunate loss of *The Titanic's* celebrity passengers completely disappeared from all newspapers, replaced by giant black type that screamed out the horrors of war.

At least the men of Belfast, most of who worked in the shipyards anyway, faced a painless transition from building luxury ships into manufacturing the weapons of war.

Not much need for fine furniture in a battle-ship but H & W was a Union Shop and Billy was given many opportunities to learn new skills whilst retaining his status as foreman. Even that privilege carried its own burdens when rationed food became scarce in Belfast, so Billy had to be careful that the neighbors did not notice the extra meat, eggs and milk his extra pay allowed him to procure. As a result of their good fortune, the McClains fared well when those around them came ever closer to starving.

Like most of the women in Belfast, Annie McClain was very proud and protective of her secret recipe for *'Boxty,'* the most popular dish of the time. A boxty was basically, a fried potato pancake but Annie always added an egg and a little buttermilk. With a couple of strips of bacon, maybe a wee sausage or two, a plate of Annie's boxty was something not to be missed.

It was under these circumstances that young Malky McClain grew up blessed with strong muscles and an equally strong constitution, managing to avoid all the otherwise inevitable childhood diseases and physical decline that befell so many families during those dreadful years. He also had the enormous advantage of a caring father with a real, paying job that kept him in Belfast instead of serving perilously in the trenches of Flanders.

Billy McClain doted on his son and the two of them took many long walks together to the tops of the hills that surrounded the city and trapped it for eternity into the Lagan Valley.

On the first of these walks, Billy had pushed a perambulator. As the months passed, he found himself holding the hand of a toddler until, almost imperceptibly, they progressed to being father and son walking side by side, sharing their thoughts of the day and singing their favorite songs:

"Boxty on the griddle, and Boxty on the pan;
The wee one in the middle is for little Mary Ann.
Boxty on the griddle, and boxty on the pan,
If you can't fry Boxty sure you'll never get a man."

Seeing them together, there was little doubt from their stocky legs and broad shoulders that they were related. If past generations of McClains had been alive to join in these walks, these common characteristics would have been obvious to any observer. Ever since the wrestling brothers who built the bridge and most likely, for many generations before, you could always count on a McClain boy to contribute his power, speed and stamina when needed in athletic competition. It was clearly in the genes and Malcolm was developing his potential to continue the family trait.

Almost as soon as he was able to walk, Malky McClain learned to kick a ball with the neighborhood kids on that vacant site opposite their front door. Street soccer in Belfast was rough and tumble to an extreme, with no quarter given to age or size. The ball was most likely rolled newspaper pages and rags tightly bound with string, Goals were often piles of discarded coats; hazards included large stones and garbage. Occasionally a neighborhood team would challenge a team from another area of Belfast to a game. In a heartbeat, this could turn extremely violent, especially if the Catholic, Falls Road boys got into a game against a team from the Protestant, Shankill Road. The hard feelings created by these donnybrooks could last for days, weeks, months or even years after the final whistle. It was just a matter of time until Malcolm's generation would be representing the Springfield Road in a territorial fight over some silly reason, and Billy was determined to protect his son from this by any means at his disposal.

Billy McClain tried to be creative in using their time together, not just to bond their relationship but to seek opportunities to lift Malky's focus away from the increasing religious friction that pervaded Belfast. In the economic aftermath of the war, grey groups of youths with nothing to do but smoke cigarettes and look for trouble could be seen at almost every street corner. But Billy noticed to his great relief that his son still seemed more interested in playing football on the vacant lot and, considering the short life expectancy of a rolled-newspaper football, Malcolm was developing speed, toughness and remarkable ball control with either foot.

Just over a mile north of Elswick Street, a Sports and Social Club had been established in 1879. Named Cliftonville, this club sponsored one of the six or seven competitive football teams in Belfast at the time. Billy McClain, a formidable and speedy player in his own right, had been captain of the team before the war broke out. With most of Belfast's finest conscripted to serve and the rest working long hours at the shipyards or Mackie's Engineering, there was a shortage of able-bodied men to make up any team, let alone form a paying crowd to watch. As such, high-level football took a hiatus during the war even though you could always find a neighborhood street game going on somewhere.

On one of their walks, Billy chose to take Malcolm by his old team's stadium. Cliftonville's home ground was known throughout Belfast as 'Solitude,' probably because the small crowds the amateur team drew compared badly with Belfast's larger professional teams. In truth, the stadium's capacity was over 6,000 but this was only met on the few occasions the Irish National team used it as a venue.

Now that the world war had finally ended, competitive football was beginning to interest the young returning warriors again so at Solitude they had cut the grass and painted the goal posts in preparation for only its second full season in the past decade.

Young Malcolm had never seen anything like it.

"Gosh Dad," the youngster marveled with wide eyes. "The pitch is enormous; flat and covered with grass!" Billy laughed as his son squeezed his hand. "The goals even have posts with hooks on the back for a net!"

A grizzled old groundsman appeared from Solitude's 'Cage End.' Every stadium in the world has an area designated as the exclusive territory of the home supporters; for Liverpool it's 'The Spion Kop' at Solitude, the 'Cage End.' Rival fans are wise not to go there under any circumstance. The groundsman aimed to question the intruders but a smile stretched across his face when he recognized Billy McClain.

"Is it yoursel', Billy? And who's this young spark? If that's yer son and he's inherited any of his father's speed, we could use a good winger next season."

"Good to see you again, Ralphy." Billy responded as he tussled Malky's hair.

Appreciative of the special situation, Ralph Kemp found a leather ball for father and son to kick about. From neighbors and friends, Billy had heard a lot of talk about young Malcolm's escapades on the vacant site although he had never really been able to see him play. Billy came home from work too late in the evenings to catch the neighborhood games. He gently kicked the ball over to his son and for the first time in his life, Malcolm faced a ball that was round and actually bounced.

"Take a shot, Malky," his dad said. "I'll play goal-keeper."

Malcolm flicked the ball up to waist high with his right foot and smashed it through the top corner of the goal with his left foot. With no nets, the ball caromed into the Cage End stands.

"Holy shit!" Billy said and then, recovering quickly, "I mean…Wow! Malky, where did that come from?"

"Holy shit!" Kemp echoed, frowning as he retrieved the ball.

"Dad, this is so much easier to hit than the ball we play with at home."

The groundsman returned with the ball and rolled it to Malcolm.

"That's dead on, Billy. What age is he? And, was that shot a fluke I'd like to know?" Ralph Kemp was now chuckling aloud.

They both turned to look at the eight-year old just in time to see him roll the ball forward, this time with his left foot, before pounding it with the outside of his right foot towards the two men. The ball was clearly going to miss by several feet until, with no time for them to do anything but duck, it curved viciously to the right, deflecting off Billy's back on its way back through the goal and into the stands for the second time.

"Not the smartest place to stand, I guess," Billy laughed but the old groundsman had a very peculiar look on his face. He left the two McClains, disappeared behind the stands and headed for the Whitehouse, a freestanding cottage where the management offices were housed.

Billy and Malcolm stayed for another couple of hours, not really paying attention to the small crowd of men that had gathered in the upper Cage End seats at the behest of Ralphy Kemp.

From that day forward, their walks never made it as far as the hills; all Malcolm wanted to do was kick balls at Solitude.

As Malcolm grew older, the players and staff of Cliftonville Football Club thought that he must live under the Cage End stands as he was there kicking the ball before they arrived and was still there kicking after they left. Best of all, he never joined a local gang or ever smoked a cigarette.

Many special conditions had influenced young Malcolm in those early years. Formal schooling had been completely disrupted by the war and its aftermath, which allowed him an unusual amount of spare time. Consequently, he developed an impressive degree of fitness sponsored by a good diet with all his waking hours spent running and chasing a ball. The stocky legs and stamina were gradually supplemented by extraordinary ball skills honed by hours of practice that had few equals in Belfast for a child of any age. And, by the time he was twelve, no kid under the age of sixteen could best him for speed over one hundred yards. As a result, he was encouraged to enter the popular Belfast Open Sprint Championship run every year at Ormeau Park.

Even though the contest was open to all comers, Malcolm still found himself winning the under sixteen age group as handily as had his dad in his day and one of his great uncles, many years before.

However, nothing was simple and uncomplicated. The kid who came in second, Paddy McBride, was competitive to an extreme and took the defeat very badly, so much so that he demanded to run the race again, even though Malcolm's margin of victory had been by several yards.

"Sorry, Paddy, you'll just have to wait 'til next year," Malcolm had retorted with a shrug.

"Then how's 'bout I fight you for the trophy," Paddy countered aggressively. He was younger than Malcolm but a big kid for his age. McClain just smiled disarmingly and took McBride's hand, shaking it as he replied.

"I'm sure we'll have another chance to go at it someday."

The young McClain's football skills began to be noticed around Belfast and, in 1927, after playing as an amateur for Cliftonville against the professional clubs in Northern Ireland, he was picked to play for his country against Scotland at Schoolboy International level. He was still only fourteen but now well known throughout the City.

Nobody blamed Malcolm when he left school after signing a professional contract with Bangor, a small professional football club located fifteen miles from Belfast Street in County Down.

Annie cried when Malcolm gave her his entire first pay envelope and, although it still didn't amount to very much, she insisted he take a few shillings back. At only sixteen years of age, Malcolm Partridge McClain had faced and conquered the rights of passage into adulthood.

CHAPTER TWO

1920 – Turbulent Times in Poland

The VII Olympiad took place in Belgium during the summer of 1920. It was a wonderful excuse to celebrate the world's return to normalcy after the Great War finally ended. However, the International Olympic Organizing Committee chose not to invite Germany to participate in Antwerp, punishment for having invaded Belgium in 1914. Consequently, when the men's gymnastics events were held in the Beerschott Stadium, the perennial European power-house was banished to watch from the stands like a child in 'time-out'.

Sitting frustrated amongst the German contingent was Albrecht Wah, universally recognized as the finest gymnast of that era. Without Wah to challenge him, Giorgio Zampori took the all-round individual gold medal for Italy, knowing in his heart that the next Olympics would be a different story.

Albrecht Wah had a magnificent physique and in his specialty, the vertical rope climb, he could rise to the ceiling as if there were electric motors concealed in his hands. His absolute supremacy in this event caused it to be removed forever from the Olympics after his continued domination in subsequent games.

The only things bigger than Albrecht's muscles were his flashing smile and ego. Wherever he appeared, women threw themselves at him, reinforcing the common knowledge that his amazing athletic prowess was not limited to climbing ropes.

Just after he returned to Germany from the disappointment suffered in Belgium, the great Albrecht Wah performed at a public exhibition of gymnastics to show the world what they had missed. Afterwards, as the adoring crowd slowly drifted back to their homes, a remarkably pretty young German girl named Josepha stayed behind; simply staring at the most perfect man she had ever seen.

"Young lady, I hope you liked what you saw," Wah said, his smooth voice loaded with double entendre. "I don't know anybody in this town and, if you can wait just a few minutes for me to shower and change, I would consider it a great honor if you would accompany me to dinner."

The dinner proved the forerunner to the happiest

week of Josepha's life as Albrecht Wah completely swept her off her feet with passion, sophistication and language she never imagined could exist beyond her impressive collection of romantic novels. She would have gladly given her life and soul for him as the tender goodbyes and obligatory promises to reunite left her in a numbing daydream that dominated her lonely journey home to Weimar. Albrecht, on the other hand, merely dismissed the encounter as another petty dalliance and returned to his busy agenda in Berlin to prepare for the next Olympics, scheduled for Paris.

However, the damage had been done and her memories turned to ashes. Nine months later, the jilted Josepha gave birth to a son. For weeks she tried desperately to reach Albrecht with the wonderful news of their child until the truth, heavy with the weight of realization, gradually began to sink in. Wah did not intend to acknowledge his son or their relationship.

Having named the child Czeslaw, Josepha found herself the sole support for a baby who seemed to require no sleep to maintain his intense energy source. The only person in Weimar remotely sympathetic to her predicament seemed to be her old boss, John Orlowski, a bookish accountant in his mid-thirties.

Weimar is an attractive German town dating back to the ninth century and it continued to be a pleasant place to live until the Nazis came to power. In 1937, the embryonic regime destroyed Weimar's benign reputation forever when they built Buchenwald Concentration Camp on the outskirts of town.

John Orlowski had not become a Weimarian until well into his twenties. He had actually been born 500 kilometers away in the middle of Poland before moving with his family to Berlin at the age of six. All his formal education had taken place in the German capital, and he gained his accounting credentials there before finally settling in Weimar to accept a full-time position with Chasnov & Harary, a medium-sized firm of accountants.

Weimar seemed perfect to John. It had a rich history based on strong cultural influences established by composers such as Johann Sebastian Bach and Franz Liszt. The town also attained nationwide fame as the signing place of the German Constitution, a document that Adolf Hitler immediately nullified after becoming chancellor in 1933. Of equal benefit to John, Weimar was situated within convenient travel distance from his surviving sister in Berlin to the north and his distant Polish family still living in the area surrounding Lodz to the east.

Ten years older than Josepha, John had been smitten by her at first sight. He acted like a love-sick puppy from the moment she started work as Chasnov & Harary's receptionist. To the ribald glee of his associates, most of John's working day was spent making feeble excuses to visit the front reception desk. In truth, he was too nervous to ever converse with Josepha and she in turn never gave any indication that she recognized his existence beyond acknowledging him as a fellow worker.

Although the community branded Josepha with the scarlet letter of a single mother, technically she had never committed adultery. Yet her situation prompted jealous scorn from all the young men her age in Weimar. It was several months before John finally plucked up the courage to visit her and the baby at her small apartment.

One morning, Josepha heard a gentle knock at the door and opened it to find a vaguely familiar face she had trouble placing at first.

"Can I help you?" Josepha inquired, her beautiful dark hair pulled back from her face into a ponytail.

"Josepha, I'm John," he answered nervously, "John Orlowski from the office?" As he stared at her, he could not help thinking once again how beautiful she was. Completely distracted, he just stood and gaped, entirely forgetting the bunch of flowers he was carrying behind his back. Josepha's first reaction, that he had sought her out for a business-related issue, confused her into taking the initiative.

"It's good to see you, John. Would you have time to come in and have some tea? :

John rediscovered the flowers, presenting them to her without explanation before sitting down timidly on the edge of the settee, rocking nervously, fingers tightly interlocked around his knees. Josepha smiled her thanks and left for the kitchen to find a vase and busy herself with the tea service. When she came back to her small living room, she found John leaning over the crib, he and Czeslaw goggle-eyed and giggling with each other. At that moment, the three found common ground for friendship.

Their relationship, initially based upon financial necessity by Josepha and adulation from John, developed slowly but surely over the ensuing months. A gentle courtship evolved until, in 1925, they married in a quiet wedding that finally bestowed a secure father figure upon four-year-old Czeslaw, an emotional anchor the boy had sorely lacked.

But this happiness was almost destined to fail. Josepha's charmed life had been shattered by her pregnancy; psychologically she never really recovered. She had been a gymnast from an early age and had shown considerable promise. In fact, her fateful visit to watch Albrecht Wah had been as a member of a German regional gymnastic team. She was beautiful, intelligent and well liked but never fully recuperated from her abandonment by Albrecht Wah. In spite of her doting husband and son, she was haunted by the past. Her health declined and then dipped into a downward spiral that ended with her death during the birth of Czeslaw's sister, Helen, six years later.

And so, by 1931 John Orlowski found himself a single man again, this time with two confused children to look after and an unstable political future looming on the horizon.

With the world in the midst of a massive global depression, a desperate German populace had wagered its only hope for economic revival on a radical group of National Socialists based in Bavaria and led by an eloquent if rambunctious Austrian.

The Nazi Party swept into power and it had not taken John Orlowski long to decide that with the new Third Reich, Germany was no longer a place he wanted to live. In fact, he soon became scared to death by the tactics Adolf Hitler employed, especially against Jews. He himself was Catholic but Chasnov & Harary was a well-known, Jewish-owned company whose principals were already making frantic contingency plans to reduce the size of the firm. Their intention was to relocate the firm to Switzerland if Hitler and his cronies were not stopped at the ballot box.

The Orlowski family made a pre-emptive move. For John, Germany had an uncertain future and a past full of sad memories, so he decided to seek a fresh start in the comfort of extended family. For once, he appeared to strike lucky. A distant cousin responded to his queries with an offer of limited accommodation—at a price. John immediately resigned his position, loaded his two young children with all their belongings into his car and left Weimar forever to embark on a new life in the perceived safety of Rekle, Poland.

Rekle was a typical small village where everyone knows everyone else, so it was only a matter of weeks before John and his family were invited to lunch at an adjacent farm owned by Roman and Tekla Wojciechowski. The Wojciechowskis turned out to be a good Catholic family with six sons and six daughters, one of whom was the recently widowed Jeanina.

Nothing, however, was quite as straightforward as it seemed, John's introduction to Jeanina being the main purpose of the lunch. If either of them suspected, they did not show it. Perhaps both were glad for the excuse to return to society. Mother Tekla masterminded and viewed the occasion as a perfect way to solve the problems of two sad and lonely people who were trying to support themselves and their children as single parents.

Like John, Jeanina had a son from her previous marriage. His name was Wlodek and he was almost exactly the same age as Czeslaw. Any other similarities with Josepha abruptly ended there. Jeanina was a large, big-boned woman with a ruddy complexion; coarse and contriving in demeanor. She proceeded aggressively with the cleverly planned courtship, treating each opportunity she met as if it were a military campaign, out maneuvering John at every turn. In his typical passive fashion, John went with the flow and they married within weeks of their first meeting. In John's defense, he perceived the trauma his adopted son was feeling from the loss of his mother and grasped this opportunity as a means to return to family normalcy.

Quite the opposite occurred.

John, Jeanina, Wlodek, Czeslaw and young Helen moved into a small cottage on the Wojciechowski farm where they earned their keep by farming from dawn to dusk. Then, after months of incessantly responding to newspaper ads, John finally managed to obtain a bookkeeping position with a small accounting firm in Krakow. Despite missing his children, the long commute and hours at a remote desk created a buffer for John's sanity against his irrational new wife.

Jeanina, left to her own devices, treated both Czeslaw and Helen worse than the wicked stepmother treated Cinderella, with Wlodek, her natural born son receiving all of her motherly attention. If somebody was feeding the pigs or gathering eggs at dawn it was most certainly Czeslaw and not Wlodek. Czeslaw never seemed to tire of hard work whereas his stepbrother was bone-bloody lazy.

On one of the few occasions Czeslaw managed to speak with his tired father, he pleaded for him to intervene but in truth, John was just as intimidated by Jeanina as everyone else was.

John Orlowski had never really recovered from the loss of his beautiful Josepha and over time his physical and mental health both declined steadily. Then, to Czeslaw's utter dismay, the man he had considered his father died after a stroke in 1938. This threw Czeslaw and his sister upon the mercy of an increasingly bitter widow who had buried two husbands and was already resigned to troll for a third.

Displaying extraordinary mental toughness, Czeslaw, now seventeen, realized his lot in life was to protect his half-sister Helen from the emotional turmoil he had suffered since birth. The two orphans experienced only fleeting fragments of the joy of youth. Most of these precious moments came from time spent with their adopted grandmother, Tekla, a kind and generous soul who treated all the children as if they were her own.

Czeslaw approached his adult years as a strong, athletic and extremely fit youth, no longer worried about the bullying he used to receive from his larger stepbrother, or anyone else for that matter. In fact, one look from Czeslaw could send Wlodek scurrying behind the skirts of Jeanina. His natural parents were gymnasts and Czeslaw was wiry, with a combination of muscle and low body fat that generated almost unlimited sustained energy on command. In addition, he possessed endless stamina and could run for many kilometers without seeming to tire.

The many grandchildren who lived around the farm adored Czeslaw. When the various families gathered for birthdays or special occasions, Czeslaw amazed them all with his tumbling and balancing tricks. Not only could he perform a one-armed handstand, he could even hop on that extended arm. Czelaw drew shrieks of delight from young cousins when he played tag, upside-down and on one hand!

His popularity infuriated Jeanina and she developed an irrational hatred for both Czeslaw and his sister. The baggage of a large family and the ravages of time upon an already dour face made her hunt for husband number three increasingly difficult, if not next to impossible. Somehow, it was all Czeslaw's fault.

By late August 1939, the Nazi Party was firmly in control of Germany. They staged an incident just across the border as an excuse to invade Poland and a blitzkrieg followed. Poland, completely surprised and out-gunned, surrendered a short five weeks later. By the middle of October, Adolph Hitler and his new best friend, Joseph Stalin, split the spoils of the defeated and now occupied country as the rest of the world argued about their obligations to enter the conflict in response.

Jeanina reacted to the regime change in Poland like a cornered rat. In a despicable act designed to protect her natural son and ensure his future, she swapped the birth certificates of Czeslaw and Wlodek without scruple, giving her son German citizenship and guaranteeing Czeslaw years of misery. To add insult to injury, Jeanina continued to abuse her two stepchildren unmercifully.

One evening everything exploded. It started with Jeanina's shrill voice.

"Helen, get your sorry tlyk down here and scrub the toilet."

In tears, Helen replied timidly, "Mother, I've cleaned the toilet three times today already. Please don't make me climb in there again." This response threw Jeanina into an irrational fury that began with her throwing a bucket at the eight-year old girl. Czeslaw, strong, athletic and about to turn nineteen, had finally had enough. He stepped in front of Helen, catching the bucket in mid-air with his left hand. With his fierce gaze never leaving the face of his stepmother, he slowly placed the bucket on the floor, crossed his arms and stood defiantly between her and his sister.

"You will never, ever lay a finger on my sister again," he growled menacingly. "If you do, you will answer to me."

The tension in the room was electric. After several seconds, the stepmother broke the silence by running out of the room, yelling and screaming all the way to the main house. There, she recast the entire event by accusing Czeslaw of attacking her unprovoked, with no warning. Or as she breathlessly explained to Tekla and Roman, "He became a mad man! He tried to kill me! I barely escaped with my life!"

Tekla listened to her daughter and shook her head in disbelief but Wlodek, believing he needed to protect his mother, jumped on his motorcycle to beg protection from the newly established Gestapo garrison in Rekle. His subsequent, panic-stricken version of the incident, richly embellished with his own bias, was duly reported and entered into the incident log. It portrayed Czeslaw as a young and dangerous Polish youth gone completely mad. The Germans returned to the farm with Wlodek and alternative explanations were not even considered. After all, Wlodek was German, why would he lie?

It took four Nazis to get Czeslaw into jail that night, breaking three of his teeth in the process.

Over the next several weeks, the dreaded Waffen Schutzstaffel swept the entire area around Rekle for cheap labor, collecting over twenty five hundred Polish youths between the ages of twelve and twenty. After brutal vetting for any diseases, these young boys and girls were transported to Germany where most would spend the rest of their short lives as slaves working in Labor Camps for the glorious Fatherland. Czeslaw was already conveniently in their custody and first into the cattle car. Although painfully aware of his birthright, Czeslaw would not have reclaimed his German citizenship even if it came with a title. He was now a passionate believer in the Polish cause.

It would be many, many months before Czeslaw managed to see the Wojciechowski farm again. After six, long and arduous months in Germany, he was transported by train, along with over one thousand older Polish youths, to an adult hard labor camp in Zagan, Poland.

Located just east of the German border, the Polish town of Zagan had Prussian heritage, but was now completely controlled by Nazi Germany. The camp was isolated several kilometers from the small town and secured by a deep valley, away from prying, inquisitive eyes that might notice the inmate population of sick and weak workers diminishing on a regular basis. Czeslaw had to be smart beyond his years and education to survive and on the one occasion that a providential opportunity presented itself, his quick wits saved his life.

The German guards were insistent about organizing the captives into two long lines that fooled none of the prisoners. Once a week, the first line had all the able-bodied workers subjected to physical and mental examination. If you failed or simply triggered arbitrary disapproval from the examiners, you were assigned to the second line. The second line was frog-marched up the valley and simply disappeared. Guards assured the inmates that those inmates were headed back to German hospitals for treatment but Czeslaw and his fellow prisoners never believed that. They knew there were no rail lines in the opposite direction from the train station and could not help but recognize the characteristic stench emanating from somewhere up the valley.

Being transferred from the first line to the second line was a death sentence, so on one occasion, as Czeslaw's turn placed him in front of the German examiner of the day, he took a risky initiative.

"Sir, I notice that your right boot has been damaged. With winter upon us, I would be most honored if you would allow me to fix it for you." He was treading a very fine line and knew it. The German guard looked up at his impudence and then questioned.

"Are you a cobbler, Polack?"

"Yes, sir." Speaking perfect German in a calm voice, he continued to lie convincingly to the intrigued guard. "My father and grandfather were both cobblers in Germany before the family moved to Rekle. I've learned the trade well."

"Get out of the line and stand over there," commanded the German guard without looking up. In that instant, Czeslaw looked his fate in the eye, certain that his own audacious stupidity had transferred him into the death line. He stood uneasily for almost three hours before the guard eventually turned, handed him his boots and said. "Have these back to me in one hour or there will be consequences."

Reprieve! Except now, Czeslaw had to learn how to become a cobbler within sixty minutes! He knew he could find another old boot in a trash pile behind one of the camp's buildings so he hurried there to cut out a circle of good leather to patch the damaged part of the German guard's right boot. He also had access to contraband within the camp, which included sturdy needles and thread. Considering the circumstances, he did a commendable job with the patch although his fingers suffered badly from his lack of skill. He mixed coal dust with grease from the kitchen trash to function as black boot polish. He buffed both boots to a creditable shine before hurrying them back to their owner.

The German guard said nothing when Czeslaw handed him the boots but the next day, he was called upon to repair more boots. Czeslaw pushed his luck to obtain supplies but quickly established himself in the eyes of the guards as a useful inmate. He never had to go down the line again and became a better cobbler with each pair of boots he repaired.

Gradually, many of the guards took a liking to Czeslaw and an arms-length relationship developed. They made sure he had his supplies and occasionally a little extra food or a blanket.

Little things mean a lot when you have nothing.

CHAPTER THREE

1927 – The Young Professional

Malcolm McClain played for Bangor Football Club for almost six years. This was much longer than he should have, considering most teams in the United Kingdom had become aware of him during that period, each one trying to figure out if he was as good as the rumors had made him out to be. Over time, almost every one of them courted him but he was enjoying his celebrity in Northern Ireland. A young man earning a significant salary during a global depression, he dressed well, had impeccable manners and a loving family. Malky was in a comfort zone that incited little incentive to leave.

Seldom fully extended by the standards of competition in the Irish League, McClain was playing well below his abilities. He enjoyed playing midfield, striker and occasionally winger to show off his blazing speed but, when he played left full back, in the traditional number three shirt, he could control the entire game. His ball skills and experience, allowed him to develop his natural propensity to read the ebb and flow of play.

As a result, Bangor developed a very simple and well-advertised tactic that none of the opposing teams could do a damn thing about. They allowed Malky McClain have fun playing wherever he wanted, maybe even score a goal or two but, if the other team began to come back, McClain reverted to the full back position to lock the game down and ensure Bangor the win or, at the very least, a draw.

In attempts to counter the *'Bangor strategy'*, most of the older, more established players throughout the league tried to intimidate Malcolm. In an Irish Cup game between Bangor and Glentoran, the *'Wee Glens'* fielded their thirty-five year old veteran, Gavin Stewart, at center forward. He had a reputation for rough play and was eager to take the younger, much-vaunted Bangor player down a notch or two. Before the kick-off he gripped Malcolm's hand like a vice and leaned in close.

"'Wee man, I plan on puttin' you in Victoria Hospital before half-time. The longer you stay on the field, the more you're goin' tae get hurt," he whispered viciously.

Malky, true to his Springfield Road roots, was not intimidated in the least.

"Thanks, Sweetheart," he replied, smiling at the man twice his age and determined not to wince as he retrieved his hand. "Don't forget to bring us some chocolates at visitin' time."

Stewart scowled a look of confusion but the hook had been set.

Bangor advanced to the next round by defeating the *'Wee Glens'* soundly by four goals to zero. McClain scored two of those goals and in the interim, had shut Stewart out of the game to such an extent that, ten minutes before the final whistle, the wheezing bully collapsed from exhaustion and was stretchered off the field.

"Nice work, Gavin," his furious teammates shouted resentfully from the Glentoran locker room after the game. "You had to piss him off, didn't ya?"

Malcolm McClain's extraordinary skills kept the once-lowly Bangor Football Club competitive with the other major Belfast teams, such as Linfield and Belfast Celtic. Their small home ground, Clandeboye Park, was packed to capacity for almost every home game, lining both the club's coffers and providing funds enough to make McClain the top paid athlete in the country.

In the short term, such financial security was in

itself enough to discourage other Northern Ireland Clubs from making any serious bid for him. However, on the other side of the Irish Sea it was a different story. The large corporate-sponsored teams of the English First Division had much larger budgets. Even the less successful, upper division clubs in England controlled funds far in excess of their cash-strapped Irish league counterparts. One in particular, Blackpool F.C., had spent the last few seasons trying to clamber out of the Second Division back up to the First. Although their manager, Sandy MacFarlane, had gotten them as high as fourth position after the 1934 campaign, only those teams in the top two positions could grab the golden ring, so even their sterling effort failed to qualify them for coveted promotion.

Under intense pressure from their fans, the Blackpool Board of Directors reluctantly voted to appoint a new manager, eventually recruiting Joe Smith for the job. Smith was charged with building a new super team; a team that would not only restore them to First Division Football but top the League and win the F.A. Cup.

Accordingly, the Board gave their new manager two specific directives: "Get Bobby Finan from Scotland to transfer here and, above all, Joe, get that McClain kid from Bangor on board. Do whatever it takes; you have an open chequebook. Catch the Heysham boat to Belfast as soon as you can."

CHAPTER FOUR

1935 – Glory Days in Blackpool

D uring that magical period in Malcolm McClain's adolescence, covert representatives from several top English teams were frequently seen in the stands at Clandeboye Park, there to watch the youngster ply his trade. Offers kept getting more and more lucrative to the point that Bangor, a relatively small County Down Football Club at the end of the day, began to find such temptation irresistible. When the pressure came to a head, it all seemed to focus on two powerhouse professional organizations, Blackpool and Celtic. Both Clubs formally approached Bangor with aggressive offers for McClain either of which would bring a record windfall for any small club. The Bangor Directors' main quandary about whether or not to accept was two-fold: would such a massive injection of capital outweigh the potential loss of their new-found fan base and, on a more personal level, would Malcolm agree to the move from Northern Ireland?

But every deal has its price and once the offers increased to nullify these anxieties, Bangor F.C. agreed to relinquish their young star to the higher level of football. Not without some trepidation, Malky resigned himself to making the move 'across the pond.'

Malcolm McClain's eventual signing for Blackpool in 1935 was daily grist for the local Northern Irish newspapers and a constant source of gossip and speculation around the province. Bangor F.C. told the officials from both Blackpool and Celtic that they could take either of the offers on the table but the final decision would be up to McClain.

The race was on.

Both teams' representatives finally caught up with McClain as he was having lunch at *Jenny Watts*, a local Bangor pub that had been serving the populace since 1780. Determined to muscle their way in to plead their individual cases, they caucused outside on High Street. Inside the bar, McClain was warned of these shenanigans by several of his friends who, selfishly but understandably, did not want to see him play anywhere except Bangor.

"Quickly, the bastards are outside," yelled Sammy Moore, one of Malky's teammates. "Get his arse upstairs and lock him in the office. Sit on 'im to keep 'im quiet if you have to."

But his friend wasn't quite quick enough. Malcolm was still bemused by the whole escapade when Joe Smith, the Blackpool manager and first to enter the pub, saw the tail end of the boys bundling Malcolm up the stairs. Smith, a quick thinker, resorted to a little impromptu deception.

"Think I saw McClain go into that toilet over there," he bellowed, flapping his right arm vaguely in the direction of a small door embellished by a cartoon man. Immediately, his Celtic counterpart, only a split second behind him, shepherded his own officials towards the downstairs bathroom. Smith jerked his chin towards the ceiling in the hope that the Blackpool entourage would realize that McClain was actually upstairs.

The rest was a done deal. The Blackpool officials crept quietly up to the first floor office, while the Celtic officials were still hammering on the toilet door. Once Blackpool tracked Malcolm down and pacified the belligerent Sammy Moore, they completed the necessary forms and escaped by way of a window, taking McClain with them.

It was not until several hours later that the disarrayed and furious Celtic officials learned what had really happened.

Blackpool lies on the east coast of England, thirty miles to the north of Liverpool. Famous for its *Seven Mile Beach* and overshadowed by a 518 ft. Eiffel Tower lookalike, the resort is visited every year by millions of hard-working Northerners. Its football team, nicknamed *'The Seasiders,'* was founded in 1887 but never commanded the resources necessary to compete with the player-buying power of Manchester United, Arsenal or Everton.

However, in 1934 a new chairman of the board was elected in the person of a self-made millionaire named Jack Parkinson. Blackpool born and bred, Jack decided that his new hobby and passion would be to make Blackpool F.C. the best team in England—and the world.

The reversal of the club's fortunes was to last for the next quarter of a century. Within two seasons, Blackpool finally won promotion back into the First Division. The Parkinson funds that backed Smith started to pay dividends as he relentlessly acquired the necessary football talent to create the world's first super star team.

As one of the key building blocks of this team, the twenty-two-year-old Malcolm McClain developed into a highly accomplished and versatile player. Using the same tactics he had perfected in Bangor, McClain would start games playing as a forward, wreak havoc with his speed, score or feed Bobby Finan to get the lead, then drop back into his familiar number three position to ensure the result. Even the English press, albeit sometimes reluctantly, found themselves forced to acknowledge him as, *A clever defender with a gift for converting danger into a counter-attack.*

Blackpool played with an attacking flair that thrilled the crowds by demolishing the conservative, defensive style prevalent with most teams of the era. Within a relatively short period, Blackpool became 'The Team.' They were the catalyst that caused home and away crowds to swell beyond their stadiums' capacities whenever they appeared on the schedule.

At this zenith of the game, Malcolm McClain's fan base grew throughout the length and breadth of England and beyond. He was just under six feet tall, solid muscle from head to toe, with a slightly receding hairline that served to emphasize his laughing brown eyes and winning smile. Quite shrewdly, he developed mutually beneficial relationships with the national print media, never ducking an interview whether it followed a win or a loss. Annie McClain must get the lion's share of credit for her son never forgetting his humble beginnings. As he once explained in a by-lined interview:

> *"Always wear a clean collar, always shake hands like a man and always get up from your chair when a woman comes into the room. What do you think of that for advice? I think it is pretty good myself but then, I think my mother is a very clever woman."*

The pivotal career game for Malcolm came against archrivals Stoke City. The Blackpool manager called McClain into his office on the Wednesday before Saturday's game.

"Malky, on Saturday, you're in the first team against Stoke," Joe Smith said seriously. "As you know, Stanley Matthews himsel' will be playin' right winger for Stoke and, no need to tell you, few would disagree that Stan is the greatest football player in the world today. No disrespect, Malky, but there's not a defender on this planet that Matthews can't mug out of their boots and leave 'em standing in their socks.

"I'm afraid I've no choice but to start you at full-back for the entire game and hope that you can keep his tally down. If you can achieve that simple task, I'll be happy. Don't worry 'bout the score. Just do yer best."

Malcolm's stomach was in knots. He had faced the best the English League had to offer but with one notable exception—the great Stanley Matthews.

"Boss, they say Matthews can open a can of peas with his right foot and that his swerve has been known to make defenders fall down without even touching the ball. Do you have any advice? Anything at all?"

"Damned if I know how to stop him," Joe replied. "If I did, I'd be the first person to figure out how he does it. Just give it your best. All I can suggest is that you never leave him. Stay close to him. When he has the ball, wait for him. Better yet, don't let him have the ball in the first place. Move to it first." Smith's voice drifted off and it was a few seconds before Malcolm realized that the manager had finished voicing his thoughts.

"Thanks, Boss," Malcolm said dejectedly and left Smith's office.

"Good luck, kid, you are going to need a miracle," the manager muttered after the door closed.

What happened that following Saturday became an instant classic in soccer folklore and, for the next decade of English football, firmly cemented Blackpool on a track to becoming the finest team in the world. Hundreds of thousands of football fans claimed to have been at that Stoke City verses Blackpool game. Those fortunate enough to number among the 23,414 in attendance watched a titanic struggle between two hugely gifted athletes. The confrontation between McClain and Matthews ended with both players exhausting themselves right up to the final whistle. When the referee brought the game to its end, the entire crowd stood as one and cheered for several minutes, all too aware that they had been privileged to witness a very special event. The result, a 1-1 tie, seemed almost irrelevant as the two weary adversaries hugged each other and swapped shirts. Then, they clasped their upraised hands together and acknowledged the near-hysterical applause from every corner of the stands.

That magnanimous gesture was to mark the beginning of a lifelong friendship. It would also open the door for Matthews to leave Stoke and join Blackpool a few seasons later.

Blackpool was now indisputably the *'Super Team'* Jack Parkinson had envisioned; by 1939, it was the top team in the English First Division. Consequently, it came as no surprise to anyone in the British Isles, when Malcolm McClain was selected at the number three position to represent Northern Ireland against Wales on the strength of his season's performances.

In fact, Blackpool's formidable roster formed the backbones of the national teams for all five of the British Isles' Countries, providing a constant stream of players to showcase the international game against European rivals. On one occasion, there were so many Blackpool players on the English International Squad that the *Daily Mirror's* sports page trumpeted: *"Blackpool F.C. is playing Hungary today at Wembley."*

Malcolm and a couple of other players on the team, Sam Jones and Jock Dodds, spent their time training, playing golf at Royal Lytham St. Anne's and regularly visiting the famous Tower Ballroom to dance to *The John Hamilton Swing Band* in the evening after Saturday's game. As these games were mostly falling into the 'win' column, when Malcolm, Sam and Jock appeared on the dance floor, there was no shortage of partners. They were living the life.

However, of all his many dance partners, Malcolm took a shine to one girl in particular, Margery Singleton. She was a devastatingly beautiful brunette with an athletic, swimmer's build and talented enough to have been accepted into the Royal College of Art in London. If that wasn't enough to rock the Belfast boy back on his heels, her wealthy father sat on the Board of Blackpool Football Club and was himself especially fond of Malcolm. This fondness was not just because of the success he had brought to the team but because he admired the very high code of morality, ethics and manners that Annie and Billy McClain had instilled into their son. The resolute, Victorian-minded Arthur Singleton promoted and encouraged the budding romance.

The future for McClain seemed golden. He was becoming quite wealthy, had a legion of fans, and he was entering the peak years of his career. Moreover, he was ready to pop the question to a beautiful girl from a well-to-do family.

However, Fate decided that enough roses had been scattered on the bed of Malcolm's future. What Jack Parkinson and his checkbook had no control over, was a maniacal little Austrian with a toothbrush moustache. He brought Malcolm McClain's career, Blackpool's Super Team and the world itself to the brink of destruction.

CHAPTER FIVE

1939 – The Beginning of the War

Adolf Hitler seemed harmless enough—at first. Nobody seriously believed that he would ever be able to breach the ancient bastions of German nobility; many people thought that he would find his comeuppance as soon the economy turned around. In the beginning, he represented no apparent threat at all and then, all of a sudden, he had total control of Germany. By then, it was already too late.

The world would never be the same again.

Once war had finally been declared, many British peacetime heroes of film and sports were inspired to volunteer for service immediately. This almost

Quixotic gesture by so many famous household names quickly evolved into an orchestrated effort to motivate able-bodied citizens to join the Armed Forces. Malcolm McClain enlisted to great fanfare as a flight sergeant in the Royal Air Force. More specifically, he was a physical training instructor assigned to No. 40 Squadron flying out of Royal Air Force (RAF) Wyton in Cambridgeshire. Margery Singleton, now his exclusive dance partner every Saturday night, also signed up with the Women's Royal Naval Service, proudly nicknamed '*The Wrens.*'

On the day Malcolm had to leave Blackpool for St. Ives, he walked over to the Singleton residence in the Fleece Hotel on Market Street to pay his respects to her parents, Arthur and Beatrice May and to spend a few last, precious moments with his beloved girl. Margery was already having trouble controlling her emotions; it clearly took all her resolve to keep from sobbing uncontrollably in her mother's arms. Her own pending war service seemed irrelevant when measured against the strong possibility that she would never see Malcolm again.

Arthur calmly took McClain aside. "Good luck, son. It will be over very soon so keep up with your football training; I honestly cannot see this thing lasting more than six weeks at the most. One thing I thought those Krauts would've learned from the last time we fought is that the British never give up!"

The middle-aged veteran of Flanders then lowered his voice and winked, adding, "I've managed to have Margery assigned to a Royal Naval Base in the Scottish Highlands. The commander is an old friend of mine and will be keeping an eye on her, so she should be perfectly safe until you return."

A fresh wind off the Irish Sea caused the seagulls to fly a little higher and further inland than normal, as if to give added privacy to the two earth-bound lovebirds as they walked hand in hand to Yates Wine Bar in Talbot Square.

The owner, Eric Horner, had known Margery all her life and was his usual, overly protective self as he shepherded her and her famous fiancé into a small private booth overlooking the square and the seashore. Eric took care to ensure their seclusion, even though throughout the long lunch, the young couple ordered no food or beverage. It was a blue rendezvous; few words were actually said before Malcolm finally gave Margery a tender kiss and reluctantly walked her back home. Mr. Horner nodded formally to both of them before ducking into the stock room to wipe the tears from his own cheeks.

Within minutes of arriving back at the Fleece, Malcolm had collected his suitcase and left for Talbot Street to catch his bus for Cambridgeshire. After what seemed an interminable journey which had included a couple of changes in drivers, the man at the wheel of this last leg finally pulled on his handbrake after stopping outside the Corn Exchange in the center of St. Ives, a small market town in Cambridgeshire. Although apparently in his sixties, the driver had obviously taken great pride in pressing his uniform that, along with highly polished shoes, indicated he had spent his share of time in military service. Opening his bus door from the inside, he stepped down, saluted smartly and called out.

"Okay lads, this is the stop for RAF Wyton. Looks like yon' lorry with the roundels on it will be your way of getting onto the base. Good luck fellows and give Jerry hell from me!"

Flight Sergeant Malcolm McClain was one of four young men who found themselves on the pavement watching the bus continue its route to the south. They introduced themselves to each other before walking towards the RAF transportation. On his way through the Square, Malcolm noted a bronze statue of Oliver Cromwell, which caused him to chuckle.

"Roast in Hell, you bastard, although I guess I do owe you something for having Taigs chase the McClain family to Belfast when you did!"

After a short but bumpy ride, all four conscripts dutifully reported to the office of Group Captain

Alfie Mairs at RAF Wyton. Nailed above the door of Mairs's office was a besom broom, the proud emblem of Number 40 Squadron, which symbolized their intent *'To sweep the Huns out of the sky.'*

Unfortunately, in these early days of the war, the Luftwaffe was proving unwilling to cooperate with the motto and Messerschmitt BF-109 fighters were decimating 40 Squadron's stock of Bristol Blenheim Mk IV's on a daily basis. McClain got jolt after jolt of reality when some flight crews he sat down with for breakfast never returned for dinner. In short order, the need to have a fitness instructor conflicted with the severe shortage of live crew necessary to fly the remaining aircraft causing Flight Sergeant McClain to be summoned to the base headquarters.

"McClain, I have good news and bad news," Squadron Leader John Elvidge started out in a lame attempt to diffuse the obvious anxiety exuding from the young flight sergeant. Elvidge, whose cheerful, rosy-cheeked face came straight off the box of Rowntrees' Fruit Gums, continued in his broad Yorkshire accent. "We no longer require a fitness instructor but we still need you. Immediately, henceforth and now, you are to undertake a fortnight course in the ancient art of direction finding, known in these parts as 'navigation.' Upon completion thereof, you will be commissioned in the rank of flying officer to help us sweep the Huns out of the sky. Any questions?"

"With respect, sir, yes! Squadron Leader, you want me to be navigator on a Blenheim crew; responsible for getting them to and from the target?" Malcolm asked incredulously. "Sir, I've never even been to high school. Two weeks just doesn't seem to be enough time to..."

"McClain," Elvidge interrupted. "All you need to know is France and Germany are over there." He pointed casually towards the southeast. "When it's time to come home, reverse course and look for Kings College, Cambridge. Very easy to find, nice turrets and all that. Shouldn't be a problem. You can do it, son. Dismissed."

Malcolm left the room in a daze and was promptly directed to the east end of a Quonset hut that had been equipped with six chairs and a blackboard. Three more men eventually joined him and the classes began.

McClain surprised himself when, at the end of the course, he began to feel quietly confident in his abilities to guide a plane around the hostile skies of Europe. He flew on several sorties over the next few weeks and, due to attrition, rose to become one of the most experienced and competent navigators in the squadron within a frighteningly short period of time.

As part of their self-imposed, public relations obligations and to kick off a little steam, all the great football players of the day participated in pickup exhibition games aimed at raising British morale and inspiring youth during those early days of the war. As a guest, Malcolm McClain played for Everton, Chelsea, Arsenal and of course Blackpool when any of these teams needed help fielding a side in the south east of England. Group Captain Mairs, understanding the benefits and prestige that these games brought to RAF Wyton, had a standing order in place that allowed F.O. McClain to receive any and all calls from football clubs that were scouring the country for available players to play in the upcoming weekend's games.

In one of the most memorable exhibitions played during the war, and arguably one of the greatest games of association football ever played during that era, McClain led the Northern Ireland National team to a 3-2 victory over a British Army team loaded with 'ringers' such as Matt Busby, Frank Swift and Tommy Lawton. The event was played at Windsor Park in Belfast, a venue where he knew every blade of grass. With this home field advantage of 20,000 fans on his side, Malcolm McClain dominated the game.

It was perhaps the finest game he ever played but would also prove to be one of his last for quite some time.

CHAPTER SIX

1940 – Staying Alive in Poland

After six months of cautiously building relationships and trust with the guards, Czeslaw Orlowski was gratified to notice he was receiving less and less scrutiny. He had always been mechanically inclined and, although he continued cobbling boots and shoes, he was now entrusted to fix watches, mend bicycles, typewriters and even vehicles. One day, against universal prison rules, a guard asked him to repair the firing mechanism of his P08 Parabellum pistol. Adopting the non-threatening demeanor of a friendly puppy as he handed the refurbished pistol back to its owner, Czeslaw knew he had made a crucial breakthrough. It was now just a matter of time until an opportunity to escape would present itself.

"Just be patient," he kept reminding himself.

"You'll only get one chance, Czeslaw. If the opportunity is less than perfect, you are dead. In their eyes, you've become as comfortable as an old jacket but remember, they still don't like you. They've nothing but contempt for you; they'd think nothing of killing you."

In due course, the German guards trusted the young Orlowski enough to run messages and collect personal supplies from the local village of Zagan. Whenever he undertook one of these housekeeping missions, he was extremely careful not to show any resentment towards his captors, nor to discuss the business of the camp when outside the gates—you never know who might be on the SS payroll. His native German with the Berlin twang helped elevate his position to servant rather than slave. Overall, the German guards treated Czeslaw well and it would have drawn more resentment from the other less-fortunate inmates had Czeslaw's contributions to the camp's contraband hoard not been considerable.

On one of his many forays into the village of Zagan, just as he was passing over the local railway crossing, he thought he heard the voice of an angel. He took pause to investigate and came across a beautiful young woman singing to herself as she polished the brass hardware on the station's front door. Completely entranced, he listened for several minutes before she noticed him. She broke off with a start until becoming aware that the young man was even more embarrassed than she was.

"Hello, I am Jadwiga Brzozowska." She was still a little puzzled that someone she had never seen before in the village, yet apparently Polish, would find himself in her railway station.

"Madame Brzozowska," Czeslaw replied respectfully as he was a few years her junior. "You have the most beautiful voice I have ever heard!"

"Oh, my goodness." Jadwiga laughed. "Calling me Madame makes me sound so old and married—which I am neither. So tell me, what's your name?"

"My name is Czeslaw Orlowski. I'm from the camp in the next valley and under instructions to obtain cigars for my superiors."

In an instant, the young lady became inexplicably defensive. Her warm brown eyes chilled to black as she folded her arms and took a half step back.

"I have heard stories about this camp. I think you had better leave. Good day, sir." Jadwiga said curtly with an edge to her voice and clearly upset.

Not understanding this change in temperament, Czeslaw, decided to play it safe. He immediately tipped his cap before retreating in confusion.

He spent the rest of that week blaming himself for mentioning the camp, at the same time contriving ways he might run into the attractive girl with the beautiful voice to explain his position with a little more clarity.

The transparent look of shock and pain that had veiled Jadwiga's face had nothing to do with the camp. It was triggered the instant she heard his name, 'Czeslaw.'

One of seven children gifted to Frank and Bernice Brzozowski, Jadwiga had been born and raised near the Russian border in a small town named Molodeczno. Their closest city was Vilnius, where she led the cathedral choir with her beautiful voice. Her father Frank held a white-collar position with the Railroad Company of Poland, (RCP) while her mother Bernice was an accomplished seamstress.

The Brzozowski children, five sisters and two brothers, lived a happy, middle class existence and did not want for anything. Even the German invasion of their town, though unpleasant, seemed like an inconvenience that could not possibly last too long. Actually, the German troops seemed more gentle than the coarse Russians, who for decades had regularly forayed across the border looking for trouble. Jadwiga and her sisters steered well clear of those Soviets whom she remembered as having foul breath and being perpetually drunk on vodka.

Immediately following the occupation, the Germans had imposed a curfew. It required everyone to be in their house by nine o'clock at night but not every resident complied; sometimes unintentionally.

One particular night, at a quarter past nine, Jadwiga's brother Czeslaw knocked frantically on their front door to gain admittance. He had been kicking a ball around with his friend and both had lost track of time. Jadwiga's sister, Zofia, recognized the familiar knock and jumped up immediately to open the door but by then her brother had disappeared. She returned to the living room, ashen faced and sobbing hysterically.

"The Germans have taken Czeslaw! I saw them carrying him to a lorry. He wasn't moving." Frank raced to the window but the street was quiet and deserted.

Czeslaw Brzozowski and his friend Vizo had been missing for several days before a friend of Vizo's mother discovered their corpses in the nearby forest. A party of grim-faced neighbors recovered them and brought Czeslaw's body home to Bernice and Frank so they could give him a proper burial. He was 13-years-old.

Life for the Brzozowski family changed forever but it was to get worse, far worse.

Inconsolable over the loss of his son, Frank suffered a massive heart attack and died on the following Christmas during dinner, in front of the entire family.

As if to compound the family's heartache, Zygmund, the youngest son, succumbed to pneumonia only six months later, just before he reached the age of ten.

Bernice was left alone to raise five daughters. Despite her brave attempts to return family life to some semblance of normalcy, there were painful reminders of the three lost males everywhere. Frank's razor still lay in the medicine cabinet; Czeslaw's coat hung in the closet; Ziggy's favorite toy was found in the attic. Their grief was almost unbearable. Several times a day, one girl or another would break down sobbing as she associated an item in the house with the loved ones so cruelly stolen from them.

Bernice knew that she had to make a change and, just a few weeks after Ziggy's funeral, the Brzozowskis packed up what treasured possessions they were able to carry and left Molodeczno in the middle of the night.

One of Frank's old friends in the RCP arranged to sneak the family into a freight car on a train headed south. The perilous journey took them through the center of Warsaw and then further south. Five days later they arrived at the railway station outside Zagan, a small farming town some 168 km southeast of Berlin, in the early hours of the morning.

The wizened stationmaster, who would later end up employing Jadwiga, instantly registered the distress on the women's faces and offered his help.

"My late husband Frank has a brother, Guidon Brzozowski who lives near here," Bernice said wearily. "We would be most grateful if you would direct us to his farm."

"Ladies, you are very close. If you walk down this road for about a kilometer, just before you reach the river you should take the lane to your left. Within two or three minutes, you'll be able to see Guidon's farm. You can't miss it. Look for the big red barn and you're as good as there…" He smiled impishly at Bernice. "…And please remind him that he owes me 10 zlotys from our Dupa Biskupa game last week."

The kind old man then added. "It is downhill most of the way and you're welcome to take this cart for your luggage. Just tell Guidon to bring it back."

The Brzozowski women arrived unannounced at the farm and following his initial surprise, Guidon was quick to welcome them. He had been Frank's older brother and his open invitation to Bernice, proffered at the funeral last Christmas, had been sincere and heartfelt, based on the love he had for his five nieces.

"Bernice, I have been expecting you every day. Welcome to your new home and girls, from this moment on, feel free to fill this house and your uncle's heart with laughter."

In an unexpected yet brilliant act of treachery, the Third Reich connived to turn on its ally Russia by refocusing most of its considerable resources into

Operation Barbarossa. A combination of bad luck, a severe winter and a gross underestimation of Russian resolve tarnished the brilliance of Barbarossa into the massive blemish of defeat.

The entire war took a noticeable turn in favor of the Allies and the world press was afforded their first real opportunity to begin researching and reporting the effect and aftermath of Nazi occupation.

In the Zagan labor camp, the heartless extermination of the weak had left but a few dozen, healthy young Poles, one of whom was Czeslaw Orlowski. If Albrecht Wah had done nothing else for his forgotten bastard son, he provided him with the genes for an amazing physique and constitution, both strong enough to help him survive while millions around him perished.

However, the Third Reich was not in the business of running a holiday camp for healthy Polish youth. After an intense period of feverishly concealing evidence of torture, experimental medicine and genocide, Czeslaw and his friends were directed to commence upgrading the squalid barrack blocks themselves.

The Poles briefly thought that the Germans were authorizing this work for the betterment of their own lifestyle, but that proved one pipe dream too far. One of the guards confided to Czeslaw that the camp was to be transformed into Stalag Luft III, a place to imprison thousands of captured Allied flyers until the Fatherland repatriated them after the victory.

Czeslaw continued to visit Jadwiga at the least excuse, never failing to stop by her railway station if he was sent to the town. At first, she greeted him with icy silence but his warm smile and cautious gifts of corn poppies eventually broke through her defenses. The poppies soon became their flower and Czeslaw would even leave one as a memento if he were unable to see her. It was on one of those lonely occasions as, resigned to her absence, he was fighting to combat the ache in his stomach when his spirits suddenly rose at the sight of a bowl of his corn poppies in a place of honor on the window sill.

Their meetings began to ignore the parameters of time, intimacy growing to the point where both mentally rejected the severe consequences that would have befallen Czeslaw if he did not return to the camp. Jadwiga found herself succumbing to good sense and responsibility as she pushed Czeslaw out of her door on more than one occasion.

An electricity coursed through both of them when they kissed and finally they were unable to resist each other, and the inevitable happened. Afterwards, Jadwiga, flush-faced and disheveled, tried to be stern as she scolded, "Czeslaw, you must go now—for many reasons. Please."

"I don't care what happens to me. I have already died and gone to heaven."

"You foolish, wonderful man," she said, softening.

She cupped his face with her hands. "I care very much what happens to you. Please, please go so we can continue to see each other."

Czeslaw never forgot that moment but always smiled to himself as he tried in futility to remember how he got back to the camp that day.

Their passionate relationship continued unfettered for many weeks until one afternoon, after he jogged back to the camp, he was surprised to find that one of the barracks contained the first of its new residents: 22 Royal Air Force Officers, captured and duly documented as Stalag Luft III's first prisoners of war.

The rules had changed for Czeslaw. Now he had to train a new breed of much more professional guards.

CHAPTER SEVEN

1941 – Stalag Luft III

During its early days, Stalag Luft III was in a perpetual state of flux. The burgeoning camp eventually stabilized to encompass six compounds: three allocated to USAF officers and three for RAF officers. Each compound was self-contained with fifteen, single-story, wooden barracks to house the POWs, plus a building for toilets and ablutions, with another to serve as a large mess hall and kitchen. Each individual barrack had a wood or charcoal-burning stove as the sole source of heat in the center of the room and housed fifteen officers accommodated in five triple-decked bunks. The population of each compound should have topped out at two hundred and twenty five but as the war progressed that number was often much higher. The camp commandant made it perfectly clear that having to sleep on the floor when bunks were not available did not constitute grounds for complaint. But then, nothing did.

As their new found co-detainees were all officers, Czeslaw and the 19 surviving hard labor camp inmates were charged with menial jobs like cleaning toilets and supplying wood for the stoves. They were at the beck and call of both German and Allied officers to do things considered inappropriate for officers under the Third Geneva Convention. It was a pragmatic arrangement between enemies and it helped ease the pressure for housing.

On the other hand, Polacks were not assigned accommodation, as their captors considered them sub-human. They were allowed to sleep under the barracks of the compound to which they were assigned, the full extent of their privileges. Access to bathrooms and even to food scraps was only possible when the guards turned a blind eye.

As with the previous German overseers, both the new regime and the POWs themselves took a liking to the personable Czeslaw, the only problem being that very few could pronounce his name. As such, he became known for the first time in his life as 'Chez.' The anonymous officer who first coined the nickname could not possibly have anticipated the fame it would engender over subsequent decades.

Security began with the three-meter high, chain

link fence that surrounded the perimeter of the camp and topped with coils of barbed wire. Ten meters inside this fence, a low strand of electrified wire was known as the warning wire. To touch this wire anywhere in the camp, immediately triggered a chorus of Klaxon horns to alert the guards. As guards were permitted to shoot any prisoner crossing the warning wire, POWs were extremely careful to give it a wide berth.

Guard towers equipped with powerful search-lights were located equidistantly along the perimeter to sweep the resultant ten meter, no man's land constantly from dusk until dawn. In addition, armed handlers with Alsatian police dogs patrolled the interior and exterior perimeters of the camp.

Despite the apparently insurmountable odds, all Allied officers, particularly the upper crust Brits, were bound by a code that imposed a moral obligation to try to escape should the opportunity present itself.

Several coordinating escape committees were set up within days of the first POW's arrival, though at times it seemed implementing their protocol was many times more difficult than organizing the actual escape itself. Plans to break out were brought before these committees but few passed even initial scrutiny. Generally infantile in concept, most approved escapes were easily thwarted by the guards with the inevitable result of the perpetrators being re-captured and locked in solitary.

Nevertheless, such pie-in-the-sky planning did serve a purpose. It became a game for almost everyone in the camp to get involved one way or another, a necessary distraction from the daily tedium. It could also prove more dangerous for some than others. Escape plans often enthusiastically included Chez and his fellow Poles, even though the risk to them was significantly higher in the event of recapture— instant execution.

In early July 1942, three USAF captains dreamt up a seemingly simple plan of escape to which Chez, who happened to be good friends with all three, had been able to contribute some practical input. The upshot was that those officers asked Chez to join their scheme because none of the Americans had ever set foot outside the camp whereas he knew every inch of the surrounding roads and valleys. As an added bonus, Chez could now converse proficiently in four languages: Polish, German, Russian and English.

As is often the case, simple ideas are best and this one followed that rule to a tee. Consequently, once the details were finalized, USAF Captain Mark Lewis, a portly man with a perpetual twinkle in his eye, presented his group's plan to the Escape Committee as required by camp protocol. Being aware that the vast majority of hare-brained escape schemes were cooked up by bored and fertile minds, Lewis did not believe for a second that their plan would be approved but, to his amazement, it won wholehearted support from the committee. Its chairman, Royal Air Force Wing Commander Todd Demetriades, had even chortled through his handlebar moustache.

"I think that this is one of the better plans we have come across. I must say one thing though, even if the planets all line up, it has to be carried out within a five-minute window or it fails catastrophically. If Captain Lewis and his compatriots are prepared to take the risk, I think we should support it."

He then paused pensively. "I trust you are aware that should you get caught, young Chez will be executed on the spot? To avoid the same fate, all the officers must take the risk of wearing their USAF uniforms to retain POW status and at the first sign of discovery, for God's sake put your hands up and surrender immediately."

"We will do that, gentlemen, and pray that Chez's luck will hold out, sir," Lewis replied. "We plan on going at 0200 hours next Tuesday. The forecast says it will be overcast with no moon. That night should be as black as pitch."

Three days later and thirty minutes before the appointed time, all four men gathered furtively behind barrack number three in the American section.

"So, where do we stand, Chez?" Mark Lewis whispered as the other two captains listened intently.

"I've de-electrified the warning wire for a five meter section right over there." Chez gestured into the black abyss. "I used by-pass wires, so hopefully, the dials in the guard house are currently showing nothing is disturbed. I've also cut through most of a section of the outer perimeter chain link. In about twenty minutes, the British section has agreed to create a simple diversion and toss a blood soaked rag into no man's land to attract the Alsatians. The dogs' yapping will be our signal to go."

"Chez, it's dark as a cave out there fer Chrissakes. How the blazes did you do all of that without light?" Dave Nichols, one of the other USAF captains whispered back. "I can't even see the frickin' fence!"

Chez shrugged in silent reply.

The next 20 minutes seemed interminable. To Lewis, the second hand on his watch looked like it was dragging through molasses. Finally, with approximately two minutes to go, it was time to prepare themselves to move from the protection of the barrack wall and take their chance with fate.

The moonless sky provided virtually no night vision as the prisoners held their breaths and turned hesitatingly to face the inexact direction of the perimeter fence. Chez was quick to notice this and brought them together.

"Gentlemen, I've got three short lengths of dark cloth. I will lead the way while you form a chain behind me. You must trust me completely. If the cloth goes slack, stop immediately until I pull mine tight. Good luck my friends."

On the other side of the camp, a raucous disturbance broke out. The Brits had switched on the lights in all their buildings and were singing a bawdy English drinking song.

> "Three German soldiers crossed the Rhine, parlez-vous?
> Three German soldiers crossed the Rhine, parlez-vous?
> Three German soldiers crossed the Rhine,
> Humped the women and drank the wine,
> Inky pinky parlez-vous."

The dogs started to yelp furiously, causing all searchlights on the far perimeter watchtowers to monitor the commotion. Chez immediately tapped the shoulders of all three captains, a signal to grab the short strips of cloth as their only guide through the darkness. He seemed to thrive in the low light and walked calmly in front, holding down the top strands of harmless warning wire with his foot until everyone was over.

Once all four were in no man's land, he tugged on his strip of cloth and resumed the lead, walking unhurriedly across the ten meters of open space to the perimeter fence.

The fence looked impassable to the three men in uniform but Chez confidently gave a sharp jerk to the one meter section he had already severed from the ground to a height of two meters. The top edge acted as a hinge as he pushed it towards freedom and went through the hole first. Once outside the fence, Chez held the section up and the captains followed, still relying upon touch rather than vision. Methodically, each man followed their pre-determined plan, careful to make no sudden movement as they headed towards the tree line, now just barely discernable as an even darker black mass, one hundred meters beyond the camp fence. Chez remained to cover any tracks by re-securing the integrity of perimeter fence as best he could.

They were almost there when some searchlights began to swing away from the rowdy Brits to resume their routine scouring of no man's land. The three captains fully expected the chatter of machine guns to open up momentarily, indicating that the game was over and Chez dead. But when they finally dived into the welcoming black blanket of foliage they were taken aback to find Chez already waiting for them.

"How the hell did you do that?"

Chez held a finger to pursed lips to indicate that they should follow him in silence. They resumed their grasps on the cloth lifelines and followed him as he commanded a brisk pace in the direction of Zagan.

With Jadwiga Brzozowska's help, all four fugitives hid in the attic of her railway station for a week.

The first morning after the escape, perhaps one hundred Wehrmacht troops blazed to and from the village, yelling and screaming, searching everyone they saw. The railway station was deemed an unlikely place for fugitives to hide, as several trains slowed through the crossing each day giving ample opportunity for escapees to put distance between them and the camp. Nonetheless, one patrol stopped to examine it anyway.

"They will not be in the station," the German Oberstleutnant shouted. "If they made it this far—which I doubt—they are already headed north or south. We will find the rats between here and the camp." Then, noticing Jadwiga brushing the floor of the waiting room, he called out, "Fräulein, kommen sie—raus. Have you seen anything unusual this morning?"

Jadwiga lowered her eyes submissively.

"No sir, nothing at all." The Germans turned to

leave. "Wait, Colonel!" she called out in a louder voice. Noting the epaulettes, she had cunningly decided to promote the German soldier's ego by one rank. "The door to the waiting room was open when I came to work this morning and there was a crust of bread on the floor. I know it wasn't there last night because I swept before I left."

"Doch! Any trains early this morning? Slow trains?" questioned the German officer with just the hint of a smile at the attractive young woman who thought he was a colonel.

"Ja, ja," Jadwiga said. She had spoken excellent German, Polish and Russian all her life and her eyes opened wide, as if solving a puzzle. "The quarter-past-five, south to Walbrzych went through on time. I heard it as I was walking to the station. It always slows down to a walking pace as it crosses the sleepers in the road at the crossing."

The Oberstleutnant spun back to his men.

"That's it. The bastards have a five-hour start headed for Czechoslovakia. Alert every unit between here and Walbrzych." Then as an afterthought, she heard him add, "Gott verdammt! They are on a slow frigging freight train and they could jump off anywhere along the line."

After three days, the search parties stood down. Only when they were certain of security, did the Polish underground arrange passage for the former

POW's in the opposite direction—north. Three heavily disguised old men were taken across the Baltic on a fishing boat to Copenhagen and eventually back to the United States by way of Scotland.

Chez did not accompany his grateful charges to freedom. Instead, he decided to remain in Poland to spend the rest of his war fighting the Nazis in defense of his adopted homeland.

His first opportunity to do so was not long in coming. Now a member of the Freedom Fighters of the Polish Resistance, he kissed Jadwiga goodbye, promising to return as he headed for the forest with his new allies.

The escape had taken the Germans by complete surprise and they never were able to solve the mystery. The inflexible SS mentality couldn't accept the fact that they might have been outsmarted, even after discovering Chez's clever doctoring of the perimeter fence. The alternative theory emerged that the escapees had perished, been eaten by wild animals, or alternatively, that they had never left the camp in the first place. The commandant became obsessed with this last idea and combed the entire camp on numerous occasions.

Though the three USAF officers never knew it,

these searches continued long after Captains Mark Lewis, Dave Nichols and Andy Pascal were safely enjoying the first of many Sazeracs on the Sunset Terrace at the Jonathan Beach Club in Santa Monica. They proudly called themselves 'Chez's Gang' for the rest of their long lives.

Their escape was a constant and major distraction for the guards and an inspiration for another notorious escape from Stalag III. In The Great Escape on March, 24, 1944, 80 prisoners made their way out of the camp by tunnel. Unfortunately, only three of them made it back to Great Britain and the rest were recaptured. Fifty of the escapees were executed by Gestapo firing squads.

CHAPTER EIGHT

1943 – The Last Flight

As fighting grew more intense all over Europe, Churchill's very tired rear guard action was now entering a phase of desperation. It was as if Britain was trying to prevent a heavy wagon from rolling down a wet grassy slope. The island nation needed to find traction or the massive, dark grey schwerwagon would roll over them as it had the rest of Europe. Eventually, sheer bloody-minded grit provided that traction and the Allies not only stopped the momentum but also began to push the wagon back to the top of the hill, the load becoming easier when, in 1941 the United States added its muscle to the mix.

Exhibition soccer games were soon replaced by an 'all-hands-on-deck' approach. Flying Officer Malcolm McClain by then had achieved significantly more importance within his squadron as an experienced navigator than as a celebrity football player, and found himself flying almost every day when 40 Squadron was relocated to the south coast.

Gosport was to be their airfield in Hampshire near the massive Royal Naval Yards in Portsmouth. As the fierce air battles continued to take their toll, the squadron's fleet of Blenheims and Wellingtons were patched and repaired. Taking off and landing on bald tires was commonplace, and using precious fuel measured in pints rather than gallons the norm, as they continued to attack targets in France, Holland and Germany.

The Squadron's code letters were 'BL,' phonetically known as BRAVO LIMA. Every day as the admin corporal walked through the long room to the blackboard to write up a BRAVO LIMA flight status, the collective breath of the squadron was held in awkward silence until the chalk finished its painful scraping. It was an excruciating ceremony. No matter how many times he notated an aircraft as being 'late, presumed missing,' there were always groans and barely concealed curses.

Considering Malcolm McClain's primary service duties had been PT instructor and 'football player,' he faced a massive sea change in his orientation. Now he was charged with navigating an aircraft constructed of wood and canvas, through the darkness of night at 18,000 feet while running the gauntlet of intense anti-aircraft fire, hopefully returning home to base to do it all again the next day. He was grateful that Gosport, located due north of the Solent strait and tucked behind the Isle of Wight, was relatively easy to find at night! On returning from a mission, Number 40 Squadron navigators would strain to identify the Isle as the largest land mass amongst the many black shapes on the friendly side of the English Channel. It marked a dramatic change in fortune for a young man who, only six months previously, had spent his nights dancing to the *JHSB* with his girlfriend in Blackpool's Tower Ballroom.

As the Allies built up their offensive, Malcolm was transferred to Number 37 Squadron, a bawdy group of battle-scarred survivors, which rejoiced in the prophetic motto of being *'Wise without Eyes.'* Within weeks, this entire squadron relocated from its base in Herefordshire to the Middle East, thereby becoming an integral part of the Western Desert Air Force. It seemed that after its disastrous start against the Luftwaffe, the Royal Air Force was now turning the tables.

Other encouraging changes were evolving. By the time McClain joined Number 37, the squadron's aircraft had advanced from wood, canvas and rubber bands to Wellingtons with armor plate and self-sealing fuel tanks. Moreover, the Allies had, slowly but surely, begun to advance north from bases secured throughout North Africa. By the beginning of 1942, the Western Desert Air Force (WDAF) numbered sixteen squadrons of aircraft, a result of the USAF and South African Air Force banding together with the Royal Air Force.

At this point in the war, the WDAF could muster twice as many aircraft as the Axis Powers and McClain was already starting to plan his return to professional football. Andy Pughe, a big affable Welshman and one of his closest friends in the squadron, used to smile tolerantly while watching Malcolm running round the base. It was a regular sight every morning, at a time when the desert air was just a little cooler.

"Iechyd da, Boyo?" he would say as he supped his ever-present cup of instant Nescafe coffee sweetened with condensed milk.

Malcolm invariably replied without slacking but perhaps running backwards for a few yards to talk with the Swansea native.

"Iechyd da, Andy. As much as I enjoy the aroma from your coffee, I smell the end of this war and need to get back in shape. I can't see it lasting more than a couple of months and Blackpool is going to want to start back up where we left off—which would, of course, be right at the top! See ya later, Boyo."

The friendships bonded by war run deep and last forever, especially after surviving long and dangerous missions in the confined space of a fuselage. Although all of the squadron knew Malcolm McClain by reputation from his playing days, in the bowels of a Wimpy he was just another reliable part of the crew.

In May of 1943, Malcolm experienced a life-altering incident. After returning from another uneventful sortie over Northern Italy, Captain Robert Scott landed his Wellington safely after six hours in the air. The regular routine was for the replacement crew to ready the plane for its next mission, while Scott's crew—including McClain, their navigator—would de-brief, eat and perhaps grab some precious sleep.

Captain Mike Summers, a thin, jocular family man from Bristol, led the replacement crew. He, in turn, hoped to be handing this same plane back to 'Bobbles' Scott in about 12 hours. However, on this occasion, Summers' navigator, Peter Wright, a pallid loner from Preston, suddenly started sweating profusely and came completely unglued in the presence of both crews. Battle fatigue struck without warning: it was generally a common condition no one wanted to admit to but, in Wright's case, it could not be ignored. Ashen faced, McClain's opposite number completely freaked out, yelling at the top of his lungs about his premonition that the coming flight was doomed.

"We're going to die! Everyone's going to die!" Wright screamed while the rest of the men backed away from him in stunned silence. It was left to Malcolm to defuse the situation with a reassuring, "Don't worry Pete, I know the way; just been there, okay? You can cover for me next sortie. Captain Summers, do you mind if I tag along as your navigator?"

What choice was there really, other than reporting the trembling Wright as lacking in moral fiber? No man wanted that stain to follow him but, as a consequence of his generosity, McClain pulled double duty and was on the Wellington after it refueled to head back north up the Adriatic Sea three hours later.

At the mid-point of the mission and less than three minutes before Malcolm was scheduled to call out the course correction for their final approach to the objective, five MC202 Folgore fighters of the Italian Regia Aeronautica swooped out of cloud cover to catch Summers and his crew completely unawares. It was the early hours of a still morning, a time in which moonlight can bewitch the glass around the cockpit into a treacherous target.

The Wellington took on a devastating burst of machine gun fire that killed pilot Summers and the nose gunner instantly. Simultaneously, an electrical fire sputtered into life from behind the cockpit controls, spreading rapidly along the interior roof of the plane. The engine pitch increased to a howl, as the unpiloted aircraft lurched into a slow, uncontrolled spiral.

Pushing back from his small desk, McClain unstrapped himself and hurried to check for survivors as the two remaining crew members, Derek Stewart and Wilson Dunlop, struggled desperately to put out the fire with little success. Within seconds, the flames spread to the outside of the plane, exploding through the upper surfaces of both wings, seeking the fuel tanks as if guided by some devilish intelligence.

Having already determined that everyone else on the plane was dead, Malcolm realized to his dismay that he had defaulted to being senior officer. In that unwelcome capacity, he gave Stewart and Dunlop the command to bail out.

"Derek, Willie, grab a couple of chutes and get the hell out of here. This plane is toast and your only hope is to follow your training. Don't forget to tuck as you hit the ground. Good luck lads, I'll be right behind you."

In escalating desperation, they searched and searched but could only locate two parachutes in the dark. Being de facto Captain, McClain realized he had little choice but to resign himself to stay with the plane. Although sick to his stomach with fear, he remained perfectly calm, even philosophical. At least his parents,

Annie and Billy would be proud he'd exited from this life by unselfishly giving his two crewmen a chance at the future.

"Could things possibly get worse?" Malcolm thought to himself as his two former crew mates ejected through the bottom hatch into the terrifying blackness of the night sky. He strained to see if their drab olive canopies had opened successfully but individual shapes were impossible to see against the dark background below. By now, the plane was engulfed by flame and moments from blowing up, the wreckage—along with Malky McClain—destined to spiral into a forest somewhere in Yugoslavia.

Almost wryly, he muttered, *"Yugo-bloody-slavia! The last place on earth I wanted to visit. Hope to God they find my body and ship it back to Belfast. Dear Lord, please have them bury me under the center spot at Windsor Park...."*

Then, racing adrenaline clarified McClain's brain and he remembered the pilot's parachute, the one assigned to the now-headless Summers. Although almost certainly damaged by bullets, it still offered a better bet than certain death in a blazing plane crash. Scrambling back to the cockpit, he fumbled to unclip the safety harness holding the captain's remains into his seat. He heaved frantically to create enough room for his hands to release the parachute pack he knew must be stowed beneath.

"Sorry Mike," he yelled as he pried it loose and strapped the pack on, unaware that a dangling strap was still looped around the seat's armrest.

The resistance pulled his legs from under him and he ended up on the floor—or at least what used to be the floor. The plane was in a dive and the floor was now a steeply sloped wall. Gravity slid Malcolm back into the back of the pilot's seat and he was able to release the strap and try again. All the time, the death scream of the plane was pitching higher and higher. With one last super-human effort, McClain climbed the floor towards a large jagged hole in the fuselage. Pulling himself through, he ejecting like a bullet into welcome, albeit freezing cold air, at extremely low altitude. What the hell, it was better than being cremated!

Less than five seconds later, the blast from the exploding Wellington thumped him hard into a somersault just as he was pulling the ripcord.

"Ohhh Jesus, the bastard isn't deploying! I must've ripped it on the fuselage " He couldn't feel the upward pull of resistance from the chute; he resigned himself for death.

Freefalling towards earth, the wind tugging his cheeks into a death mask, he simply closed his eyes and concentrated on Margery's smiling face. He put every fiber of his being into summoning that memory, praying that God would communicate his final message of love to her over the thousands of miles of separation between Yugoslavia and northern Scotland.

However, God apparently had other plans. The increasing air pressure of his descent finally tugged his chute open just enough to cushion the final three hundred feet.

He landed, very hard indeed, in a pine forest somewhere in northern Yugoslavia.

CHAPTER NINE

1943 – Capture

McClain had absolutely no idea how long he'd been hanging unconscious in the trees. He vaguely remembered bailing out of the blazing Wellington at an extremely low altitude. His terminal velocity should have been more than enough to splatter him into a very dead pancake over the surface of the first immovable object he encountered. But, as luck would have it, he fell between trees in a dense hillside forest; his parachute snagging on the flexible branches to arrest his fall before he hit the ground. The laws of physics then reversed his motion and he had blacked out with whiplash caused by the tree's elastic resistance to his fall.

A combination of pain, harsh morning sunlight and, what sounded like dogs barking in the distance, slowly brought the reality of his helpless situation to him as he hung suspended by his harness. A fluttering white object caught his left eye's peripheral vision, so he turned his head to bring an identification tag into focus as it quivered from the cotton webbing that had saved his life. It read, *'IRVIN AIR CHUTE CO: MADE IN LETCHWORTH, ENGLAND.'*

"Well, thank you Mr. Irvin and everyone in Letchworth," Malcolm mumbled in a short prayer. His head, back and groin ached severely but nothing seemed broken as he cautiously began to move his extremities in an attempt to restore circulation.

The barking dogs, now accompanied by shouting, were definitely getting closer. His mind finally began to clear as he asked himself, *"Where the hell am I and what am I doing in this tree?"*

Then it all came flooding back. There'd been a few jokey comments about Pete's premonition when the engines of the Wimpy had coughed and spluttered during taxi followed by massive relief when the twin nine-cylinder Bristol Pegasus engines roared healthily just as Summers rotated the aircraft. Some memories were as mundane as the boring run north up the Adriatic when he'd noted that the Irish linen lining of the fuselage was stamped *'Made in Belfast.'* Others, such as the surprise whine from the attacking Italian fighters and the sudden staccato as they thumbed their canon, elevated into nightmares.

He remembered panicking as the plane lurched and caught fire; the broken photos of Pete Wright's wife and two kids above his navigation desk; the slumped, headless body of Mike Summers; Stewart and Dunlop diving into uncharted darkness. Finally, his own leap of faith with a borrowed parachute and seeing Margery's smile just before the trees suddenly appeared out of the darkness.

His groggy mind returned to the family photos, happy for Pete's premonition but sad for Mike's family even though he had never met them. Mentally exhausted, he started to weep until, like a roller coaster, his spirits lifted yet again as he remembered the two young crewmen who had bailed out before he had jumped. He hoped they'd made it safely to the ground.

By now, he could definitely hear branches cracking under someone's foot and perceived different sounds from the dogs as their barking changing into excited yelping. He guessed that they must have picked up his scent. Eventually he made out the voices of men clearly enough to know they were not speaking English or German. So, there was at least a chance they were friendly and could extricate him from this bloody tree.

"Those voices have to be speaking Yugoslavian," Malcolm thought optimistically to himself. *"Hopefully they're partisans but, they could also belong to the side of the country that has bet its future on the German Reich!"*

However, the men who finally stood below him did not look friendly at all. Saliva dripped from the bared fangs of dogs as they stared up at the helpless navigator, no doubt anticipating Irish steak for breakfast. One of the handlers raised his shotgun and appeared primed to shoot when abruptly, the unkempt peasants stepped aside as five Wehrmacht soldiers materialized from the forest behind them. Malcolm's spirits plummeted as he re-assessed his situation. He was now absolutely certain he was going to be shot where he hung, high above the ground.

The German officer in charge had two studs on each epaulette, indicating to McClain that he was a captain.

"Cut him down before you shoot him. He might have documents that could be useful to us. I do not want bullet holes or blood on any RAF battle strategies, if that is what we find!" The captain was actually laughing as he spoke with a clipped, affected, German voice.

Getting McClain down from his perch onto the ground was not without pain. Two of the Yugoslavs climbed up into the tree and cut the branches that held his harness, thereby causing him to free-fall six meters to the ground. As he lay groaning, the Germans searched his pockets and delivered everything they found to the captain. McClain tried feigning unconsciousness but could not help wincing involuntarily from the foul smell of body odors emanating from his captors who, for their part, quite casually awaited the command to put a bullet through his head.

Gradually, the fetid pongs were replaced by the smell of sweet cologne and McClain's eyes snapped opened to stare into those of the German captain.

"Welcome to Yugoslavia, Flying Officer McClain, or should I say, Irish International, Malcolm McClain! Allow me to introduce myself. I am Hauptmann Volker Richter and you, sir, are in my custody as a prisoner of war." He spoke in a calm voice, showing off his almost-perfect English before reverting to German as he turned to his men, "Mein herren, we've captured a celebrity. This is Malcolm McClain, the famous British footballer."

The other Germans and a few Yugoslavs moved forward to stare into Malcolm's face before recognition registered with them.

Richter pointed down at McClain. "In 1937, I was standing on The Spion Kop and saw this man play for Blackpool against Liverpool in the English First Division. He was a key member of their famous 'Super Team.' I think we will get some excellent publicity with this one!"

It was a very jovial group that escorted McClain back to their parked truck for the short journey to a nearby Durchgangslager. More commonly known to Allied airmen as Dulags, they served as transit camps through which all Allied POWs passed before being processed for reassignment to permanent camps.

The German captain practiced his English with Malcolm for the entire journey, apparently remembering every minute of his pre-war visit to Anfield. "Malcolm, do you recall your second goal; the left foot drive from twenty meters that bounced off the back of the Liverpool defender's head. Forgive me but surely that must've been accident; it couldn't have been by design?"

"A complete accident, Volker, but I think it would've gone in the top corner anyway. The deflection took the goalkeeper by surprise. By the way, that Red's defender, Mike Beale, has a knack for blocking shots and always caused me problems. I just got really lucky that time."

After more, almost obsequious flattery, which Malcolm was happy to encourage for his security and well-being, Hauptmann Richter asked for, and received, his prisoner's autograph before delivering his somewhat confused charge to Stalag XVIII-D in Maribor.

Infamously known as Stalag 306 by its Allied occupants, the German prisoner of war camp where Malcolm was eventually sent was located in the Drava Valley of northeastern Slovenia in Yugoslavia. Over its brief existence, the camp hosted nearly 4,500 British and Commonwealth prisoners who had been shot down and captured along this section of the Adriatic Coast. When the camp first opened, just after the Nazi occupation in 1941, the accommodations were terrible and the prisoners were jammed into tents, resulting in inevitable outbreaks of typhus throughout early 1942. However, by the time McClain arrived in early June, 1943, the prisoners of war had inherited healthy benefits from the newly constructed raised huts which had airflow underneath to create dry floors.

In the same spirit prevalent throughout all European POW camps, including Chez's Stalag 3 in Poland, officer inmates considered it their paramount duty to create ways of disrupting the regimen of their German captors. To help combat this, along with the inherent POWs' commitment to escape, the Maribor camp successfully used the reward of off-site work details as a means of occupying the fecund minds of all bored young men within its barbed wire.

Three days after McClain arrived, a new convoy rolled in from a different Dulag. Amongst others, this one contained Wilson Dunlop and Derek Stewart. McClain's two crewmen had landed safely and evaded capture for as long and as best they could until a local turned them both in for the going rate of thirty Reich marks.

Malcolm greeted them warmly. "Thank God! Somebody was watching over the three of us. Hopefully, we will all have a tale to tell our children when we get home."

"We certainly never expected to see you again, Malcolm," Derek responded in wide-eyed wonderment. "You pushed us out with the last two parachutes and we were both certain that you went down with the ship. We saw the Wimpy blow up in the night sky just as we landed."

With all three aviators from the Wellington now safely accounted for and ensconced, Captain Volker Richter asked Camp Commandant Kappel if they might discuss a matter of some importance over dinner. Richter heavily implied that there might be great benefits to both their careers; something that always appealed to Afonso Kappel.

The meeting between the two officers was indeed interesting and, after a few days of deliberation, Commandant Kappel sent 'his' idea by way of a communiqué pouch to the Ministry of Propaganda in Berlin.

Dr. Joseph Goebbel's department responded positively and with enthusiasm within a week.

CHAPTER TEN

1942 – The Bracia

I n April of 1942, German troops had unleashed another patented Blitzkrieg to invade Yugoslavia, their practiced efficiency overwhelming that country's defenses in less than two weeks. With the same familiar, disingenuous goodwill offered to Austria, Poland and even the ungrateful British, Germany used extensive propaganda to try to convince the Yugoslavs that their reluctant invasion was to unite the Saxon, Slavic and Germanic races for the good of everyone. Half the Yugoslavs bought into the lie while the other half resisted fiercely.

The Yugoslavian Partizani were among those who refused to accept the subterfuge. As a result, the Nazis were harassed for the rest of the war. Over the course of the next two years, the Partizani slowly but inexorably regained many occupied portions of their country, causing huge global humiliation to the Nazis' propaganda machine.

In Yugoslavia, wherever the Third Reich implemented their proven terror strategies to eradicate any resistance, the reverse occurred. The youth of the hillside villages and towns determined there was little choice but to join the Partizani and fight back. As Nazi pressure increased, so did the level of resistance and support for the secret groups. For the first time in a Nazi-occupied country, Gestapo intimidation tactics proved overwhelmingly counter-productive. The more the jack-booted thugs tried to impose their will, the stronger resistance they encountered. The oppressed Yugoslavian people chose fighting back over submission as their best option for survival.

The initial scattered groups of Partizani soon evolved into a passionately united militia against both the invaders and their Yugoslavian puppet collaborators. In a stroke of good fortune, a fearless man, Josip Tito, emerged as their leader. Now a cohesive force of resistance confronted the Nazis, something they had never planned on or encountered in occupied territory.

When the Partizani slowly began to take their country back village by village, valley by valley, the word filtered back to the rest of Europe like a tonic…a catastrophic side effect the Third Reich had never anticipated.

Starving prisoners in the camps thrived on the news and the guards began to notice an increase in resolve, duly reported back to Berlin. A furious Hitler elevated defeat of the Partizani and the capture of Tito to the top of his priorities. Despite half-hearted objections from his general staff, critical German and Italian resources were diverted into a grudge campaign to stamp out the Partizani resistance.

By February of 1943, the momentum of the Second World War stalled completely for the Third Reich when they suffered a ruinous reversal at Stalingrad and the Allies successfully invaded Sicily. All the resources of the powerful Luftwaffe were diverted to repel ensuing counter attacks on both fronts, a consequence being that resistance fighters throughout occupied Europe found themselves on a more level playing field.

The Yugoslavian Partizani was quick to exploit this with audacious raids against German troops.

Back in the forests of Poland, Josip Tito became Chez Orlowski's super hero. One of his fellow rebels, Vedran Bozic, had been born in Slovenia and his mother still lived there. Chez constantly pumped Vedran for information about the Partizani, most especially how they created mayhem and disruption for the Nazis.

"Vedran, my friend, the Nazis have training and sophisticated weapons, even tanks. How can your Partizani possibly hope to win against such odds?"

"All I can tell you, Czeslaw, is that professional soldiers generally fight their battles against other professional soldiers. There are accepted practices in warfare that even Germans adhere to, the Geneva Convention for instance. However, the Partizani aren't hindered by convention; they're fighting for the very existence of their families and country. So they fight without rules; they attack under cover of a white flag; they poison water supplies; mutilate their prisoners and leave the bodies displayed as a clear message. Czeslaw, when a stone is your only weapon, even a Panzer Tank becomes scrap metal if that stone finds its way into the engine."

Chez's group was still based in the forest surrounding Zagan but even there, he found himself inspired to emulate Vedran's Partizani comrades as they fought to free Poland. Despite having German blood in his veins, the young man's loyalties, energies and life had become implacably focused on destroying anything and everything associated with the Third Reich.

His comrades felt much the same. With hatred of the Boche their sole driving force, this particular band of Polish freedom fighters became famously known as the Bracia—the Brotherhood. Fervent, patriotic villagers who lived everyday lives in the surrounding districts, were an extension of the Bracia who could be counted upon when needed to provide valuable information about the occupying forces.

The Bracia leader, a tough-as-nails young Pole named Jan Kowalski, exploited this intelligence to great effect, always seeming to know well in advance, what the local garrison was doing, although his task was made all the easier knowing that Germans were predictable by nature.

Meanwhile, the Bracia lived as vagabonds. The price they paid for patriotism forced them to abandon their homes and any contact with family. The Gestapo would torture any Pole in order to gain information about the whereabouts of Resistance fighters. Yet, despite the jeopardy, the Bracia could always count upon brave Polish people to support them.

The Bracia gradually migrated south towards Krakow by which time, Kowalski had a substantial bounty on his head. For a period, the group operated from the area where Chez had grown up as a child. He had now risen to second in command but the Germans had still not realized he was alive; certain the verdammt Polish kid had long-vanished following the escape from Stalag III.

One night, Jan gave Chez permission to leave their camp to visit the Wojciechowski Farm in Rekle. His adopted Grandmother, Tekla, woke the next day to find a giant bunch of flowers at the foot of her bed accompanied by a short note.

"Love from Czeslaw."

Despite being unable to explain how the flowers got there, a thrilled Tekla kept the note hush-hush even from the family. However, she did share her secret with Czeslaw's sister, Helen, who had been adopted by the kindly old lady and for several days around the farm, both women wore big smiles, knowing that Czeslaw was safe.

The lithe, 22 year-old was now as accomplished with a gun and knife as anyone within the Bracia but it was his remarkable athletic and mechanical skills that set him apart from the rest of the Freedom Fighters. If the Germans left any vehicle unguarded overnight, Chez capitalized on his abilities to move in silently. Once he had crawled beneath the vehicle, all he needed was five minutes to ensure that vehicle would become worthless scrap. Sometimes a vehicle might mysteriously catch fire when started, sometimes a small bolt found its way into the engine. Only two things were certain; they never saw or heard Chez, and they had an extraordinary number of mysterious, mechanical failures.

Jan originally came up with the idea. "Czeslaw,

you move like a spider in the night. It is uncanny and downright scary. Forget the anonymous attacks and start leaving a calling card. Those bastards won't be able to sleep at night for wondering what's going on."

"Do we have business cards with 'Bracia' printed on them?" Chez laughed.

"They are already scared of the Bracia. You need to leave a logo all Poles can copy when claiming responsibility for sabotage. I suggest a simple circle with eight legs—a spider!"

Jan Kowalski and the Bracia began to consolidate their near-mythical reputation. While the German units around Krakow hated them with savage passion, the Polish population lauded them as the bravest of protagonists. At last, the Poles were successfully mimicking their Yugoslav comrades; they were demonstrating that an occupying force, no matter how cruel, will never force a proud nation to capitulate.

In no time, the occupiers become very aware of Chez's existence as a thorn in their side. As the Polack terrorists' second-in-command, a bounty was put on his head too but this only enhanced his fame, adding to the folklore he had already engendered. Soon, he became known all over Poland as *'Pająk,'* or spider, a soubriquet that brought further comfort to an oppressed population desperately yearning for heroes.

Chez might have personally disabled twenty German vehicles during that summer, but the Pająk legend adopted a mystique of its own. The Spider would be credited with sabotaging every Wehrmacht and SS vehicle that broke down anywhere in Poland for the next three years, despite his having moved on from that benighted country long before.

"Do you know why the Germans can never catch Jan and his Bracia?" young boys heard from their elders. "Because in less than thirty seconds, Pająk can climb the tallest tree in the forest to see where the Germans are located. He uses the branches like a web."

Within days, these stories had the Spider climbing the same trees in 10 seconds. Such wistful thinking was providing great solace to a people who believed they had sunk to their lowest point.

Meanwhile, Jan commanded a core group of twenty men but, more crucially, their exploits inspired hundreds of other 'Bracias' to wreak havoc and mayhem on the hated Nazi forces wherever they found them.

One evening in mid-July, a message to the Bracia was dropped off by way of a train driver. It passed through a dozen trusted hands before finally reaching Jan Kowalski himself. Originating from the Yugoslav Partizani, it was addressed specifically to him, care of V. Bozic. Kowalski called for Vedran and asked him to translate the unexpected letter into Polish.

Apparently, the Partizani had devised a plan to devastate German morale by sabotaging months of carefully planned Nazi propaganda. Key to their plan was the recruitment of a dedicated freedom fighter who spoke fluent 'Berliner' German. They had heard of the Spider through Vedran's family and considered him a prime candidate. The Yugoslavs hoped he might be available to help them.

Having carefully considered the content of the message, Jan turned to Chez.

"Well, Pająk. It seems your heroes in Yugoslavia could use a little help. Are you interested in creating some international pandemonium for our jack-booted friends?"

Chez did not need to think long. Since his first incarceration in the hard labor camps, his life had revolved around generating as much bedlam for the enemy as possible. He had little to lose apart from his life. Except for Helen, he possessed no blood family and no home, only the memory of a young beautiful girl back in Zagan and that, he could take with him across every border.

"If it sits well with you, Jan." Chez shrugged. "I

just need a few more details." Jan simply referred him to Vedran for a repeat of the translation.

The message described an assault the Yugoslav Partizani was planning on a work camp in Southern Austria. The operational details would be explained to him at a subsequent meeting with the Yugoslavs in Semic... provided he was willing to take on the colossal risk of traversing half of Nazi-occupied Europe.

Both Kowlowski and Orlowski had heard about the small market town of Semic, even though it was almost 600 kilometers southwest of Krakow. Tito's Partizani had recently pushed north to recapture the area of Yugoslavia known as Bela Krajina from the occupying Germans who, despite having mounted a savage counter-attack, failed completely and to enormous embarrassment! Semic, the regional capital of Bela Krajina, was now firmly and resolutely Yugoslavian again, functioning as the forward headquarters for the victorious Partizani. It had proved a crucial victory; devastating enough to jolt Hitler's already faltering determination. Yugoslavia was relegated to being a lost cause as Hitler reluctantly realized that his stretched forces would be better mobilized for the defense of Berlin.

Kowalski immediately suggested that Vedran

accompany Chez; after all, he spoke the language and was intimately familiar with Slovenia, the northerly province of Yugoslavia formerly known as the Dravska Banovina. Vedran's home turf was the current stage for several epic battles between David and Goliath: Tito's ragged group of men verses the Third Reich.

But Chez demurred. He suspected he would be better served by undertaking this mission alone. Confident in his own abilities, he did not need the added responsibility of looking after a guide, even if it was a tough old bird like Vedran.

The Bracia gave their blessing to the mission but it took almost two months for a second message to arrive from the Partizani. This one assured Chez that his route to Semic had been established and secured.

CHAPTER ELEVEN

1943 – The Pipeline

There was a distinct possibility that the whole escapade could be an elaborate trap, baited by the Nazis to catch the Spider. Secrecy was deemed paramount and details of the mission were known only by Jan, Vedran and Chez.

A heavy storm had been stationary over southern Poland for three days, providing soaking discouragement against travel to any sane person. So, seizing this opportunity, the three comrades shared a silent hug before Chez quietly left the Bracia camp and disappeared into the heavy rain.

The recently received message from the Partizani instructed that his directives would all come from closed cells. The cell before would have no knowledge of instructions from the cell after. This added a comforting degree of security to the journey, as alternative plans could be substituted when there was any suspicion of a breach.

To satisfy his first directive, Chez had to make his way to Gilowice, a small bucolic village about a day's journey southwest of the Bracia's current camp. Once there, he would receive his next directive from a confessional located within the village's small wooden Catholic Church.

The appalling weather worsened and, while it virtually eliminated his chances of running into an enemy patrol, it took Chez almost two days to walk to Gilowice. When he finally did arrive, he was soaked to the skin, pausing to shelter under a tree canopy to change his shirt and trousers; wringing the water out of his travel clothes as best he could.

The pretty little church proved easy to find as it highlighted the main square. If the entire mission was a trap, this is where it would be sprung. Chez was now on his own, unprotected by his friends and entering an unfamiliar town. His senses were on full alert as he approached; looking for signs of normalcy as much as disconnects.

The Germans, especially the Gestapo, created abject terror wherever they went; honest, regular Poles could not mask the fear from their eyes if something was amiss. Chez's antennae were seeking clues, but there were none. He heard the sounds of laughter from one side and the friendly admonishment of a mother to her son from the other and he knew in his heart that Gilowice was safe.

Chez stopped at a small café on the opposite side of the square from the church and took a strategic seat at a small, outside table. He was comforted that the owner was suspicious about his strange appearance. "My bicycle is in a ditch about ten miles to the north. Knowing what I had ridden through, I thought I could walk away from the storm by heading south but the rains followed me. I'm going to give my thanks to Mother Mary in your church before I start my long walk back."

The owner was relieved and almost friendly so, ordering coffee and some local kolachke, Chez remained there for over an hour to air out his damp clothes and casually observe the mood of the village before chancing a wander towards the church.

Eventually, the nettle had to be grasped. He left the café and after casually climbing five stone steps, he pushed open the left-hand leaf of the church's pair of gothic-arched, heavy wooden doors. Pausing to benefit from the outside light now flooding the nave, he surveyed the inner gloom. Chez could make out only one confessional; the small church seemed deserted. Closing the door behind him, Chez waited for his eyes to adjust to the dim light before slipping inside the ornately carved, oak kiosk. Within this dark confined space he searched for his next message, frowning uncertainly when rewarded with absolutely nothing.

Then, from behind him, a soft Polish voice cautioned, "Be careful of spiders, my child. This old church has quite a few." The sentence contained the mission's agreed secret password so Chez backed slowly out to confront an old man dressed as a parish priest.

"Thank you, Father. I am the Spider." Chez cautiously identified himself.

"I expected you yesterday, my son. I was getting worried," whispered the priest. "But, listen carefully as this directive is verbal: You must stay here until the sun goes down. You can dry your clothes on the old boiler behind the vestry while you wait. For the next leg of your journey, one of my flock will arrange for a special box car to be added onto tonight's freight train to Bratislava. You should be under the east platform by eleven, where another parishioner will contact you and reveal a secret compartment that will serve as your luxury accommodations. This man will tell you what to do after that. Good luck, Pająk."

Chez blinked. That was it? He watched uneasily as the old priest turned away without another word and disappeared into the darkness of the church.

The young Pole spent the remainder of the day hiding in the vestry behind the church, relieved that a Nazi trap had not materialized, yet nervous to be faced with a long and perilous expedition to Yugoslavia. He trusted his own instincts but no one else's so the prospect of being confined to a secret compartment in a train for a 250 kilometer journey through the Nazi-occupied Slovak Republic, was starting to make the hairs on his neck tingle but, he had little choice but to go along with the plan.

Eleven o'clock that night found Chez crouching below the small platform at the station which served Gilowice. Nearly an hour dragged by before he heard a train approaching, yet he still had not been contacted. Then he became aware of movement on the other side of the tracks. A little bit further down the line, two railroad workers were swinging red lights to slow down the approaching engine. The night air soon filled with squealing, clanking and a great gushing of steam as the train braked to an unscheduled halt. His ears picked up the engine driver shouting in Polish above the steady chug of the train. "What's the problem, my friends?"

"We had to replace the fishplates in this section. One was completely cracked all the way through," another Polish voice replied. "Give us five more minutes to tighten the last bolts."

Suddenly, Chez whirled and whipped out his knife as he sensed another person under the platform. The visitor, shocked by the cold steel against his throat, held both of his hands open-palmed to show Chez that he meant no harm, before nervously gagging, "Spider?"

Chez nodded and relaxed the knife. The stranger let out a sigh of relief before motioning for him to follow him under the rear of the stationary train.

By the time Chez caught up, the man had already opened a trap door for Chez to climb up and into the space above. It revealed itself to be no more than one meter deep but mercifully more spacious in breadth and height. Apparently, the Resistance had retrofitted a false wall inside the rear of this particular freight car. On feeling around within the cramped space, he found a small bench. Prompted by his guide, Chez was passed an envelope, some bread, sausage and a bottle of beer. The claustrophobic space was completely without light.

"God speed, Pająk," called a voice, as his unknown accomplice pushed the hinged floor back into place. Chez was instructed to bolt it from the inside and, serenaded by the hiss of steam, his six-hour journey through the Slovak Republic began.

He ate every crumb of bread and the sausage was delicious. Most particularly, he enjoyed the beer, which relaxed him enough to take a nap. His vulnerability in this wooden coffin, surrounded on all sides by battalions of Nazis caused a wry grimace as he drifted off and the next thing he knew, he was waking up to a change of cadence as the wheels began to slow.

Having no watch, Chez had little idea how long he'd slept but daylight had begun to seep between the horizontal cracks in the wooden sides of his hideout. He suspected, by the clatter of points, that the train was entering a freight yard somewhere but that alone offered no clues as to whether he had yet made it to Bratislava, Slovakia's capital on the Danube River.

Once his eyes had adjusted to the light, he was able to tear open the envelope and read the next instructions. This directive was short and to the point; his next contact would occur in the railway freight yards of Bratislava.

The daylight faded to late afternoon before the train eventually stopped moving. With a series of squeals from the steel wheels of the engine, he felt the crash, smash, and bump, as un-braked freight cars caught up with each other.

After months of living in concentration camps and the forced intimacy of a forest, Chez had no social hang-ups about relieving himself as and where he crouched. The beer proved potent and, after six hours in this small space, he began to feel concern that the putrid smells he had created could well trigger his discovery by inquisitive guards. Having suffered several hours of silence and immobility, even Chez was becoming paranoid that he had been abandoned, until he heard movement from below.

"Any spiders?" whispered a voice, this time in German. "Any spiders?"

"I am Spinne—the Spider," Chez responded in the same language. There came a double knock from below and Chez released the trap door.

"Whew! Come on Spinne, before we both die from your stink." Crouching low, Chez followed the hunched back of a small man dressed in dark clothing who was already scuttling crab-like to ease himself from under the train. They maintained their crouches for several meters, before ducking into an abandoned tool shed.

The small man, who appeared to be in his late forties, turned to whisper, "My name's Ernst. We must keep very quiet; the Germans patrol these yards every hour." Ernst pricked his ears at the sound of a clang but then continued, "Herr Spinne, listen carefully. We're two kilometers away from the river and I plan to get you onto a barge which we control. We've only thirty minutes to get there, so we'll have to move swiftly without drawing attention to ourselves. Carry this tool bag, put this plumber's cap on, stay stum and follow me."

As they walked away from the freight yards, Ernst began to talk in a manner that inferred they were simply two friends sharing a joke.

"One of my colleagues will take care of cleaning up your last hiding place, so we can use it again for our next smuggling operation. Your boat ride will be more comfortable than the train but it'll still take over eight hours to get you downriver to Gyor in Hungary."

The two men strolled confidently through the older parts of the city and Chez realized they were headed for a magnificent house on a ridge that over-looked the north bank of a wide river. Within five minutes they reached it and Ernst knocked loudly on the front door. A maid answered almost immediately.

"Is this the Krupkova Vila?" After she nodded, Ernst continued. "I understand you've got a plumbing problem?"

"Thank goodness you've *finally* arrived," the maid retorted haughtily and loudly, quite eager for the occupants to hear her. "Could you *please* take your equipment around to the basement door? I'll meet you there and let you in."

The two plumbers walked around the side of the house and down two flights of steps to a service door. When the maid opened this door from the inside, Ernst promptly pecked the girl on both cheeks causing Chez to widen his blue-gray eyes in surprise.

"My sister, Lisl," Ernst explained with a grin. It seemed the Bratislav resistance movement was a family affair. Lisl left the two men to themselves and disappeared back upstairs into the cavernous house.

"I helped build this house about ten years ago," Ernst announced, still smiling broadly, "– and know every inch of it. Most useful to us, is a secret tunnel down to the river. Follow me."

The secret tunnel turned out to be a one-meter diameter, drainage pipe that the original owner, a prominent and justifiably paranoid Jewish banker, felt necessary to install in case he had to make a rapid retreat from the Nazis should the worst happen and they came to power. A decade ago, with that escape provision in mind, Ernst had bolted short strips of metal angle iron every six hundred millimeters across the floor of the pipe to aid his employer's potential rapid flight.

Tying a light rope around his waist, Ernst unraveled the loose end and motioned for Chez to grip the final knot. Connected by this lifeline, they abandoned the plumbers' tools and trudged cautiously into the total darkness.

After ten minutes negotiating the downward-sloping, cramped space, the two men emerged onto a narrow exterior, concrete ledge. Chez had counted eighty makeshift steps, which meant they had covered about fifty meters. For every treacherous step, the inside surface of the pipe had been slick with wet algae.

"Hey Ernst, without your strips of angle iron, we could have slid down here in about five seconds!" he chuckled softly.

CHAPTER TWELVE

1943 – A Cruise on the Danube

As Chez's eyes adjusted to the dusk, he estimated that they were about two meters above the surface of a wide, unexpectedly pitch black river. Ernst read his thoughts and whispered,

"Yes, Spinne, this is the Blue Danube. But it is only blue in paintings and occasionally on a bright summer's day. Please remain very still and quiet."

"I have to ask you, Ernst. Did the banker escape by the way we just came?"

"No, Spinne, he was shot in his living room by the Germans during the first days of occupation of our city in late 1939. The current occupant is an SS General but Lisl is confident he has no knowledge of the tunnel. Now, we must be quiet; sound travels a long way over water."

There was a considerable amount of traffic on the river even this late in the day as Bratislava was a major garrison for German troops. Control of the River Danube allowed Germany to transport massive numbers of men, munitions and supplies from Regensburg in the Fatherland all the way to the Black Sea. The river passed through 'The Four Bs': Bratislava, Budapest, Belgrade and Bucharest.

Chez was concerned at first as he registered a couple of patrol boats sweeping the river banks with searchlights but there was no apparent urgency to their movements. Then, a long, low black shape emerged out of the gloom and began to approach much closer to the shore. A sound emanated from a deep voice somewhere on the river.

"Tic, Tic, Tic."

To which Ernst immediately responded, "Toc, Toc, Toc."

The barge slowed appreciably, coming close enough alongside the drainage pipe to enable Chez to leap aboard at Ernst's urging. Turning quickly to whisper thanks, he found his guide had already silently disappeared back into the drainage pipe, returning to his bogus plumbing assignment.

As he landed on the deck, a massive hand caught him by the arm and forced him briskly and firmly under the cover of some sacks of beans, where a comfortable void had been created. The vessel then resumed speed and its course down the starboard bank of the river.

There was no attempt at communication with Chez until after dawn some six hours later. A man wearing a black balaclava pulled the bags off him. Squinting at the harsh daylight, Chez covered his eyes with a forearm.

This giant growled through a bushy black beard that seemed part of his headgear. "We have crossed the border into Hungary, Herr Spinne. No roads run beside the river on this stretch and I can see for miles upstream and downstream. Would you like some coffee and pastries?"

His name was Hans Freidmann, an Austrian who had lost his mother and father to the Gestapo in 1938. Like Chez, he was understandably bitter and dedicated to exacting his revenge at any opportunity. They spoke in German for three or four more hours before Hans stood up and looked downriver.

"Back under the beans, Herr Spinne," Hans said. "I'm instructed to get you to a small landing on the South side of Gyor. I do not wish to know what you are up to but you must keep very quiet for the rest of the cruise. A large number of Gyor's residents are already enjoying the hospitality of Auschwitz. This city's commandant is a first rate bastard."

Chez heard the city sounds of Gyor as they passed by on the Danube. Hans Freidmann, a regular and easily recognizable figure on the river, seemed to attract no undue attention.

Gyor is at the confluence of three rivers that generate complex, swirling currents, but the big man handled his ungainly craft with the casual aplomb of a professional bargee, eventually negotiating a swing to starboard which enabled him to direct the barge upstream into the Raba Valley, where he held the new heading for a further five kilometers.

Near an outcrop of weeping willows, the barge edged towards the bank and bumped gently alongside. Hans removed the bags for the last time and encouraged his passenger to stand and stretch. Immediately, Chez's keen eyes picked up the slight figure of a man, hiding behind the vertical branches of the beautiful trees.

"Auf wiedersehen und viel glück, Spinne!" Hans said gruffly. "Go with that man, his name is Kardos."

The man identified as Kardos had already moved to the edge of the bank and extended a hand for Chez to grab. As soon as his feet left the worn deck planking, the barge slid effortlessly back into the middle of the river, turned through 180 degrees and was gone as if it had never stopped.

Kardos performed the obligatory check.

"Any spiders from the barge in your clothes?"

"I am the Spider," was the dutiful response as the two men left the landing, heading swiftly for the cover offered by the next copse of trees, located some two hundred meters inland.

"I know it must seem tedious but your route has been designed as deliberately circuitous to avoid the Gestapo and limit you to travelling only on transportation controlled by the Resistance."

The Hungarian reached into his satchel and handed Chez a peasant's sandwich, a jug of water and an envelope as they continued their brisk walk, conversing in German for Chez's benefit.

"I've not been told where you came from, but I do know where you're bound for. The next leg should be a lot easier and all is explained in this directive." Chez quickly slid the envelope inside his coat.

"We have papers for you to travel as a train passenger from Gyor directly to Ljubljana in Yugoslavia. The border crossing from Hungary will be at Murska Sobota and is lightly manned by the Wehrmacht. We've paid our local agent well to grease any occasions that the Gestapo might drop by for a surprise visit!" He continued by explaining, "Currently we're heading for a farmhouse about three kilometers from here, where you'll be able to shower and shave. You'll meet some loyal, dear friends of mine who own the farm and they'll make the final adjustments to your new wardrobe and go over your papers."

After walking along backcountry roads for almost

forty minutes, they eventually approached an unassuming yet typical Hungarian farmhouse where they were greeted by a man and two women. As Chez could not speak Hungarian, Kardos handled the translations.

"Herr Spinne, for the next day or so, your new identity will be that of a German student with bad lungs: You regret not being able to serve the Fatherland. Your father is Doctor Klaus Heber who has a medical practice in Vienna; you are here in Hungary to bring him some medications that he ordered from the Leipske Labs in Gyor to try on some of his patients. You are twenty-four years old and your new name is Günter Heber."

Chez nodded, desperately trying to file the information in his head; his life could well depend on it.

"Here are your papers; memorize and guard them well. You'll be catching your train in Ikreny instead of the main station in Gyor, because your distant cousin, Kardos, insisted that you have lunch with him." He smiled at this little touch, proudly tapping himself on the chest to establish authorship.

After Chez had cleaned up, the two women went through the articles contained within an expensive, brown leather suitcase that carried the monogramme 'GH', making sure that he recognized each article as Kardos identified them. Also included within, was a slab of lard wrapped in wax paper that they hoped would pass for the salve noted on the receipt from the Leipske Labs.

Expert hands had tailored the clothing and, once the suit and shirt proved satisfactory, Chez posed confidently for a photograph. The other Hungarian man took the camera to a corner desk where he developed the film in order to complete the travel documents, while Kardos continued to grill Chez on the details of his cover story until he knew them backwards.

"Time to go," Kardos said. "The train will be arriving in ten minutes." Chez then asked Kardos how to say 'thank you' in Hungarian and said a sincere *'Köszönöm szépen!'* to his new friends. His last memory was of them waving goodbye from the door of the farmhouse.

Suddenly, a throaty roar from a powerful engine caused Chez to retreat into the farmhouse for fear of a patrol until Kardos appeared through the barn doors on what appeared to be a brand new Hungarian BMG motorcycle. Chez cautiously reemerged and eased astride the rear seat with suitcase squashed between his stomach and Kardos's back.

Ten minutes later, they pulled up to the railway station in Ikreny. As tutored, Chez produced his return ticket to Vienna by way of Ljubljana and presented it to the stationmaster. Once authenticated, he turned and waved to his 'cousin' with a big smile.

"Danke, Kardos. Auf wiedersehen."

Another friend re-consigned to the shadows, another leg of the journey completed, another unknown adventure ahead.

In no time at all, the train pulled into the station. It was not full so Chez carefully selected a seat as far from any other passenger as he could without being too obvious.

However, about an hour into the journey he decided on a better plan and nonchalantly strolled the corridors. When he heard German being spoken by a couple of middle-aged ladies, he sought them out and asked if he could join them in their compartment. They were delighted for the company, no doubt because of his good looks and charm. When the German guard assigned to patrol the train passed through their carriage, all his papers were deemed in order. Chez was in the middle of a tasteful joke, and all three were laughing merrily.

He was not bothered until they stopped at Murska Sobota.

CHAPTER THIRTEEN

1943 – Yugoslavia

M urska Sobota is the most easterly of Slovenia's eleven directorates and its namesake town forms a popular border crossing point for road and rail between Hungary and Yugoslavia, the gauge of both railway systems being the same. It was not uncommon to find passengers destined for Austria and Germany skirting the Alps by this route.

Chez, anticipating only a routine, five minute stop at Murska Sobota, was shocked when ten heavily-armed Wehrmacht soldiers boarded the train and began systematically checking every passenger's papers. Looking uneasily out of the window, he saw that there were at least ten times that many soldiers patrolling the platforms and looking under the train.

"Holy shit! They must be looking for me. I'm a dead

man." Unable to hide the concern written on his face, he began to ponder, "*I wonder who betrayed me? It could only have been that bastard, Kardos.*"

Chez's two female travelling companions glanced nervously at each other when they saw his distress but remained calm.

After a seemingly endless wait, a Wehrmacht Staff Lance Corporal and two squaddies entered the compartment where Chez and the German ladies were sitting.

"Papers?" the Stabsgefreiter barked, eying all three with suspicious distain. Then, somewhat unexpectedly, he checked both ladies' documentation first. Chez sensed a glimmer of hope, realizing that he might not be the center of attention. Meanwhile, the squaddies began to rummage behind curtains and under the seats.

"*They must not be specifically looking for me,*" Chez was beginning to think optimistically to himself, when the overly officious lance corporal snapped his fingers in his direction.

"Young man, bitte."

Chez had his papers ready but as he handed them over, he started to cough violently and excused himself. The German backed up, fumbling for a handkerchief to cover his mouth and protect himself from any flying sputum. Nevertheless, the corporal still dutifully scanned every line of the proffered identification pass.

"Herr Heber," he noted. "I see here that your lungs

denied you the opportunity to serve the Fatherland. What was your business in Hungary?"

"My father treats arthritis in his patients by using a salve made at the Leipske Labs in Gyor." He pointed up at his suitcase indicating that the balm was inside. "Once a year, we need to restock. Normally we use a courier but this year it was more expedient for me to make the trip. Everything has to be paid for with cash nowadays."

Chez then experimented with another bout of coughing that doubled him over. That last paroxysm did the trick. The Germans no longer wanted to expose themselves to this pathetic weakling and the entourage hastily left the carriage without further ado.

Less than thirty seconds later, there was excited shouting from the rail yards and Chez switched his gaze to the window just in time to observe two men making a desperate break from the cover of the train. A volley of shots rang out and both men fell, their prone bodies soon surrounded by the pursuing German troops.

"We have the bastards," one shouted. "Just where we thought they would be hiding."

Still, Chez did not completely relax until the train was allowed to continue its journey west. Much later than expected but without further incident, it finally pulled into the Ljubljana main railway station, located just northwest of the city.

As he followed his two lady travelling companions onto the platform, one of them turned to him and whispered conspiratorially, "A convenient cough, Günter; we both wish you a speedy recovery."

And with that, they were gone.

Initially considered a mere annoyance, the Yugoslavs were now a force to be reckoned with as they stubbornly continued to generate problems for the Third Reich. In an act of desperation, the occupying German army encircled Ljubljana with kilometer after kilometer of coiled barbed wire in the form of a fence two meters high. This barricade was officially intended to prevent co-operation between the Liberation Front of the Slovenian People—an underground resistance movement based within the city—and the Yugoslav Partizani, who operated and controlled most of the surrounding countryside. However, by late 1943 this fence was serving more to protect the Germans troops within from the increasingly aggressive, marauding Yugoslavs. Much to Hitler's chagrin, his vaunted occupying force was on the defensive.

With a firm grip on his brown suitcase, Chez walked confidently out of the main hall of the station and into Osvobodilne Trg, Ljubljana's main square. Having memorized the most recent set of instructions given to him by Kardos in Ikreny, he had torn the note into shreds and scattered them from the train's corridor windows during his recent journey.

"Head south to the River and wait by the Dragon Bridge." Chez added a silent apology to his 'cousin' Kardos as he began to walk. The street ran downhill, so he knew he was headed in the right general direction and after barely 500 meters, he caught his first sight of the beautiful River Ljubljanica. On its eastern bank, an outcrop of forested rock had forced the river to alter its course millions of years ago and the crest of this hill was the site for a stunning castle from which a red and black Nazi flag drooped languidly.

Two bridges came into his sight. The one upstream had three arches and the other had four dragon statues guarding the span. He smiled to himself before casually turning in that direction. It seemed his brown suitcase acted as an identifier for the Resistance because as soon as Chez veered towards Zmajski Most, the Dragon Bridge, a man in a trench coat—a man he recalled having seen at the Railway Station—walked by him muttering quietly in German, "This city is as confusing as a spider's web!"

The strange man stopped at the Dragon Bridge, seemingly to assess the traffic. As Chez caught up with him, he whispered tentatively, "I am the Spider."

It was a brief encounter and the man immediately adopted the pretense of giving directions. He pointed dramatically to the right of the castle while slipping a piece of paper into Chez's pocket. In a blink, he had walked away without a backward glance and disappeared. Chez continued across the bridge towards the castle before fishing in his suit to retrieve the note.

"Café Antico in Stari Trg. West side of the castle."

Rather than risk attracting attention by asking further directions, he decided to continue in the general direction of the west side of the castle and was rewarded in less than five minutes by street signs for Stari Trg. Upon arriving at the square, he easily identified the Café Antico.

Under a vaulted ceiling, most tables in the cafe were occupied by Wehrmacht soldiers. Chez hair prickled with nervousness but suddenly, he felt a helpful hand cup his elbow whilst brushing his shoulder assiduously.

"Please excuse me; you had a small spider on your coat. Would you mind sitting over there, Mein Herr?" a smiling waiter suggested. "I'm sorry to ask you to share a table in the corner but, as you can see, we're quite busy."

Still somewhat bemused, Chez found himself seated beside a man in his late fifties who sported a salt and pepper beard. Through these whiskers, the man was smoking a hooked, Alpine style of pipe, the type carved out of bone with an ornate silver cover hinged to close over the bowl. He seemed oblivious to all around him, preferring to puff intently on his pipe as he scoured his newspaper.

A moment later, without looking at Chez, he surprisingly whispered quietly in German, "Welcome to Yugoslavia, Herr Spinne. Those Krauts have to be back on patrol in five minutes and then we will be able to talk."

Chez ordered a coffee and played his part by completely ignoring the man.

Heralded by the squeals of chairs and tables being pushed across the bare wooden floor, the German soldiers arose, adjusted their uniforms and left, waving thanks to the friendly waiter. As soon as the door closed, the bearded man got up without a word and made his way towards the bathroom. He had a pronounced limp and it took a while, but a moment later, the waiter caught Chez's attention, motioning with his eyes for him to follow.

"Mein Herr, let me look after your suitcase while you visit the bathroom." He took the suitcase from Chez and placed it safely behind the counter as Chez headed for same door in pursuit of bearded man.

On the other side of the door, he found himself faced by a steep flight of stairs. At the top, an open door led into a small room occupied by his table companion and two, very tough looking Yugoslavs. A hitherto concealed fourth man gently closed the door and pursed his lips with a finger to indicate silence. The beard parted into a broad smile as the obvious leader held out his hand, "You are the famous spider, Ja?"

Chez nodded cautiously as he continued. "My name is Milo. What a long journey you have had my friend. Uneventful I trust?" At this point, the other men came over one by one to shake hands, whereupon the room's atmosphere relaxed noticeably.

"Meet Goran, Ladislav and Florin. They speak some German but only poorly," Milo continued. "I will be your translator but, as you have probably figured out, my gammy leg means I cannot lead the mission we're about to describe to you. Goran is my second in command, however, you can trust all my men to protect you like a brother."

The hirsute Milo continued to speak softly as he pulled on his pipe. "This is one of our safe houses; the waiter downstairs is my son. Change into these clothes as swiftly as you can and then leave with Goran. He will take you to Semic where you will meet my brother, Josip. The rest of us will be following close behind to cover you and bring your suitcase."

The rough clothing transformed Chez into just another local peasant before he and Goran left unobserved by the rear door of the Café Antico. As they strolled out of the back alley and into Stari Square, Goran talked to Chez in Yugoslavian. He was a tall handsome man with an infectious smile who embellished his conversation with animated arm movements. To any casual observer, they would have looked like old friends sharing a memory as he steered Chez towards a battered, green truck, though the young Pole had very little clue as to what Goran was saying. Nevertheless, he kept nodding in agreement, injecting the occasional, jocular "Ja, Ja" for the benefit of passersby.

After driving for about ten minutes, they found themselves approaching one of several German control points, established in the city's barbed wire perimeter fence to serve as gates. Two Wehrmacht guards armed with Schmeisser sub-machine pistols manned the barrier. Goran apparently knew both guards and, as one of the soldiers scanned the street, the other ducked low through the truck window to be rewarded with an apparently customary bottle of expensive vodka that he surreptitiously slipped into his tunic.

"Your friend?" he was obligated to ask, pointing at Chez.

"My cousin," assured Goran in poor German but with a smile. They were waved through and entered, what was technically no-man's land, unpatrolled by Germans and unoccupied by Partizani. However, after several kilometers, Goran prodded Chez and pointed to his mirror.

"Milo and the others are behind," he confirmed. It was at that moment Chez realized Yugoslavia truly was being successfully retaken and the German Reich was inexorably headed for defeat.

"Just a matter of time until Jan Kowalski becomes the new President of Poland," he thought to himself in satisfaction, as they finally entered the town of Semic ninety minutes later.

With no reason to fear the Luftwaffe any more, Semic was under complete control of the Partizani. They continued to be wary of potential long-range bombardment from big field artillery but basically, it was a safe haven and even had its own grass airstrip.

"Welcome to the Free Democratic Republic of Yugoslavia," Milo greeted Chez when the rest of the group reunited. "Come and meet my brother, Josip, the leader of this disreputable band."

Milo led Chez to a beautiful church adorned with a series of steep red tiled roofs. The building dominated the main square of Semic and apparently, it now served as the Partizani Headquarters, as evidenced by the giant Yugoslavian flag attached to its ornate, lead-clad steeple.

This prompted Chez to consider the Yugoslavs yet again. "*These brave men must have no fear at all of the Third Reich! I hope Poland will be able to hang our flag on Wawel Cathedral in Krakow before too long.*"

Once inside the church, they found themselves confronted by a handsome man who stood and turned to greet them with a warm smile. "Czeslaw Orlowski, the famous spider? A legend and yet so young! I welcome you to our country and thank you from the bottom of my heart for making such a difficult journey based upon nothing but faith," he said in heavily accented Polish for their guest's benefit.

It was what he added that rocked Chez back on his heels.

"Please allow me to introduce myself. I am Josip Tito."

CHAPTER FOURTEEN

1943 – The Partizani

I n early August of 1943, Malcolm McClain celebrated his thirtieth birthday with a bowl of cold bean and potato soup as the sole inhabitant of Barrack Number 18 in Stalag 306, Maribor. He had been confined in that solitary state for almost nine weeks, designated as a prisoner of war who required 'special attention.' For the first few days of his capture, McClain had been treated as a regular POW, sharing a barrack with other RAF officers including his friends, Derek Stewart and Wilson Dunlop. Then quite suddenly, he had been isolated from everyone else and kept under guard in that squalid building.

Malcolm McClain had no innate gift for languages. As he awoke each morning, he spoke English to each guard charged with his custody, in the forlorn hope that one would respond and give him a clue what the hell was going on. Alas, they either could not converse or were under strict orders not to.

He had never been so miserable in his life.

Malcolm could not possibly know that a young man called Chez Orlowski was the dinner guest of Josip and Milo Tito, joint leaders of the Partizani that controlled the vast majority of Yugoslavia.

The young Polish Freedom Fighter was faring much better than McClain in that his meal that day included slow-roasted pork accompanied by some excellent red wine from France that a recently routed German garrison had involuntarily contributed to the Partizani cause.

As it happened, a connection was already being forged between the two, as Malcolm McClain was currently the main topic of the after-dinner conversation in the transformed Semic church. The Partizani and Chez had decided that German would be the best way to converse, even though the young Pole, a natural linguist, was already starting to pick up a few phrases of Yugoslavian. Josip could speak commendable Polish but Chez's German was perfect and it allowed Milo to participate in the briefing by translating everything back to the men.

"Herr Spinne, I should first like to relate a brief history which might explain why you and I are eating like kings in this beautiful church instead of sucking gruel in a Nazi concentration camp."

The curious diners lit cigars and nursed snifter glasses of celebratory brandy as Josip Broz Tito continued. "First, why you, Spinne…? Well, our good friend, Vedran Bozic, the small wiry Slovenian who has fought with Kowalski's Bracia since early 1940 became a great admirer of the Spider and passed along some wonderful tales to his mother who, by the way, lives over there, right here in Semic."

Josip gestured vaguely beyond the door of the church. "So, that was how we became entranced by your exploits over the past years." Tito smiled wryly, "And while I do not doubt for a moment that you have performed every single one of those incredible deeds, I have to say that I too find myself credited with super-human acts—albeit sometimes, I hear about them for the very first time from the mouths of our children! We must both be cognizant of the importance of propagating hope in the hearts of our youth."

Chez blushed and the men laughed as Tito continued. "Even more important to us than your bravery, Chez, is the fact that you spoke nothing but German for the first few years of your life; perfect German with a Berlin accent thanks to your father, John."

A brief pause allowed Milo to catch up with his translation before Josip asked. "And I also understand that you are…ah…extremely familiar with Nazi hospitality?"

Chez was now becoming somewhat uneasy. He had a growing feeling of vulnerability, caused by being amongst strange men who seemed to know everything about him. Tito continued by laying out a brief history of the Partizani, as if to balance things out.

"Basically, the Germans were able to overrun my country by blitzkrieg; it took only ten short days. I am ashamed to admit that half my fellow citizens, the Chetniks, decided to roll over in front of the Nazis like puppies. However, the other half did not. Instead, we Partizani fought back ferociously, as I understand you are doing in Poland. Slowly but surely, we've beaten the bastards back, causing them to regret ever setting foot in our country. I have no doubt they would leave Yugoslavia tomorrow if they could find a way to convince that egomaniacal asshole, Adolf Hitler, that we are invincible."

He paused again for effect, prompting the other men in the room to murmur their approval. Then, after another sip of cognac, the volume of his voice rose. "The rest of the world has been watching our insurgency closely. We have refused to let these pigs take over and it seems that every week, I hear of another group in France, Belgium and of course, the Bracia in

Poland—all inspired to emulate our path to freedom. So you see, Herr Spinne, ultimately it will not be the Allied Armies that defeat Hitler, it will be the People."

At this moment, our main base is in Drvar, 170 kilometers to the southeast; it has only been a few weeks since we captured Semic. Of course, no Luftwaffe to worry about; Patton and Alexander preparing to charge up Italy made a big difference. A few more weeks and we *will* have our flag flying from the castle in Ljubljana. They cannot win and we cannot lose."

On this note, Josip Tito had no choice but to pause, his voice drowned by the deafening cheers in the church. It was enough to persuade Chez, if proof were needed, that Tito possessed the powerful gift of oratory. Every man in the room would follow him through fire if asked.

Josip continued at center stage, this time looking directly at their guest.

"So now I come back to you, Spinne and the part I hope you will play in this grand strategic design. About three months ago, I was wounded and almost captured at the Battle of Sutjeska. My men were understandably distracted, so it was not until later we learned that a Royal Air Force Wellington had been shot down in the forests near Tolmin, just North of Ljubljana. Three of the crew managed to bail out and were subsequently captured by the Wehrmacht. These men are now being held in the POW Camp at Maribor, which is not far from Semic. In fact, your train passed within five kilometers of this camp as it journeyed from Murska Sobota to Ljubljana yesterday. Why is this so important that we would risk compromising our pipelines to bring the Spider all the way from Poland…?"

Tito used another patented pause for effect. "…Because, Spinne, one of those captured flyers is none other than Malcolm McClain!"

If he had expected a reaction from Chez, he was disappointed. Chez maintained an uncomprehending stare, forcing Josip to explain patiently, "Malcolm McClain is one of the world's best known footballers. He plays for the greatest team in Britain and millions of Britishers, especially the kids, worship him as a hero on and off the field."

Chez was caught up in the moment and, trying to second guess the secret mission and its raison d'etre, he made a silly joke. "So you are telling me that I've come all the way from Poland to rescue a flying football player and get his autograph?"

The weak joke elicited not even a glimmer of reaction from Josip. He simply stared at Chez in silence for a few seconds; leaving no doubt that this foolishly youthful remark was being tolerated but not appreciated, before he continued.

"One of our sources works as a waiter in a café in Maribor. This café is a popular place with guards from the POW camp, so we pay close attention to any loose conversation. About three or four weeks ago, Volker Richter, the captain who captured McClain, was having dinner with Stalag 306's Commandant Afonso Kappel, who is, incidentally, a fat corrupt pig. Lubricated by several bottles of wine, they started to brag about having devised a brilliant piece of propaganda for the Third Reich. Their plan revolved around McClain and how, by exploiting his capture, they might even receive personal commendations from the Fuhrer himself."

"Exploiting?" Chez muttered, the relevance still lost.

"From what we can glean, this scheme involves turning the famous Malcolm McClain into a cheap propaganda vehicle, one intended to demonstrate to the world that the British people have been grossly misinformed about Adolf Hitler and the Third Reich. That now the great McClain has personally experienced the loving hospitality and kindness of the German people, one of Britain's greatest sporting legends has decided to switch sides, transferring his allegiance to the Fatherland. As part of this misinformation campaign, he will be seen photographed beside Sepp Herberger, the current coach of the German National Team. They will both be smiling at Hitler over a caption saying something to the effect:

"–McClain has defected; he has already committed to play for Bayern Munich and to coach in Germany after they defeat the British."

Tito, aware that the brave young Pole in front of him was still having trouble understanding why all of this was so important, lowered his voice to emphasize the potential ramifications of such a plan if executed.

"Since the beginning of this year, Germany has been beaten back on all fronts. Their new vulnerability has spawned increasingly bold resistance to their tyranny. They are desperate to reverse the tide of anti-Germanic sentiment. Dr. Josef Goebbels, director of Nazi Lies, has convinced Hitler that British morale will plummet when this admittedly-dangerous ploy to expose McClain as a traitor, is unveiled." Tito smiled thinly, then added. "We're dealing with men on the brink of madness, Spinne; men clutching at straws. They might even imagine, in their paranoid desperation, that the British people will rise up in revolt against Churchill himself." The Yugoslav leader then shrugged. "Either way, British Intelligence is not only aware of the McClain situation, it is taking it extremely seriously. Brigadier Bryan Zumwalt of the Balkan Air Force has asked me personally to extract McClain from Stalag 306 as soon as possible, hopefully before he disappears forever into the bowels of the German Ministry of Propaganda. If we time this right, it will turn the tables on the Nazis and cause the German High Command massive embarrassment."

Now that he could see all the implications, Chez frowned. "But why would McClain go along with such evidently treacherous strategy? He must realize that his life and reputation will be worthless back in Britain after the Nazis are defeated."

"We believe McClain is being blackmailed—that the Gestapo threatens to torture his two surviving comrades from the Wellington crash. The Nazis are masters of psychological warfare; take my word for it, whereas McClain never had any formal education. After all, he's been a football phenomenon since he was nine or ten—intellectually, he does not stand a chance against the likes of Doctor Josef Goebbels."

Milo chimed in to allow his brother to refill his glass.

"Frankly, Spinne, if we were just fighting for our own survival we wouldn't give a shit but we have these bastards on the ropes in the fifteenth round and every man here is prepared to keep hammering them right up to the final bell, perhaps even beyond. We will allow them no victories at all!"

At this key phrase, the Partizani in attendance stood up as one and chorused the mantra in agreement, "No victories at all!"

Josip smiled and relaxed the room by adding quietly, "I am honored to have you here with us, Spider. Believe me, you are essential to this mission's success. I thank you again for all the dangers you have faced in order to be part of our team.

"Now, go and get some sleep and in the morning,

we'll go over the details of how we propose to bring Mr. McClain to Semic. It's a solid plan and I think you'll appreciate it."

The next morning Goran knocked on Chez's cottage door but there was no reply. After a third knock, he cautiously peered in to find an exhausted young man spread-eagled on his stomach and deep in sleep on a bed for the first time in years. Fatigue had finally caught up with the Polish hero. Goran backed quietly out of the door and, after reporting to Josip and Milo, they decided to defer the meeting until lunchtime.

Chez finally surfaced, hustled to get dressed, then hurried over to the church. Embarrassed, he immediately apologized but the men just laughed, beckoning him to join them and enjoy the spread of pastries and fresh coffee laid out in the middle of the large room. Josip started the conversation with an unusual question.

"Chez, why do they call you *The Spider*,' my friend? I have heard so many stories and, if you will forgive me once again, most of them strike me as either ridiculous or plain impossible."

Chez said nothing as he stood up and flexed. High above them, the vaulted roof of the church had been constructed with exposed wood trusses, one meter apart with bearing almost five meters above the stone floor where he stood. The old walls were built from rough-hewn stone and were at least a meter thick. He took it all in within seconds.

Taking three very deep breaths, Chez turned and ran straight at one of the side walls. His speed allowed him to plant three steps up the vertical face of the wall, creating enough leverage to execute an effortless vault upwards, putting him within reach of the lower chord of a truss. He used arm strength to continue his upward momentum until he was standing on this lower structural part of the structure. Without any perceptible pause, he moved horizontally across the church, jumping the meter between the chords in an angled, forward direction to arrive at the opposite wall of the church in less than twenty bounds. Once there, he dropped down to catch the lower chord again, executed a perfect backward somersault and landed softly on his feet facing the men.

The demonstration had taken him less than thirty seconds and was virtually completed in silence. All the Partizani, including both Tito brothers, stared, their mouths hanging open in shocked silence. It was several seconds before Josip cleared his throat.

"I have never seen anything like that, nor would I have believed it possible by any creature other than a cat—or perhaps a Spider!"

After the buzz died, they got back down to business.

The Partizani knew exactly where McClain was incarcerated. An inside source confirmed he was isolated in Barrack Number 18, Stalag 306 in Maribor, one hundred kilometers to the north. The flyer was closely guarded night and day. With McClain having attained such strategic importance, they would be well advised to anticipate even that high level of security would be stepped up.

"At first, we considered raiding Stalag 306 with everything we've got, but determined that the chance of McClain and all the POW's being killed was simply not worth the risk."

Josip was all business as he outlined the plan. "However, every morning at seven, the Germans send some one hundred selected POW's on a well-guarded, thirty minute train journey to a work camp in St. Lorenzen. It's just on the Austrian side of the border and about fifty kilometers from Maribor. A cook at the camp reports it is relatively poorly guarded by non-regulars."

"Why do they send a daily dose of POW's there in the first place?"

"It's part of a daily work camp program designed to pacify the POW's propensity to go stir crazy. The site at St. Lorenzen is being used to build the Third Reich a desperately needed munitions factory. For the record, Spinne, we fully intend destroying this factory before a single shell is produced. But that must remain a pleasure delayed; for now, we must focus on current events."

"Meaning?"

"Meaning, every evening at seven, the prisoners are returned to their barracks at Stalag 306 in Maribor. We're confident we can overpower the work camp guards and spirit the entire work detail back to Semic via our escape pipeline through the Drava Valley before reinforcements arrive. With luck, we will have all the POW's back here before the SS realizes they are gone."

This time, Chez hesitated until he was certain Tito had finished, before asking the obvious question,

"If Adolf Hitler himself needs this McClain character for his stupid propaganda scheme, why is he not already under armed guard in Berlin?" As he thought more about it, he added, "Hell, even if he is still in Stalag 306, there's absolutely no way the Boche are going let him go on a day trip to Austria. The man's probably handcuffed to his bed with a couple of SS bullyboys standing over him."

Josip nodded for his brother to reply.

"A good question, my friend. McClain is indeed being kept under close guard and is the only prisoner in his barrack. The bastards daren't risk leaking any part of their propaganda plan until Goebbel's spin doctors are ready.

"He's denied all communications with any other POW and has a Schmeisser MP40 in his face even when he goes to the bathroom. So, you are absolutely correct. McClain is indeed the least likely prisoner in the camp to be selected for inclusion onto the daily work detail." After a pause, he added, "What's more, we have recently learned that an SS escort is scheduled to take McClain to Berlin next week, perhaps sooner. Josip?"

Chez continued to frown dubiously; the answer he sought had not come from Milo but from Josip as he seamlessly took over,

"As soon as word gets back to Stalag 306 that the Partizani have humiliated them by emptying the work camp at St. Lorenzen, Commandant Kappel will panic. That despicable piece of shit will be very aware that his is the fattest and most likely neck to be chopped. All his resources will be frantically redeployed to recapture the prisoners before heads begin to roll.

"I can buy that," Chez smiled. "He'll be one very pissed Nazi."

Josip returned the smile. "And we intend to exploit the bastard's weakness to the limit. In the midst of the confusion, the SS escort detailed to take McClain to Berlin will arrive at the Stalag gates and present its credentials—an unfortunate additional pressure on a man desperately trying to keep the lid on a major screw-up."

Chez frowned, "How can you possibly know that McClain's Berlin escort will arrive at that precise moment?"

"We know much more than that, Spinne. We even know that a large official Mercedes—license plate SS136152—will provide the transport. It will be carrying a certain Hauptsturmfuhrer Günter Heber and his SS driver."

Chez grinned as the audacity of Tito's plan dawned on him. Bluff and counter-bluff.

"Under the circumstances, Commandant Kappel will be falling over himself to get Malcolm McClain out the camp with all haste, before his escorts become suspicious about the escape crisis and report back to Berlin."

A tense silence fell over the church while every set of eyes focused on Chez; the key to their whole operation. He surprised them all with his plausible Yugoslavian.

"Like all really good plans, it is amazingly simple," he pondered straight-faced. Then he let out an explosive belly laugh. "It is also friggin' brilliant!"

Shortly afterwards, Josip, Milo and Goran walked Chez to a large barn a few meters from the church. Inside, a bulky object was covered by an old tarp.

Goran pulled it carefully aside to reveal a pristine 1938 Mercedes 170-V German staff car. It was a gray convertible with an SS flag attached to the driver-side headlight. The license plate read SS136152.

"Goran has been practicing driving this car for a week," chuckled Milo. "He will be your driver and already has his uniform. We have one for you too but we had to guess your size; better make sure it fits. Goran's German is somewhat limited so you will have to interrupt into any conversations they direct towards him."

The rest of the day was spent going over every detail of the operation, after which Josip drew Chez aside.

"Currently, I am the most wanted man in Yugoslavia, Spinne. After you've pulled off this escape, you will most likely take over that title. All available resources of the Third Reich from here to Berlin will be focused on getting McClain back or, at worst, killing you both. You are about to kick open up a hornets' nest, my friend, and I wish you Godspeed."

"Perfect," Chez responded softly.

The intensity of hatred in his cold blue-grey eyes sent an involuntary shiver up Josip Tito's spine.

CHAPTER FIFTEEN

1943 – The Escape

Having analyzed all details of the proposed twin escapes from Maribor and St. Lorenzen, Chez found himself reassuringly impressed by the thoroughness shown by the Tito brothers and the Partizani. Not only had the main plans been worked out thoroughly; several contingency plans had been put in place should any part of either operation go awry.

Following a further two days of intensive training, every participant in the mission was as ready as they could ever be. No one was permitted to leave Semic during that period, the Partizani being ever mindful of the danger from quislings. Milo made every single one of them read a pamphlet, passed to him by his son, the waiter in Ljubljana. It read:

"Persons offering effective aid in apprehending escaped prisoners of war may be granted financial awards, applications for which must be directed to the respective prisoner of war camp.

The reward herewith provided for are to be paid out of Reich funds... The reward of one individual shall not exceed 30 marks even when several prisoners of war are apprehended. The amount is fixed by the Commander of Prisoners of War having jurisdiction over each respective prisoner of war camp."

"Trust no one, my friends, and watch each other's back. Yugoslavia appreciates your bravery. *Veliko sreče; Varno potovanje!* Good luck and travel safely."

"*Bomo. Hvala*—We will. Thanks, Milo," Florian replied quietly. Milo had entrusted him to lead the Semic Freedom Fighters so it was he who turned to the men and ordered. "Move out."

The fifty Partizani left Semic in small groups. Their orders were to rendezvous later that afternoon at a stated location outside Dravograd. Once there, they would travel en masse to a hitherto secret location where they would be supplemented by fifty of the local Drava militia for the assault on St. Lorenzen.

Dravograd is situated near the Austrian border. A small, compact town in the Carinthia Province, it is strategically located on the banks of the River Drava, one of two rivers that flow eastward from Italy before entering into the Danube River basin. Although still occupied by several thousand German troops, Yugoslav resistance was strong in this area and the entire Drava Valley was heavily pro-partisan. The navigable river, with its numerous villages en route, always provided excellent surveillance and intelligence reports back to Semic.

With no German patrols reported, it took less than three hours for Florian's disparate groups of Freedom Fighters to arrive at their initial destination, a large barn between Dravograd and the Austrian border. Once assembled, Florian conducted a roll call to confirm all were present and correct.

"Okay, my friends, it will get a little more difficult from here on and I must demand that absolutely no communication take place outside this group. Not even with your closest family as too many precious lives are at stake, including those of the POW's. I will immediately shoot anyone who disobeys this direct order.

"Our next point of reference will be several kilometers further east."

Florian turned to the silver haired stranger standing beside him. "Meet my good friend, Tomaso Langovic. He knows these trails like the back of his hand and will be our guide. We leave after dusk."

That evening found the group hiking east on scarcely perceptible back trails known only to Tomaso, eventually arriving at Muta, a small, remote Slovenian village located on the Yugoslavian side of the border with Austria. It was in Muta that their force doubled, swelled by the Drava militia.

Now numbering almost one hundred armed men, such a gathering in a small village was certain to invite attention but, as Florian noted when he and his group approached, multiple lookouts had been posted around the perimeter to secure this forward base. Without asking the reason, the regular Muta residents had taken convenient trips to visit relatives. In effect, Muta had been locked down and the Partizani militia had the village to themselves for as long as needed.

Ladislav had been in Muta for the previous three days but was not there to greet his compatriots when they arrived that evening. He and his childhood friend, Savo, the swarthy, curly-haired commander of the

Drava militia, were spending time in the hills that overlooked the target work camp at St. Lorenzen. They had been there since noon the previous day, carefully assessing the situation through binoculars and waiting for a pre-arranged signal from Savo's sister, Darja, who worked in the camp's kitchen.

"I see a large building and five smaller buildings, surrounding a concrete square," Ladislav reported to Savo while panning the work camp with his Carl Zeiss, Kriegsmarine binoculars. "Any idea what they are, Savo?"

Savo was lying on his back, a flat cap covering his eyes and a stalk of sweet mountain grass between his teeth. It looked like he was trying to take a nap.

"I know exactly what they are, Ladi," he replied in a bored voice. "The large building is the factory where they plan to assemble the munitions; the smaller buildings are the administration, guards' quarters and toilet block. The building closest to us is the kitchen where Darja works. By the way, the tallest building with the clock on its tower is the railway halt. You might not be able to see it from here but the siding track from Maribor sweeps in from the east and terminates at the buffers." Rolling over to be alongside Ladislav, he pointed. "Right there, see it?"

"Perfectly," Ladislav replied.

Savo rolled back again and soon began to snore.

At about three o'clock that afternoon, Savo's sister,

Darja, appeared outside the kitchen and stretched as she surreptitiously scanned the hills surrounding the camp. She wiped her brow with a brightly colored scarf, the signal to Savo and Ladislav that the guards were taking their daily siesta. The two men backed away from their observation location and cautiously moved downhill towards the camp. For the entire descent they carefully followed a pre-selected route, which shielded any movement from the camp's view.

A major miscalculation by the Wehrmacht involved the lack of fencing around this work camp. In their arrogance, they had assumed that one hundred foreign POWs could not possibly escape into these hills dressed in allied uniforms without certain recapture within days. This misconception would return to haunt them.

Darja saw her brother wave to her when he was about twenty meters away. At this, she turned and signaled a small group of seven POWs she had befriended to walk calmly around the kitchen building and towards his hidden location. Access to the camp bathrooms, being restricted to guards only, the POWs were expected to relieve themselves in the surrounding bushes anyway, so even had a guard woken up at this critical time, it would not have triggered undue alarm.

After the seven men sauntered towards the bushes, Darja returned to the kitchen to keep an eye on the sleeping guards through an adjacent window.

Savo and Ladislav showed themselves and beck-
oned to the men, now technically outside the camp
and in peril of being branded escapees. Using the
same convenient ridge to retreat to the other side of
the hill, the POWs followed the two Partizani until
they were safely out of sight and earshot of the camp.

Since Savo's father had worked in Ireland for three
years before the war, he and Darja spoke reasonably
good English. For the next thirty minutes, he grilled
the POWs about the guards' routines, translating on
the fly to Ladislav.

"As you've probably figured, gentlemen," Savo
said, "you seven and the rest of today's Stalag work
detail are not going to escape this time. That privilege will fall to tomorrow's lucky lads. Your turn will
come, I promise."

"No worries, mate," chipped in Flight Lieutenant
Andy Hungerford, an affable, lanky Australian.
"Strikes me that unless there are considerably more
than just the two of you, we might be considered the
lucky ones tomorrow. But, cheers anyway. Glad to
help."

The two Partizani escorted their POW charges
back down behind the ridge and waited in the
same general area where they had all met. Almost
immediately, Darja gave the safe signal, whereupon
the men casually returned to the camp buttoning
their flies.

As far as the guards knew, they had never left.

Twenty minutes later, Ladislav and Savo were back in Muta briefing Florian and what seemed like an entire army of disreputable looking, unshaven Partizani.

"What a fine upstanding group of men I see before me," Ladislav announced with a sardonic laugh. "You don't need weapons, my brothers. You look so damn fierce, you might just scare the bloody guards to death.

Here is what we have learned. Tomorrow's work train will arrive as usual at half-past eight in the morning. The guards on duty in the work camp are old, retired and out of shape. The guards that will accompany the POWs on the train are a different story. For them, we will be applying a different solution."

By dawn's first light, the Partizani were completely camouflaged and stationed in various positions throughout the hills overlooking the camp. The majority of them had grown up in these very hills, hunting rabbits as young boys. In the unlikely event that a wayward hiker was to stray through this location, he would probably have noticed nothing amiss, each guerrilla blended so well into the landscape.

Savo made his way to the work camp by the same

route as the day before. As soon as Darja appeared with her scarf, he signaled back by relay to Florian and Ladislav. Fifteen minutes later, all eighteen camp guards were dumbfounded to find themselves rudely prodded awake by the muzzles of various assorted weaponry.

Even the youngest guard was well into his fifties and, since there had never been evidence from Darja that any harsh treatment had ever been inflicted on the POWs, the old veterans were not harmed.

Instead, the shaken Volksturm were stripped to their skivvies, bound and gagged. Then, they were placed under armed guard in the factory building. As the Austrian civilian overseers began to arrive from their homes at eight o'clock, the silent, efficient routine was repeated. Finally, the bemused local suppliers were surprised, bound and treated the same way as the guards to complete the first phase of the operation.

Right on time, the soulful sound of a train whistle was heard in the distance. Sending out billowing clouds of grey steam, an engine drawing four freight carriages pulled noisily into the siding with a long hiss, clattering to a halt beside the clock tower. To underline the German penchant for precision, the large timepiece indicated that it was exactly half-past eight.

As intelligence had indicated, the train was protected by twelve armed Wehrmacht guards; one on the roof; one on the front and rear of each carriage. In turn, these guards saw exactly what they expected to see: ten uniformed camp guards waiting for the train to stop. None of the armed guards from the Maribor Camp noticed that the work camp guards were younger than usual and wearing ill-fitting, baggy uniforms. In a matter of seconds after the train halted, the Maribor contingent jumped down from their guard posts to assist with the opening of the freight doors thereby allowing today's fresh POW work detail out and onto the ground. Florian waited until all the Maribor guards were facing the train and then called softly,

"Entschuldigen Sie mich bitte, Herren."

The guards swung around uncertainly to find themselves facing one hundred guns aimed steadily at their heads. There ensued a momentary hesitation before all twelve looked at each other, thought about loved ones, laid down their Schmeissers and raised their hands. Even without their over-abundance of firepower, the Partizani looked much too tough to mess with.

The train driver and fireman were invited to join the guards. Both were Yugoslavian but they were on the German payroll and the wellbeing of their families depended upon them being treated the same as the freshly captured guards. Savo called out in English to the captured Allied officers inside the train,

"Gentlemen, you are now the honored guests

of Josip Tito and the Free Democratic Republic of Yugoslavia."

The POW's simply stared out in blank incomprehension as the doors were opened, wondering whether it was a trap. Their trepidation lessened as Savo continued, a peculiar Irish brogue flavoring his English. "Please, jump down and briefly stretch your legs, then get back aboard. We are taking this train back to Maribor but this time we are not going to stop. This time, we are going to race to the Hungarian border where we have a flight of BAF aircraft waiting to take you home."

This was a complete fabrication for the benefit of the German guards with heavy odds betting that more than a few of them would be able to understand English.

The Maribor guards were dutifully bound and gagged before joining the eighteen puzzled work camp guards, the local overseers and suppliers on the floor of the kitchen. The doors of the kitchen were then securely locked. But before the Partisans left, Ladislav called to Florian in Yugoslavian for additional insurance that his message would be overheard.

"Let's get going quickly; it will take a while to get to Murska Sobota and into Hungary."

The bound, gagged but unhurt guards could clearly hear the sounds of the train being reloaded with prisoners and Partizani. It sounded as if some had to climb on to the roofs of the freight cars or hang precariously onto the sides but within ten minutes, there was the chug-chug-chug of steam as the train backed slowly out of the siding.

In the front cab of the engine, the driver and fireman had Savo, Darja and Ladislav for company so there was little thought of disobedience. It was now well after nine o'clock in the morning and, as the sounds of the locomotive receded, the guards feverishly attempted to escape their bonds so they could warn Stalag XVIII-D to intercept.

Although Florian had guessed thirty minutes, it took the first guard closer to forty-five minutes before he was able to escape his ropes and commence freeing his companions. After he started this chain, that first guard then scrambled for his radio and contacted the camp.

In reality, the train only travelled about three kilometers from the St. Lorenzen work camp before it stopped out of earshot. Everyone except Savo, Ladislav and the crew got off and followed Florian and Darja to a waiting assortment of trucks, the same armada that had ferried Florian's men from Semic.

Once loaded, they headed south by various routes to arrive without incident in Partizani territory by early afternoon.

Meanwhile, the now passenger-less train chugged back into motion and, with every worn valve exuding dense clouds of steam, it was passing through Maribor station at full speed just as the frantic radio call was being received in the communications room in Stalag XVIII-D.

"*Achtung! Achtung!*—Priority! All work detail prisoners have escaped and are on a train headed for Hungary!"

As Tito anticipated, tremendous confusion and concern compounded into near-panic at the Maribor Camp when the train had let loose three shrill blasts of its whistle as it caromed through the town, scattering all in its path.

When a disheveled signals officer raced across the compound to the commandant's office with the news, an already ashen-faced Kappel dispatched every available Krupp Boxer to try and intercept the speeding train. He also called ahead to the Wehrmacht Garrison at Murska Sobota to block the border crossing.

"When I apprehend them, those prisoners will go straight into solitary," he snarled. "The Yugo Rats and the train crew will be shot in front of their families. I'm putting every one of those imbecilic guards at St. Lorenzen on that shit list too."

Four hours later, when the rattling, disparate caravan of trucks successfully completed its journey to the square outside the church in Semic, the Tito brothers were there to greet 132 RAF, ANZAC and USAF officers. The flyers were understandably ecstatic, albeit their relief was tempered by thoughts of their less fortunate comrades still penned in Stalag 306.

The first part of Tito's Partizani mission could not have concluded with greater success. But the second part—the seizing of Flight Officer Malcolm McClain from the clutches of the SS—would not be as easy.

CHAPTER SIXTEEN

1943 – Deception

As the Partizani were commandeering the train in St. Lorenzen, Goran and Chez were preparing to leave Semic on their leg of the mission. It was first light and the two men were dressed in worn Yugoslavian work clothes, drinking strong coffee as they watched eight hefty Partizani maneuver the Mercedes Staff car up an incline of planks and onto the back of an old Hungarian Raba flatbed truck. They used the powerful motor to ease the strain but could not afford to 'gun it' for fear of ramming the back of the driver's cab. Goran climbed up onto the flatbed itself and walked around to make certain the car was stable and centered. A dirty tarp was thrown over the car to protect it before ropes were looped through anchor points, securing the entire cargo.

In their new personae as mechanics, Goran and Chez had papers that certified the SS Staff Car needed a new carburetor and was scheduled for repair in Maribor. Their Waffen SS uniforms were well hidden, sewed inside a potato sack tucked behind the seats. Once the planks were removed, there was nothing left to do but head towards Maribor and the unknown.

Josip and Milo personally walked Chez and Goran to the front of the Raba. There was a distinct possibility that the four men would never see each other again. This weighed heavily upon the two brothers and caused Josip's usually taciturn voice to crack as he bade farewell to the two young men.

"Goran, I have known you since you were a small child; Chez, for just a short week…however, what I see before me today, are two of the bravest human beings I have ever met in my life. You're both fearlessly walking into the lion's den to take away his meat…*Sretno*, my dear friends, *Good luck!*"

There was nothing more to be said. The antiquated lorry spluttered into life after two turns of its starter handle and wheezed out of Semic on the road north to Maribor.

Their itinerary was much more likely to place them within the range of German patrol activity than the route to and from Dravograd and, sure enough, after just over an hour, the truck had to stop behind a line of cars that had been pulled over to the right hand side of the road. Ahead, four Wehrmacht soldiers were meticulously examining papers before allowing any vehicles to proceed in either direction. After a nerve-racking wait of some twenty minutes, the flatbed Raba came to its turn, rolling slowly up to the checkpoint. Goran noticed that Chez had positioned a 9 mm Mauser within easy reach but out of sight.

"Alt!" the Gefreiter barked, holding out his hand for papers. As he dug into his pocket, Goran caught a glimpse of a strangely familiar car in his rear-view mirror. It was a light blue Fiat 514 and he was certain it was from Semic; in fact, five years ago, he and his brother changed the color of the old car from black to blue as a favor to his Uncle Zori, the car's owner. Suddenly, the 1930 Fiat saloon backed up, performed a dramatic about turn and roared off to the south with a squeal of tires.

"*Achtung! Achtung!* the Gefreiter yelled to his three stunned companions. In a commendable imitation of the Keystone Cops, the German soldiers immediately leapt into their Opel Olympia and began to pursue the Fiat, abandoning the check point and most likely forgetting that Partizani occupied territory began only ten kilometers to the south.

"Thank you, Uncle Zori," Goran murmured softly as he pushed the Raba gear lever from neutral into first.

In less than two hours, the Raba reached the village of Bohova on the outskirts of Maribor without further incident. Now, they had to look for a small farmhouse, recognizable by a yellow scarf tied around a tree at its entrance. Chez saw the scarf before Goran, who in turn swung the old flatbed left onto the dirt road which he followed cautiously for a further five hundred meters until the actual farmhouse came into view.

Almost immediately, an old woman came out and waved her right arm up and down three times, a pre-determined safe signal for them to pull up and park outside the open doors to her barn.

Chez located the readied stack of solid planks for a makeshift ramp as Goran untied the ropes and hauled the tarpaulin off the Mercedes. Then ever so cautiously, he backed it onto the ground and continued reversing the gleaming staff car until it was inside the barn.

A farm hand dressed in overalls emerged from the house just as they were closing the barn doors and spoke to Goran. Satisfied, he threw his bicycle up onto the now empty flatbed and drove it away. Goran explained that the old Raba had originally come from Bohova, and would be left in the village for its owner to pick up later.

The two men washed, shaved, and changed into

their black Waffen SS uniforms. Their new look scared the old lady almost to the point of hysteria. Goran tried to calm her down but her empty eyes fixated on the silver skull above the peak of Chez's black crusher hat and she began to shake uncontrollably. Such was the power of suggestion inspired by her Nazi oppressors. Chez immediately removed the hat.

"Why don't I just throw this in the back seat of the Mercedes until later?" He said quickly.

After about thirty minutes, just before quarter past ten, they heard the anticipated three blasts from a train whistle somewhere in the distance.

"Well done, Florian!" Chez whispered as they went to the barn and re-started the Mercedes. They were rewarded with a powerful, throaty growl from the 170-V's engine.

The final part of their mission to rescue Flying Officer McClain had begun.

It was pleasant enough weather that fateful morning but they decided that the roof of the car would be better up than down. Assuming their new identities, SS Sturmmann Schenck held open the rear door and stiffly saluted as Hauptsturmfuhrer Günter Heber got into the rear seat without a glance of acknowledgement. The old woman watched the drama from behind her curtains, knowing that such SS arrogance was usually not an act.

They arrived at the main gate of Stalag XVIII-D just a few minutes before eleven in the morning. Goran cranked down his driver's window and impassively showed their orders to the sentry while Chez relaxed in the rear passenger seat, looking bored. When the guard asked Goran a question, Chez aggressively leaned forward, quick as a rapier, to interject sardonically, "Oberschutze, do you have difficulty in reading? At your convenience, direct me to the office of Commandant Kappel."

The guard hesitated, nervously fingering the papers. Raising his voice a tone, Chez interjected sharply, *"Unmittelbar, Oberschutze. While I am still young."*

The guard quickly returned the orders to Goran and slammed to attention, raising his arm in the Nazi salute.

"Heil Hitler!"

"Heil Hitler," Goran acknowledged with a stony expression, inwardly grinning to himself that it was one of the few German phrases he spoke perfectly.

The grey Mercedes staff car entered the compound, crossed the parade ground and swung parallel to the short flight of wooden steps leading up to the commandant's office. Goran jumped out and walked smartly around to open the rear door for his important passenger.

Chez stepped out with practiced arrogance. He stretched his legs, as if he had just completed a long journey, taking the opportunity to survey the compound. Without staring, he noticed that several grey troop transporters were filled with guards and getting ready to leave the camp.

Chez walked up the steps purposefully and entered the office, leaving Goran standing beside the Mercedes with the engine running. Once inside, he noticed the humped back of the commandant's clerk, head below the desk, stuffing papers into what appeared to be a floor safe. Upon hearing the door open, the corporal started and banged his head painfully on the edge of the desk before finally focusing on the youthful SS captain who had burst into his anteroom demanding to see Commandant Kappel. The adjutant promptly moved his attention from the safe and grabbed his phone to contact the inner office.

"Commandant Kappel, I have SS Hauptsturm-fuhrer Heber here who wishes to see you immedia…?" the corporal broke off in mid-sentence, blinking as the captain's broad back disappeared into his comman-dant's office without waiting for an invitation.

On any normal day, the commandant would have objected but this time he restrained his temper: it was just possible that the SS might have already discovered the screw up in St. Lorenzen. His anxiety diminished, however, when the extremely fit looking SS captain clicked his heels and raised his arm.

"Heil Hitler, Herr Kommandant," Chez snapped in the fashionable Berlin accent affected by the SS. "I am charged by these orders to escort your prisoner, Flying Officer Malcolm McClain, to Berlin, where he has a personal audience with Reichsführer Himmler: possibly even with our glorious Fuhrer himself."

Conscious of the need to push Kappel hard before the fat man had time to think, Chez slapped the orders onto the desk before him, challenging the commandant with his stare.

"Have him brought to my car immediately." Holding one of his SS-issue, black leather gloves in his left hand, he fastidiously flicked imaginary dust from Kappel's desk as he spoke.

Kappel hesitated, thought better of extending the confrontation a moment longer than necessary—and then picked up the phone.

"Oberschutze Stossel, have the prisoner McClain found and brought to the front of my office immediately." As soon as he replaced the receiver, Chez turned up the pressure.

"Have him <u>found</u>, Commandant? Is he lost? I did notice a flurry of activity in the yard and several Krupp LH2's preparing to leave the compound." He paused as he saw Kappel's eyes darting to the window.

"A clumsy figure of speech on my part," Kappel said.

"I hope you are sure. If you have lost McClain, I need to inform the Reichsführer immediately." Chez held out his black-gloved hand. "Hand me your phone."

Afonso Kappel diffused the moment with a smile. He felt more comfortable now: it seemed certain that the SS did not yet know about this morning's escape. If he could just get this arrogant bastard and McClain out of his camp quickly, he would have all his prisoners back by nightfall. Then he stiffened, relieved at what he noticed outside.

"Ah, my dear Captain, I can see McClain being escorted to your car from Barrack 18." He even risked a little cockiness. "You were not due until noon. That is why we were a little unprepared...Have a safe journey to Berlin. Guten tag, Hauptsturmfuhrer Heber."

"Guten tag, Herr Kommandant – Heil Hitler," Chez rapped, accompanied by the inevitable rigid Nazi salute. Nothing in his arrogant exterior betrayed the pounding of his heart as he swung abruptly and left the office without so much as a glance at the disheveled clerk.

Once outside, he marched purposefully to intercept the two guards headed towards his Mercedes with a tall, manacled RAF officer between them. The guards halted instantly, snapping to attention. Chez snatched the hand-over documentation rudely from one, returning it with his scribbled signature.

"Put him in the back seat behind the driver," Chez barked. "Handcuff him to the inside door pull then give me the keys." He got in beside Malcolm then rudely slammed the door in the faces of the guard before barking, "Let us be on our way, driver."

As they headed for the gate, it was clear that the guard he'd abused fifteen minutes earlier wanted no further entanglement with the SS. He went straight to the counterbalanced armature, lifted it skywards, and stepped aside, saluting rigidly as the staff car accelerated past.

Not three kilometers from the camp, they encountered another SS staff car, this one headed towards Stalag XVIII-D. Chez avoided eye contact with the SS major inside but noted how unusual it was for such a high-ranking Nazi to choose the front passenger seat.

As soon as the cars had crossed, Chez realized that they had avoided McClain's genuine escort by mere minutes and all hell would be breaking loose momentarily. The safety cushion he had hoped would be measured in days, was about to vanish. He quickly explained all of this in animated fashion to Goran, who immediately floored the accelerator.

The powerful car leapt forward, adding to Malcolm McClain's mounting confusion. Confusion that peaked when the SS captain turned to him, unlocked the handcuffs and said in Polish-accented English, "Malcolm McClain, my name is Chez and this is Goran. We have been charged by the British government to look after you as a guest of the Free Democratic Republic of Yugoslavia until we can return you safely to Great Britain." He smiled at McClain's puzzled look of apprehension as he continued. "You must keep your uniform on for your protection as a prisoner of war under the Geneva Convention. If caught, Goran and I will be shot as spies for wearing these Nazi uniforms. Come to think of it," his smile broadening into a laugh, "they'll certainly shoot us anyway when they find out what has just happened, so I'm going to change into my Partizani clothes. This Nazi garb makes me want to throw up anyway. Unfortunately, that staff car that just passed us was the real thing and our cover is about to be blown. I think we only have about ten minutes head start, so Goran'll have to wait before he can change." Chez stripped off the black uniform and pulled his old clothes from the potato sack stashed under the seat. Goran, continually glancing in his mirror, noticed a worrying cloud of dust behind them and called to the back seat.

"They're on our tail, Spinne," he called, almost matter-of-factly.

"And probably road blocks being set up ahead," added Chez. "Plan B, Goran."

Turning to Malcolm, he asked. "Mr. McClain are you as fit as they say?"

"Eighty per cent," McClain replied, still confused. "But please, call me Malcolm. I guess we're best friends now, huh?"

Chez climbed over into the front passenger seat, "Okay, Best Friend Malcolm, get ready to follow me... on my count."

At the next opportunity, Goran swung a hard right, leaving the main road for a narrow dirt track that meandered up a valley. For a hundred meters, the bumpy road gradually curved to the right, concealing the car from the main road. Goran slowed the car enough to allow Chez and Malcolm to jump simultaneously out of both right hand doors and sprint for the forest tree line. He then picked up speed again and headed deeper into the valley.

The Germans behind saw only the dust and followed, now a slight sixty seconds behind. None of the SS in the car following had any idea that the prisoner McClain and the bogus SS captain were crouched behind bushes watching them race by in pursuit of the dust cloud ahead. After a count of five, the two fugitives moved deeper into the forest, heading back towards the farmhouse in Bohova that Chez had left just over two hours before.

Goran, a skillful driver who knew the local roads well, was able to stretch the sixty-second gap considerably as he barreled up the valley. He was actually starting to enjoy the hunt; even grinning to himself as he swung the car into a blind left-hand corner.

Shocked to the core, Goran stood on the brakes with all his strength, bringing the big Mercedes skidding to a halt in a cloud of dust and gravel, no more than ten meters from a Wehrmacht-manned road block.

"Shit—I'm dead!" Goran muttered as he stared down the barrels of a dozen-plus guns trained on him. The trailing SS eventually caught up and a haughty SS major got out of the front passenger door to confront Goran. The Yugoslav had already been forced into a kneeling position beside the Mercedes, hands clasped behind his head. Choosing to ignore him for the moment, the major addressed the soldiers at the roadblock.

"Where are the other two?" he screamed. The soldiers shrugged and looked dumbfounded, responding that their orders were simply to apprehend the grey staff car and this driver had been its only occupant.

Turning to Goran the SS man repeated harshly, "Where are McClain and the captain?" Goran said nothing.

Sturmbahnfuhrer Abelard Hans von Keller put his Mauser to the base of Goran's neck and repeated the question for a third time. Goran took a last deep, glorious breath of Yugoslavian mountain air. Then, ever so deliberately, he lowered one hand to raise a middle finger towards von Keller.

He smiled characteristically before spitting, with all the hatred he could muster, *"Majku mu ga!"*

The Sturmbahnfuhrer did not speak or understand Yugoslavian. He didn't need to.

A gun butt smashed Goran to the ground, whereupon the major shot him twice in the back of his head.

CHAPTER SEVENTEEN

1943 – Pursuit

Although Goran's murder took place in the middle of nowhere, Jefta, a twelve-year-old boy out chasing squirrels with his dog, heard the shots. He knew they hadn't come from a hunting rifle, so his instincts caused him to duck low into the underbrush as he edged through the trees towards the noise. He had a clear view of the bizarre sight—a dozen Wehrmacht soldiers involved in—of all things—the execution of an SS trooper at the rear of a big Mercedes staff car.

Prudently lying low until the Germans left, the terrified youngster then retreated, making it safely home to stammer out what he had seen to his uncle. The man could see that his nephew was telling the truth. Nevertheless, he crouched down, put his big hands on the boy's trembling shoulders and asked for confirmation.

"Jefta, do you swear on your father's grave that you could not be mistaken in what you saw?" The boy's eyes welled with tears while he slowly nodded. "I am sure, Ujak Drazan."

Drazan Horvat and his late older brother, Andro, had grown up in Zagreb. It had been almost fourteen years since Andro had fallen in love with a beautiful Slovenian girl, ultimately following his heart to Maribor where they had married and borne a son, Jefta.

Still a single man himself, Drazan doted on his nephew; so much so, that he'd continued to visit his filial family every summer, even after the occupation began. When Andro had been tortured and killed by the Gestapo, Drazan had immediately left Zagreb for Maribor to offer his support.

"Jefta, you're a brave boy; every bit as brave as your father was. I need to contact a couple of friends, so look after your mother. Lock the door and wait for me to return. I'll be back before dinner."

On the previous day, Ladislav and Savo had taken the empty commandeered train through Maribor at reckless speed.

After a further 15 kilometers of steam-billowing madness, they called for the train to slow down and ordered the driver and fireman to jump off. Ladislav joined the terrified crew while Savo stayed aboard until the last possible moment before jamming the steam valve in the wide-open position. The train derailed at the next curve in a snaking, piling roar of disintegrating steel and wood.

By the time the pursuing Germans caught up with the empty diversion, Savo had already made his way back along the track to rendezvous with Ladislav. There, they had engaged in animated and loud discussion, with much arm waving and pointing north, before the two had headed in that direction. They left behind a confused train crew to await arrival of their Nazi employers.

Bluff and counter-bluff. Another simple deception to be related to the enemy. Once out of sight, they doubled back south to await their expected rendezvous with Chez, Goran and, hopefully, the now-freed Malcolm McClain. This was scheduled to take place in the town of Dogose, another Partizani stronghold on the Drava River.

Upon arriving there next evening, their faces betrayed immediate concern when they discovered that, not only had Chez's team failed to arrive, but one of Savo's men informed them of the inexplicable shooting incident young Jefta had witnessed further down the Drava Valley. The four Partizani shared a bad feeling as they drove to the boy's village to investigate, leaving optimistic instructions for the Dogose Brigade to protect the obviously delayed fugitives, should they show up before they returned.

The leader of the village resistance group quickly introduced the worried Partizani to Drazan Horvat who recounted his version of the incident. Within five minutes of arriving at the uncle's house, their worst fears began to unfold as, just before nightfall, Jefta recognized his uncle's knock on the front door. Although he seemed alone, Drazan immediately hurried through to the kitchen, opened the back door and let out a series of low owl hoots and minutes later, Jefta found himself relating his extraordinary tale of the shooting once more, this time to the village head and four grim-faced strangers. Two of those strangers were Ladislav and Savo.

"The person Jefta saw being shot was wearing a Waffen-SS uniform but he was almost certainly not Schutzstaffel," Ladislav explained. "Combined with the description of the staff car, we can be pretty certain that the victim had to be either Goran or Chez."

"Jefta only heard and saw one person killed; the 'double tap' typical of an SS execution," Savo supplemented quietly. "Goran would have been driving and the last to leave, so most likely it was he who got caught. Typical Goran, stubborn and brave as a lion. I suspect that once they'd determined they could get nothing out of him, it was all over."

Ladi sniffed. It was a long sniff, accompanied by a painful grimace that expressed more than words could ever do.

"I guess we'll find out soon enough," Savo said quietly while putting a comforting hand on Ladi's shoulder. Then, he turned to the local Partizani. "Of course, we cannot tell you of our further plans, for your own security and because there are other brave Yugoslavs involved. Now, we must leave immediately…Drazan, you have an extraordinary nephew. Andro would have been very proud."

Drazan nodded, grateful that the leader of the Drava Division knew about his brother's sacrifice. Then Savo added an afterthought, "… if the Spider and McClain do turn up in Dogose tomorrow, just tell them to follow Plan B. They'll understand and we will be waiting for them at a certain farmhouse."

After sending the other four men back to Dogose with the car, Savo and Ladislav waited until long after nightfall before leaving Drazan's house.

Travelling west to Bohova from the small village was only four kilometers as the crow flies. However, they were not crows and it took Savo and Ladislav almost two hours to traverse the valleys as they took great care to remain unobserved, pausing under cover at the slightest untoward sound. This was Savo's home turf, he being the person who had originally suggested the farm outside Bohova as a way point for Chez and Goran to change into SS mode. The leader was now feeling uneasy; using the same location was an extremely risky contingency he'd hoped they would never be forced to use.

By the early hours of next morning, they found that the yellow tag was back on the tree, meaning that Plan B had been implemented. Again, their fears for Goran surfaced as they walked slowly to the rear door of the farm. Savo knocked three times quickly, followed by twice slowly. Iva peered nervously through her curtains before opening the door.

Once she had ushered Savo and Ladislav into the tiny kitchen she announced, "Chez? It's Iva. It's safe to come out."

There was the sound of boxes scraping across a floor before the figures of Chez Orlowski and Malcolm McClain emerged slowly from their hiding place beneath the stairs.

The reunion with Chez proved a sombre affair. Despite the valiant Pole's crucial importance to the mission, Goran had been one of their own and a friend since childhood.

"It is good to see you again, Spinne…while you

must be Flying Officer McClain?" was all Savo said, without emotion.

For his part, Chez felt no less uncomfortable. The fact that Savo and Ladislav had been pressured to deviate from Tito's plan; being here at the farm instead of waiting for them in Dogose, represented their first major setback. But there was little time for reflection as they swapped each other's accounts of the previous day's perils, with both Savo and Chez taking turns to translate into English for Malcolm.

"So from young Jefta's account," Savo eventually summated, "Goran encountered a large group of Wehrmacht and at least one very pitiless Schutz-staffel major. Himmler will probably court-martial that bastard when he returns to Berlin empty-handed but, of greater immediate concern is what will happen now. The SS is going to pull out all the stops—torture and kill anyone suspected of being associated with us—in a concerted effort to recapture Malcolm McClain.

At the moment, they think they are also looking for a rogue Nazi captain. If and when it leaks out that the Spider is here in Yugoslavia, we will be up shit creek without a paddle!"

"Then call it off now. I'll walk into Maribor tomorrow and give myself up," Malcolm interrupted grimly. "No one else should die on my account."

"Malcolm," Chez explained patiently. "This is

not about you anymore. The best way we can honor Goran's memory is to complete the mission by denying them your celebrity for their propaganda."

"He knew the odds were against success. Goran will be smiling in his grave when you get safely back to England," Savo added. "Believe me."

Chez and Ladislav nodded agreement. "So now, Iva," Savo continued by addressing the old woman. "If you could spare us a little food and water, we must leave immediately. This farm can never be a safe place for you until we are far away from here and deep in the forest. I thank you and your husband for your unselfish bravery with all my heart."

Within thirty minutes, the four men were back at the main road. Savo removed the yellow tag along with any traces he could find that might indicate they had ever visited the farm. After checking for any sound of approaching traffic, they crossed and headed for the safety of the trees.

Sturmbahnfuhrer Abelard Hans von Keller was the stereotypical Nazi; immaculately groomed, he wore a monocle in his left eye and riding jodhpurs. However, more sinister than those harmless affectations, he was a passionate follower of the Party line and cruel to a fault.

Earlier that afternoon, and within an hour of

having executed Goran, he came to the realization that his two prime targets, Malcolm McClain and the treacherous SS captain, had apparently vanished. His patrol backtracked and searched but found absolutely no trace of the fugitives. This forced the now increasingly apprehensive Sturmbahnfuhrer to regroup for a strategy meeting at Stalag XVIII-D.

Kommandant Kappel's day had been equally disastrous. When SS Major von Keller explained his own experience, Kappel gained little comfort from the fact that the SS man also faced the dreaded prospect of sharing Himmler's wrath.

Von Keller chaired the meeting, announcing that henceforth, he would be taking control of the pursuit and recovery of Malcolm McClain. Kappel, of course, did not object for a moment. *'Never volunteer when someone else is foolish enough to risk taking the blame,'* had long been the obese officer's mantra.

"Clearly, this was coordinated; a Partizani plan to distract the camp guards from guarding McClain effectively!" von Keller said, staring directly at Kappel. "Fallen for hook, line, and sinker by you, Herr Kommandant."

"I strenuously deny...!" Kappel began, rivulets of nervous sweat already turning his once-white collar a dirty grey.

Von Keller ignored the protest. A career intelligence officer who played a high level of chess for a hobby, his brain was trained to assemble facts and then exploit them. He continued to pursue his coldly succinct analysis.

"It is logical to assume that McClain, and whoever had the effrontery to pass himself off as me, are going to reunite with the Yugoslav rabble and the St. Lorenzen prisoners—safety in numbers. Thereafter, all of them will most likely attempt to reach the relative safety of Partizani strongholds to the south. My guess would be…Semic."

Once again, von Keller focused a cold, contemptuous stare on the fidgeting, nervous Afonso Kappel, who cringed noticeably. "No bodies were found at the site of the train crash, so we must assume it was derailed deliberately with nobody aboard. Having permitted such a disaster to occur was a serious dereliction of duty in itself, Kappel, but then to believe the fugitives would have allowed the train crew to overhear their plans to travel north was stupidity beyond comprehension. Yet you committed all your resources to this wild goose chase without question!"

This time Kappel didn't even try to protest.

"You are an idiot, Kappel. Interview the driver and the guard again and again. Use any method needed to encourage them to tell you where the prisoners got off."

Von Keller held the reins on his mounting fury with a deep breath before proceeding.

"I have one hundred elite SS troops at my disposal. I intend to commandeer at least that number of your Wehrmacht guards and every single troop transporter you can find. I want road blocks set up thirty kilometers south of here on any road that can be used to get to Semic. Nothing gets through…"

However, this time his anger got the better of him and he raised his voice to a shout as he repeated. "Do you understand me—NOTHING! Get going. There are over two hundred fugitives out there on foot, most of them wearing Allied uniforms. I expect every single prisoner, including our two main targets, to be back in this camp, dead or alive, by morning."

After a hasty mapping exercise, the troops regrouped into squads before speeding off to their assigned interception points.

Von Keller's mind, fueled by adrenaline, throttled into overdrive as he reverted to one of the SS's more practiced areas of expertise.

"Kommandant Kappel, get a raiding party together. Have your men arrest any suspected Partizani in the Maribor area for interrogation…." He hesitated, pondering. "You mentioned a girl in the camp at St. Lorenzen, kitchen staff I believe? Bring her in too. If she's in on this, if the Partizani had some traitor within to direct them, I intend to find out who it was within the hour."

The search for Darja in St Lorenzen provided a further frustration. Savo had wisely insisted his sister escape along with the POWs in one of the trucks now safely returned to Semic. However, three scared-looking workers from the Maribor region and their immediate families found themselves under armed guard in Stalag XVIII-D. They were isolated in separate rooms, waiting to be interviewed by Sturmbahn-fuhrer von Keller. Fate was no longer solely favoring the Partizani. Now the heat was being turned up on both sides.

One of the rooms contained a tall, rough-bearded man in his mid-thirties. This suspected Partizani had been brought to the camp accompanied by a pretty, four-year-old girl with wide, frightened blue eyes. The youngster was seated beside him, racked with fear and refusing to release her hand from his.

"I do not care to know your name, only if this child is your daughter?"

As the interpreter spoke to the man, von Keller stared straight into the detainee's eyes without a trace of compassion. He could actually smell the man's fear and, he noted idly, the experience left him somewhat aroused. On an apprehensive nod, the interpreter continued at von Keller's behest, asking how much the man knew about today's escape.

"Nothing, sir, I know nothing! And please…I beg you not to hurt my daughter."

"I actually do believe that you do not know about today's incidents. However, I strongly suspect that you *do* know the current codes that the Partizani are using to denote safety and danger."

The major could tell by the Yugoslav's body language that his bluff was working and, Sturmbahnfuhrer von Keller was now a man on a mission. With theatrical deliberation, he produced a pocketknife and opened it.

"You will tell me these codes immediately or your daughter will lose the sight of both blue eyes within the next sixty seconds."

Six minutes later, SS Major von Keller slipped into the front passenger seat of his staff car and left the camp to follow his men, armed with the knowledge that yellow scarves were being used as indicators that a house was safe for the fugitives.

CHAPTER EIGHTEEN

1943 – The Noose Tightens

M alcolm McClain may have been a sturdy city boy from Belfast but his three comrades were much, much tougher, having lived their entire lives under extremes of adversity. Hardship had not featured strongly during Malcolm's charmed upbringing and the disparity between the men showed clearly.

The flyer was damp and sparkling with dew when he awoke the next morning. He had an uncomfortable ache in his back, caused no doubt by sleeping on a root or a rock. He was more tired than he had ever felt in Barrack Number 18.

In contrast, Savo and Ladi were up and alert before the first birds had anticipated the dawn. They exchanged smiles as Malcolm blinked and looked around, attempting to get his bearings. The slopes surrounding them helped him little. His companions had shrewdly chosen this depression within the thickly forested area so no movement against the horizon could be observed from the road.

"Good afternoon, Malcolm," Savo joked. It was just a little after seven in the morning.

"Where's Chez?" Malcolm asked uncertainly in response. Savo glanced upwards and the Ulsterman's eyes followed. He did not immediately notice anything but continued to look skyward. Then, at the top of one of the tallest trees, he detected an almost imperceptible movement among the branches. Next, he saw a human form dropping down from the top of the tree effortlessly and in complete control.

True to form, the Spider landed softly beside his companions and nodded briefly to McClain.

"Well, at each of the three road blocks I identified, I saw them relieving their overnight forces with perhaps twenty fresh troops. There may be more checkpoints but I could not see into the next valley. Their positions are all south of here, so I suspect they're on to our ruse to send them north and now figure we are, in fact, intending to return to Semic."

"I agree, Chez," Savo nodded. "The Nazis will cover the roads south to Starse, Podlehnik and Slovenska Bistrica. I suggest we head southwest and stay in the mountains. There's a safe house in Zrece we should be able to reach by nightfall."

"Not only does that mean departing from Tito's plan, going in that direction gets us no closer to our next objective," Chez said dubiously. "I don't like it but it seems we've got no choice."

"Not necessarily," Malcolm interrupted with a thoughtful look. McClain, at thirty, was the eldest in the group and, foreign fish out of water or not, the others turned to him respectfully. "The belief that the Germans will not shoot me because I'm wearing an RAF uniform is, quite frankly, ludicrous. … Savo, could you take my RAF tunic and plant it somewhere as bait to create another false trail?"

"You sure you want to do that?" Chez interjected. "Ludicrous or not, it means you can kiss goodbye to any chance you have of staying alive under the protection of the Geneva Convention."

McClain blew him off with a grin. "The trick, of course, is to hide it somewhere it won't be found, then to make sure the Nazis are clever enough to find it…Does that make sense?"

"Perfect sense," Savo mused, thoughtfully studying McClain's light blue tunic. It even had an 'F O McClain' name tag on it.

"If I can get this east to Ptuj, which is a large city on the River Drava, my men will make sure it is discovered quickly and in a fortuitous manner. Once the Boche congratulate themselves on their lucky break, they'll be convinced we have made it that far—to a city situated like the hub of a wheel, from where we could have gone in any direction. If they run true to form, as they invariably do, the Nazis will move all their search operations to Ptuj."

Savo then turned to Chez. "Did you see any movement on the west side of this forest?

"None," Chez confirmed. "All the roadblocks are currently to the south."

"Okay then. Malcolm, give me your tunic but put my jacket on. It gets even colder on the mountains where you are going. I'm used to this weather."

Then Savo talked to Ladislav in Yugoslavian for several minutes. "Ladi, do you remember the high hunting trails to the west, the ones that lead to Zrece? We played there together when we were young boys."

"I remember every stream, every tree, every rabbit burrow."

"Good. Then if I keep up a steady pace while you guide our new friends to Zrece, I should be back to meet you at the safe house tomorrow morning after dawn."

Savo described the safe house and urged them to be alert to danger. Then, he shook hands with everyone and swiftly disappeared, carrying Malcolm's RAF tunic in a bundle under his arm.

Careful to stay within the cover of the forest, the Irishman, the Yugoslav and the Pole travelled west for several miles until Ladislav halted and pointed at a deep gully formed over time by a fast-moving stream on the opposite side of the road. This gully headed north to the top of a range of hills that the men would be able to use as cover once they left the forest.

They stopped before crossing the road so Chez could shimmy up a tall tree and check for German patrols.

"I don't like what I see. Let's go but we'll have to be quick," he said as soon as his feet hit the ground. There was about fifty meters of open space to cross from the forest to the gully but before they even reached the road, all three heard the roar of approaching motorcycles.

They froze for a moment at the edge of the road then sprinted back towards the forest, diving the last few paces into the cover of some tall bushes. Only a few seconds later, two Wehrmacht motorcycles hurtled around the corner from the direction of Maribor. The gears shifted down as they began to slow, eventually performing slow circles in the road not twenty meters from the bushes where the fugitives were hiding.

The three held their collective breaths, suspecting that these two soldiers were an advance party. Sure enough, within five minutes four Krupp Boxer Troop Carriers, loaded with about thirty Wehrmacht soldiers had arrived and immediately began to set up a roadblock.

Worse, they seemed prepared to stay for quite a

while as a couple of tents were erected and a fire lit to boil water for tea. One tent was pitched so close to the escapees that Chez could clearly make out the stitching in the canvas.

All three fugitives were sufficiently well hidden, but they didn't dare move a muscle for fear that any noise from the surrounding brittle bushes would attract attention.

"We must wait until nightfall," Chez mouthed to the other two. As it was only about eleven o'clock in the morning, appalling tedium, tempered by moments of potential terror, lay ahead of them. At various times during the day, each of the men needed to urinate, prayerful that any sound or smell would not catch the attention of the troops. Even worse, after hours of fighting a growing discomfort in his stomach, Ladislav winced and farted long and loudly, no longer able to hold back. There would have been other occasions when this act could have drawn a chuckle from his companions but all three tensed, knowing that the sound, which seemed to stretch out interminably, had the potential to be life threatening.

A soldier frowned and glanced over at the bushes; he stood up, paused for a moment but then shrugged and continued the game of doppelkopf with his companions.

Just before nightfall, the patrol received a radio call and when the Oberstleutnant in charge of the troop was handed the transcript by the radio operator, he immediately began to bark orders. Everyone jumped up, packed up, and engines were started.

"*Schnell, Schnell!*" The vehicles re-organized themselves into a convoy that created clouds of dust as they sped off back in the direction they came from.

After waiting five more minutes to make certain they were safe, Chez climbed back up the tree, estimating that the contingent must by that time, be about two miles away. As neither Malcolm nor Ladislav spoke German, when Chez returned to terra firma, both men turned to him with raised eyebrows. "Well?"

"Savo's been quick," Chez announced before adopting an expression of mock regret. "It seems that unfortunately, the RAF prisoner Malcolm McClain, has been located in Ptuj. His tunic has been positively identified…"

"Jolly good show," Malcolm grinned. "I wish him the best of luck."

"Over the course of our enforced rest in the bushes, I caught a few more snippets of information," Chez continued. "The Boche still haven't a clue where the POWs are, so hopefully Florian got them all safely back to Semic. In addition, the SS are now totally focused on catching two men in the area around Ptuj: McClain, in what is left of his RAF uniform, and a traitorous German posing as an SS captain. That would be you and me, Malcolm," he added proudly.

The three men, their clothes now badly soiled, finally made it across the road and into the relative safety of the deep gully. Once there, they took the opportunity to bathe in the cold, sparkling water of the stream. Unfortunately, they had to put their dirty clothes back on before climbing to the top of the hill. Wet clothes would have been a catastrophic mistake, as the three men faced a freezing cold night on the mountain trails.

Fortunately, with Ladislav as their guide, the small band made much better time on the old hunting trails between the Drava and Sava river valleys. It was early September, and the tops of these hills were cold enough to carry snow. But they didn't dare risk traversing the slopes at a lower altitude even at night until they finally reached the valley that protected the village of Zrece, early the next morning.

Although Ladislav made a positive identification of the safe house, they still approached it tentatively, concerned about a small baker's truck parked outside the barn. This area of Slovenia had mined marble for hundreds of years and continued to do so at the nearby Cezlak Quarries. The safe house was set back from the road, on a level area that had been chiseled out of an ancient marble outcrop. By the look of the mature vegetation surrounding it, mining must have ceased many years ago and both house and barn used the vertical stone backdrop of the former quarry as part of their structure.

Ladislav approached alone for a further fifty meters before gesturing for the other two to join him. There should have been a yellow ribbon tied within proximity of the house but there was not. This caused further concern but, before the three had crept any further, they heard a low warning whistle from inside the dark recesses of the barn. Savo appeared in the door, motioning first for silence and then to follow him into the old structure.

Once safely out of sight, Savo whispered in English, repeating only the main points in Yugoslavian for Ladislav's benefit.

"I got one of my Ptuj group to plant Malcolm's tunic with the local police by having a young boy pretend he found it on a boat in the river. I'm not sure how long it will take for the SS to get the word."

"Don't worry, Savo, it worked like a charm. I imagine every SS and Gestapo thug within fifty kilometers is headed for Ptuj," Chez reassured him by relating the conversations he overheard at the roadblock.

"I actually entrusted planting the tunic to one of my men in Maribor. I learned from him that a certain Sturmbahnfuhrer von Keller was in charge of finding you and that he had taken several Partizani into the camp for interrogation. Normally, these tactics fail to extract any useful information, because we are careful to compartmentalize our cells for security, but this particular major was very interested in learning something for which I fault myself. I hadn't attached any significance to the safety color and codes for our operation, but it seems von Keller did."

"That bastard maimed a four-year-old girl, right in front of her father, just to learn about our safety codes…Her name is Biba and I actually attended her last birthday party. I'll live the rest of my life blaming myself for every tear she shed."

Chez's expression went as stony as the cold marble that surrounded them.

"Considering the counter attacks they're experiencing on the Russian and Italian fronts, it makes no sense to have such a high ranking Schutzstaffel officer here in Yugoslavia. *Unless* he's also the one who came from Berlin to pick up Malcolm. This arsehole has to be the same bastard who murdered Goran."

"Then I have two reasons to want to meet him in the worse possible way," Savo retorted fiercely. "I arrived here about two hours ago and was actually inside the farmhouse when a two-man motorcycle patrol drove up. I was hustled into the barn to hide but the soldiers didn't even knock on the door. Why…? Because they were alerted to stay clear if they came across a yellow ribbon, that's why! It told them this is a safe house ready to receive us, but that we hadn't yet arrived. Otherwise, it would have been removed."

"Suggesting that all the SS in Slovenia will be descending on this farmhouse within the hour," said

Chez but then reflected. "No. Wait a minute…Let's try and get into the mind of that murderous pig. This von Keller can't be certain that we intended to use this particular safe house but, it's probably the only yellow ribbon that has been found."

"We'd identified three possible escape routes, Spinne," Savo said. "Each route offered one safe house for tonight only. My men know which route we're following so the other safety markers have probably been taken down already."

"But the major won't *know* that, so put the yellow ribbon back" Chez insisted. "To him, this one's merely the first clue to come his way since Malcolm's tunic was discovered. If I were him, I'd send a squad to check this place out just in case, but keep his main force searching Ptuj, still his strongest lead by far. If the squad sees that the ribbon is still in place, they will think we never came this way!"

"So what is our plan now?" Ladislav muttered in frustration. "We could hide in the hills but that won't achieve getting Malcolm to safety. Meanwhile the noose is tightening, Chez."

"You're right, Ladi. We have to assume the Germans will have troops here within the hour, meaning we have to evacuate right now and head for Semic… Which raises another problem. As a precaution, I suspect they will also have set up a road block between here and Vojnik, that being the most likely route we would take."

Ladislav spoke rapidly to Savo while the others frowned, not understanding. Eventually Savo turned.

"Ladi believes he can take this bread truck and run towards Ljubljana before cutting south to Semic. It's about the same distance but on very bad roads. However, with luck he could be at our headquarters within two hours. As the owners, the Brodniks, can't risk staying here now, he'll take them with him to safety. If they're stopped, it is just a baker, his wife and son making a delivery. Assuming they do make it, Josip and Milo will send help."

"Let's do it," Savo decided, moving to knock on the door. An extremely nervous Baker Brodnik opened it and hustled the four men quickly inside.

The old man and his wife were shaking with fear but agreed the plan to take the truck and flee with Ladislav was much better than facing certain death. The baker trusted no one but Savo and demanded he have an immediate, urgent, private conversation with him. After they were finished, Savo returned to his friends grinning.

"Mr. Brodnik has entrusted me with an old family secret, which might buy us some time. Let us show you before they leave."

As Mrs. Brodnik and Ladislav clambered into the front of the bread truck, Mr. Brodnik and Savo led Chez and Malcolm back into the barn. A large vintage wine vat dominated the space against the rear, rough-hewed marble wall. Following Jan Brodnik's terse instructions, Savo slid the hinged, lower portion of the vat to one side, revealing a narrow stone passage into darkness.

"Behind this wall, there's a fault gap between two marble outcrops which transverses all the way through to the next valley. About two hundred years ago, the Brodnik ancestors roofed this gap with heavy timbers and time has subsequently filled in the void above with debris, soil and vegetation. It is virtually undetectable if you don't know about the two entrances.

"Our friend the baker apparently had relatives that used to make illegal liquor in this very barn. This was their emergency escape route!" Savo explained. "I plan on hitching a ride with Ladi. Jan will show me how to find the other side of this passage and then take me to Dravograd.

"We are forgoing trying to get to Semic. It's only twenty minutes to my base where I'll make sure the Brodniks are safe before Ladi and I return here with as many Partizani as I can roust up at this time of night. We'll save time and should be back here within ninety minutes."

Savo paused and ordered the others. "When the Germans come here, retreat through this passage. After we treat them to a little Partizani hospitality, we will search for you at one end or the other," he finished grimly.

Ladislav had already started the truck but got into the rear with Jan Brodnik so Savo could drive. Once loaded up, they turned left onto the main road and sped off up the valley. After five kilometers, they slowed almost to a stop to take a very sharp and treacherous turn west onto a barely visible and little used dirt road. Savo stopped the truck after only twenty meters and, for several minutes, used a branch to erase any tire tracks that might betray their diversion. This dirt road eventually led to Mislinja, after which they continued north on the main road to Dravograd.

Chez and Malcolm reentered the front door of the farmhouse unaware that only one of the motorcycle advance patrol had gone for reinforcements. Concealed behind trees across the road, the other corporal had been observing everything that had happened at the Brodnik house through his 6 x 30 Dienstglas. He had duly noted the futile attempt to fool the hunters by re-installing the yellow ribbon.

The SS noose was indeed closing fast on the two left behind.

CHAPTER NINETEEN

1943 – Revenge is Sweet

L eft alone with Malcolm in the Brodnik living room, Chez calmly summarized their predicament.

"The Germans will be here shortly, my friend. You must hide in the passage and wait for Savo and his men. They'll get you to Semic and freedom by tomorrow."

"Sounds like you're not coming with me," Malcolm said, frowning.

"If we both leave now, the Nazis will be suspicious of an empty house and might search and find the passage. There might not be enough time for Savo to get back here and rescue us. I'll keep them occupied here for a while before I…"

He broke off abruptly, swinging to squint into the blaze of headlights that suddenly flooded the interior of the house.

"…join you in the tunnel," Chez finished calmly.

"Shit! Time to scramble!" Malcolm said

They both headed upstairs to get a better view from the front bedroom.

"You sure you want to play the hero?" McClain said uneasily. But then, he'd never looked into the eyes of a close combat adversary. Flying Officer McClain had been used to killing his enemy from 20,000 feet.

The odds were not insurmountable as far as Chez was concerned. Outside, on the flat forecourt only two Krupp troop transporters had drawn up, joined by the two motorcyclists; a patrol of fourteen soldiers in all.

"Hardly a full magazine load," Chez judged coldly. He'd been up against worse odds, and '*The Spider*' had always managed to survive.

Then suddenly, the odds against them lengthened as another pair of headlights materialized behind the Krupps. One of the bikes revved up and turned back towards the new arrival, its headlight clearly illuminating a staff car with an SS major in the front passenger seat.

"Well, well, well," Chez mused softly. "It looks like our favorite Sturmbahnfuhrer has decided to follow this lead himself. That makes it personal for all of us… and in turn, leaves me rather looking forward to the next few minutes."

The soldier who had remained to observe the house was reporting to SS Major von Keller who remained seated, ramrod straight, in his Mercedes.

"Herr Major, two elderly people and two younger men headed up the valley in a small bread truck about twenty minutes ago. I judge that at least two other men remain inside the house."

Von Keller then stepped from the staff car with careful deliberation.

"Corporal, take the other motorcyclist and one troop carrier. Catch that damn bread truck! If it's headed up the valley, they must be climbing over the top of the mountain to Rogia and then back down into the Drava Valley and Maribor. They have a twenty-minute start but there's only one road. In the meantime, I'll radio for troops from Maribor to block that road at the river. They have no escape. *SCHNELL!*"

While the pursuers sped off up the valley, von Keller turned sharply to address the remainder of his patrol.

"Until I can determine whether our prime suspects have remained here or taken flight in the bread truck, we will stay to interrogate the two inside. I rather suspect that McClain will be trying to escape in the truck but he will find himself back here anyway."

"In your dreams, Sturmbahnfuhrer." Chez grinned. "The chances of them finding—let alone catching—Savo in those mountains are somewhere between slim and zero."

Then it was time to focus on the immaculate bastard in the polished black boots and jodhpurs as the major raised a megaphone and addressed the house. Simultaneously five Wehrmacht soldiers trained their headlights and machine pistols on the windows, a sixth manning the MG-42 light machine gun mounted on the troop carrier.

"I know there are at least two of you in the house. You have five minutes to surrender and step outside."

The surrounding facets of the old marble quarry gave von Keller's already amplified voice an added quality of menace. Malcolm thought back to the movies he'd watched at the Arcadian on Albert Street, goggle-eyed as a kid in Belfast. No money needed from those who had none; two jars of jam had been enough to get a front row seat. He smiled.

"Seems this is another fine mess you've got me into, Ollie," he said.

Chez looked blank: going to the cinema had never been part of his childhood prison camp experience but he thought, *Damn, this Irish guy has ice in his veins. I like that!*

Regardless, their survival time was shortening by the second.

Malcolm blinked as, without warning, his companion suddenly ripped a sheet from the Brodniks' bed then pulled up the casement and proceeded to hang the linen outside.

McClain was about to blink even harder when the Spider's shout in German took on a most uncharacteristic whine.

"I have Flying Officer McClain here. He's badly wounded and the occupants of the house were sent to get medical help. We surrender! Allow me a minute to get him downstairs…but please don't shoot."

Malcolm spoke no German but the meaning was easy to follow. "What the <u>hell</u>…?" McClain began to blurt before Chez whirled urgently.

"Shut up an' follow me to the Wine Vat in the barn."

Without waiting, Chez turned and led the way downstairs, navigating each flight in one effortless jump. On reaching the ground floor, he darted left into the kitchen where a rear door led directly into the barn. By the time Malcolm caught up with him, the young Pole was already holding open the Wine Vat's secret access to the passage. He gestured for Malcolm to enter. With the Irishman inside the void, Chez started to close the secret door from the outside.

"You go ahead, Malcolm. There is one small detail I need to take care of before I catch up."

Sturmbahnfuhrer Abelard Hans von Keller was exceedingly pleased with himself. Although he had not expected it to be this easy, he had the two bastards he'd wanted and could leave it to others to apprehend the Partizani bit-players in the bread truck.

There was no hurry, therefore he had time to savor

his coming rehabilitation in the eyes of his superiors. While the knowledge that McClain was virtually back in the bag with no harm done to his career, von Keller would also be able to exact retribution on that still-mysterious traitor to his Fuhrer's beloved Third Reich: the man with the Berliner accent who had almost pulled off the successful kidnapping of his prize.

Walking briskly back to his staff car, he could already feel the adrenaline coursing through his body. He vividly imagined himself placing his gleaming jackboot between the bastard's shoulder blades before shooting him in front of McClain.

Sliding into his car seat, von Keller reached into the glove compartment, retrieving a short, black ebony cigarette holder into which he carefully pushed a Balkan Black Sobranie. He'd never permitted himself to become an inveterate smoker—the Fuhrer would have disapproved—but there were occasions when one could justify a brief, discreet deviation from the SS model of perfection. He thumbed the flint of his silver, monogrammed lighter, drawing the rich, satisfying smoke deep into his lungs. He smiled a very cold smile and murmured out loud, "As you stagger through that door, you treasonous cretin, appreciate your last few moments on this earth..."

The major felt a slight pinprick, the irritation of a mosquito biting his neck. It was a curious sensation in itself. As he swatted it, a dark spray splattered the inside of the windshield in front of him. Puzzled, Hans von Keller slowly raised his warm, wet left hand until he could see the sticky glint of what could only be his own blood. While he was still frowning in confusion, a strong hand clamped across his sagging jaw and he heard a soft Berlin accent from the back seat,

"I am not a treasonous cretin, Herr Major, because I do not consider myself a German. I am Czeslaw Orlowski, a proud Pole and one of those resistance fighters you hold in such contempt. You might know me better as *'The Spider'*?"

As von Keller's carotid artery continued to pump out warm blood, his body involuntarily began to shut down. With a supreme effort, he compelled his brain to focus on analyzing the facts. Unmistakably, he had just heard this same voice from the upstairs window. He'd detected neither movement from the house nor the slightest sound since returning to his car. He hadn't even felt the blade slice his throat. He still felt little pain. It made no sense, and for the analytical mind of Sturmbahnfuhrer Abelard Hans von Keller, that came as a terrible revelation.

"Spider, Spinne …? But you're a myth. You don't exist outside the pipe dreams of your filthy Partisa …"

Nevertheless, before he slipped down to the eternal flames of Hell, Sturmbahnfuhrer Abelard Hans von Keller heard the voice softly utter the last earthly words he would ever hear.

"With fond remembrance of Goran…and Biba!"

Chez slid silently out of the car and dissolved into the shadows but his luck finally ran out as he returned to the barn and was swinging hand-over-hand between the roof trusses. Suddenly, a powerful flashlight snapped a fix on him. He had little option but to freeze.

"Come down now, whichever one you are, or you'll be shot," demanded Corporal Manfred Gimmstadt, one of three grey-uniformed Wehrmacht troopers in the barn.

But then, a most unexpected event occurred.

"I believe you may be looking for me as well?" Flying Officer Malcolm McClain called almost conversationally from behind them.

Without understanding his English, the three soldiers whirled in shock. Gimmstadt re-directed his torch towards the new challenge. Then, the confused corporal briefly re-shone his flashlight back into the rafters, which were now empty.

"Verdamnt!" he snarled, quickly returning his flashlight back to illuminate McClain while a second soldier trained his Schmeisser on the seemingly nonchalant British flyer. The third slung his machine pistol across his chest and motioned for McClain to step forward, hands above his head, to be searched.

Commendable standard practice, only Gimmstadt didn't realize he was dealing with a man from Belfast.

McClain's demeanor transformed into a whirl of action as he took one step forward to grab both lapels of the German's uniform. In a crisp motion, he pulled the soldier towards him, simultaneously smashing his forehead into the bridge of the trooper's nose. A brutally unsophisticated but extremely effective tactic known colloquially as giving *'a stitch'* by those fighting for survival around the Falls Road.

Allowing his victim's semi-conscious body to slump to the floor, Malcolm swung on the second soldier and in a continuous, flowing movement, launched his right foot straight into the man's crotch. With this foot still airborne and the unfortunate soldier already doubling in agony, Malcolm completed the scissor kick with a round-house left foot to the soldier's right temple.

When kicking a leather ball, a professional football player's boot can travel at over 75 miles per hour, and McClain had perhaps the most lethal left foot in the game. The second guard was brain-dead before his body hit the floor. Two down in as many seconds, McClain was already pivoting to dispatch the last captor when he suddenly stopped in his tracks.

Before his eyes, the beam of light that had started the debacle, began to rise steadily towards the rafters. Then the torch dropped with a clatter to the accompaniment of a strangled gasp.

McClain could just make out Corporal Manfred

Gimmstadt's knees hovering in front of him, shortly to be replaced by frantically kicking jackboots as Gimmstadt continued to swing higher. Malcolm recovered the lamp to observe the elevated soldier dangling helplessly, his neck pinioned in the vice-like grip of the Spider's thighs. Hanging effortlessly from the rafters, Chez rotated his hips savagely, first to the left and then right. There came a snap and Corporal Manfred Gimmstadt's corpse joined his inert comrades on the floor of the barn.

"Well done, Chez," Malcolm announced almost matter-of-factly as the Spider landed like a cat in front of him. The young Pole's respect for his foreign charge had tripled in the last few seconds.

"Now for the rest of those bastards!" McClain said.

"Enough, Malcolm. Remember, my prime mission is to get you safely out of here. Though, I'm starting to think you are looking after me!"

Just as they were ready to close the secret passage door, they heard urgent shouting from the courtyard.

"Hold on here for now, Malcolm," Chez grinned as he caught the gist of the guttural conversation. "If they've found what I suspect they've found, then we might not need to negotiate that long damp passage."

It seemed the three Wehrmacht soldiers remaining outside in the yard with von Keller's increasingly nervous SS driver, had become restless while awaiting Chez's promised surrender.

Even more unsettlingly, Corporal Gimmstadt's party who had entered the barn to prevent any back door escape had not reappeared. Nor had they heard the reassuring sound of shots from within. Direction was needed…but where the hell was Major von Keller when the arrogant bastard was needed?

They soon found out. The panicked shouting Malcolm and Chez had heard provided evidence enough. To compound their disarray, the soldiers then ran back to the barn to locate the missing men and tripped over three bodies, only one of which retained any signs of life.

The decimated squad's leader, a grizzled veteran of the Russian front, stared at the seemingly vacant farmhouse and made a battlefield decision.

"Load the bodies into the Krupp, leave the staff car for now, and we'll return to Maribor for orders!"

Only while they were carrying the dead major to the troop carrier, did one of them see the salutation pinned to Sturmbahnfuhrer von Keller's chest by the Thiers Issard cut-throat razor Chez had commandeered from the Brodniks' bathroom.

The square of paper showed the infamously feared caricature of a spider. Beneath the eight legs was a terse message in German.

"To the Führer. With the compliments of The Spinne!"

CHAPTER TWENTY

1943 – Back to Semic

C hez and Malcolm only left the refuge of the stone passage when they were certain the last of their enemies were long gone. Still wary of a trap, the two men slipped cautiously from the barn into the dark, deserted courtyard.

There was no moon but thousands of stars filled the vast expanse of clear black sky, framed by the high night cumulous. They both shivered. At this elevation, the temperature had dropped significantly and the edge of the forest across the road sealed them within a darkominous arena.

Malcolm McClain looked up into the sky almost wistfully; he had become accustomed to seeing it through the cockpit window of a Wellington bomber. It was an odd feeling, being so exposed out there and although they knew that the danger had receded, each sensed an indefinable presence.

Chez proved to be first to shake himself free of the paranoia. "You did okay for an old man," he shrugged, barely concealing his grin. "I must remember not to mess with anyone from Belfast."

"Very wise, Chez," Malcolm retorted. "One of the great lessons my dad, Billy, taught me was: *'There's always somebody tougher, better and faster than you out there.'* And, if you think Belfast lads are hard, you definitely don't want to mess with anyone from Glasgow!"

"I'll remember that, my friend. Let's try and clean up the Major's car so we can ride in style back to Semic."

There was blood—a lot of blood—soiling the front well of the Staff Mercedes. While they were both cleaning the car with hot soapy water from the farmhouse kitchen, Chez's sixth sense again picked up danger again. Frowning, he gestured for McClain to act normally while he surreptitiously slid the late major's 9mm Mauser within easy reach.

Then he smiled.

A low, familiar owl hoot heralded the sight of Savo, carrying a British Sten gun, materializing through the edge of the forecourt. He skirted the two fugitives cautiously, looking for the slightest indication of a warning signal: a frown, wink, a raised eyebrow. What the hell were they doing cleaning a car when he was expecting a fight with a German patrol?

Only when they'd made it apparent by their smiles that the danger had passed did he approach. A brief hug for each comrade and Savo turned to raise his right arm, making a circular motion above his head.

At this signal, some fifty heavily-armed Partizani led by Ladislav appeared from the surrounding forest, like an army of silent ghosts. Savo turned back to Chez and Malcolm and remarked casually, "Call it overkill if you like, but we just ambushed eight Wehrmacht who were driving here from Rogia. We've hidden their two motorcycles and a Krupp further up the valley. Apart from that, all the fun seems to have taken place right here. What the hell have you guys been up to since we've been gone?"

"Tell you on the way back to Semic," Chez shrugged while passing von Keller's box of Black Sobranie around as a token gesture of appreciation for their intervention. "What *would* be a good idea, though—Do any of your men have a Yugoslavian flag we can borrow for this fine Partizani Mercedes we have commandeered?"

Meanwhile, Malcolm had been studying the grim faces of the guerillas. "Those four soldiers we scared back to Maribor are the luckiest bastards this side of Africa," he whispered to Chez. "These Slovenians would've chopped them into pieces, then fried 'em for

supper! I've never seen a scarier group of hard men…
and that goes for the worst in Belfast or Glasgow."

"They're not just hard, they're also charged with
hate, Malcolm," Chez retorted bitterly. "Those men
have all lost family members over the past few years,
thanks to the Nazis. Now they have only revenge to
live for: They would have jumped at the chance Savo
offered them to unleash their fury on our mutually
detested major. It's the message von Keller and his
sub-human ilk are just beginning to take onboard,
loud and clear…*'As ye shall sow, so shall ye reap'*."

As monitored by Savo's Partizani, courtesy of the
radio left undamaged in the recently acquired troop
carrier, German signals traffic between Maribor
and Ljubljana focused almost entirely on what had
happened to Sturmbahnfuhrer von Keller. A prompt
Staff decision was made to consolidate all patrols
behind barrack lines for the night.

So the trip from Zrece to Semic was undertaken
in almost surreal conditions. Savo had instructed
Ladislav and a dozen of his Partizani to use the Krupp
and motorcycles as an escort for the Mercedes, a move
that made the erstwhile caravan appear uncomfortably
German. Except perhaps for the loud singing and a
hastily fashioned Yugoslavian flag.

Before they parted, Savo shook hands, briefly hugging Chez, Malcolm and Ladi, before leaving to spirit his remaining band of fighters back to Dravograd.

"Spinne, Ladi, get this crazy Irishman safely back to Britain, then meet me at the Café Antico in Ljubljana. The beers are on me."

After a couple of hours into the drive, the convoy encountered a seemingly impassable boulder right in the middle of the road. The singing stopped abruptly; the clatter of weapons being cocked took over.

"Easy," Ladi warned. "Take it easy …"

This proved a good call when, within seconds, a voice with a heavy Slovenian accent called out from the surrounding darkness.

"Gentlemen, ease your triggers and raise your hands if you want to live. You are completely surrounded by over a hundred Partizani."

"Do as he says," Ladislav snapped tightly.

The voice continued ominously. "First, explain why you are led by a German Staff car that is flying our national flag?"

Ever so carefully, Ladi eased onto the road and walked forward, halting by the large boulder still illuminated by the headlights of the staff car. He was acutely aware that if this was a German trap, he would be the first to die in the ensuing hail of bullets.

"In this darkness, I cannot tell if you are Germans or Yugoslavs but I am just a humble chauffer named Ladislav," he responded in Yugoslavian that precisely matched the dialect of the hidden accuser.

"You claim to be Ladislav?" the voice from the darkness retorted. "Tell me a little about Josip's brother."

"I wouldn't mess with that SOB, even though he favors his left leg. Is that you, Josko?" Ladislav responded, beginning to smile. This marked the moment when the voice became a man who stepped forward to embrace him in the illumination of the headlights.

"Welcome back to the Free Democratic Republic of Yugoslavia, Ladi," he announced, as several others emerged to slide the 'seemingly impassable boulder' to the side of the road with remarkable ease. Malcolm, left alone in the rear seat of the Mercedes, noticed that the large boulder had rested on tree branches that acted as rollers.

At the first signs of the ambush, Chez, armed with his knife, had disappeared from the car. Now, he walked silently into the circle of light from behind Josko and frowned quizzically at those moving the rock.

"One *hundred* Partizani?" he queried dubiously. "I only counted eighteen."

Josko's eyes went wide and he shook his head in

amazement. "We thought you were the Boche," he responded. "It is okay to tell lies to the Boche."

The escorts peeled off to return to Dravograd and the Mercedes continued its journey south through Partizani territory.

The heroes clearly had been long expected, for when they finally rolled up to the church the next morning, Milo and Josip were waiting on the steps. For the last couple of hundred meters, cheering POWs and Yugoslavs—men, women and children—lined the road on both sides.

Josip invited Chez, McClain and Ladi inside for breakfast. There he was able to fill them in on the latest news.

"Chez, my friend, to say you have over-achieved the mission we imported you for, might well prove the greatest understatement I'll ever make." But then his expression became grave as he laid his hands on the Spider's broad shoulders.

"However, it is my sad duty to pass along some very bad news. Last week, during a daring raid by the Bracia on the Nazi headquarters in Krakow, your friend Jan Kowalski was killed. He insisted on fighting a solo rear guard action in order to allow his men to escape. I'm afraid it cost him his life. Please accept my assurance that all your Yugoslavian brothers feel for your great personal loss."

Chez was still shaking his head in disbelief, unable to help reflecting that perhaps he could have saved Jan had he stayed in Poland, when Tito returned to addressing his men.

"Barely eight months ago, the Third Reich controlled an area of the world almost twice the size of the United States. Now our Allies are poised to take it back. Accordingly, they have prioritized the liberation of our beloved Yugoslavia, in order to provide the Balkan Air Force with secure forward air bases from which to harry the retreating Nazi forces."

Josip Tito paused then, aware that he was taking a risk by revealing top-secret information, but equally sure he could trust every man in the assembly.

"In absolute confidence, gentlemen, I will be leaving Semic next week for Jaice on a crucial mission. Within two months—assuming I'm still alive—I shall be appointed president of the Yugoslavian National Committee of Liberation. At that time, Milo will take over from me in Semic, as military commander of the Partizani. His orders will be to take Ljubljana."

Normally undemonstrative men, on this occasion, everyone in the room stood and cheered.

When the raucous shouting died down, Chez, who still struggled to cope with the news of Jan's death took the opportunity to address the men.

"Josip, Milo…each and every Partizani gathered here. I couldn't be more proud of the small role I played in rescuing Malcolm McClain from Maribor and I can only apologize for some of the dumb remarks I made before we left on the mission."

He turned to smile at Malcolm and despite his RAF friend's obvious discomfiture, added. "Although I had no idea of how famous this man is as a footballer, I've now seen him in action. I now fully appreciate why every kid in Britain adores him because by God, I do too."

Seizing Malcolm in a bear-like embrace, Chez hugged the embarrassed Ulsterman for a full 10 seconds before continuing, "However, unlike his, my fight is not even close to being over. I must return immediately to Poland and assume leadership of the Bracia. The memory of Jan Kowalski deserves that much."

"We anticipated nothing less from *'The Spider,'*" Tito responded.

He hesitated then, eyeing Chez speculatively.

"But before you decide to take overall command of the Armia Krajowa, I would ask you to consider engaging in a little…ah, diversion before you return to Warsaw."

"A diversion?"

"The Balkan Air Force has been charged with carrying out a crucial mission in Poland. In brief, it will call for the incursion of a specially trained team into a classified area of the Carpathian Mountains. Precisely what that mission entails will be explained later but I can assure you, Spinne, if successful, it will deliver a hammer blow to any Boche hopes of holding their ground in the face of the Allied push.

"Should you choose to accept the mission, several of our courageous Partizani have volunteered to visit Poland with you, in an attempt to repay, at least in part, the great service you have performed for us."

Chez hesitated. The temptation to have another major confrontation with his hated enemy was extremely appealing. Meanwhile, Malcolm was whispering urgently to Ladislav who, in turn, translated it for Tito's benefit.

"Malcolm McClain tells me, that if Spinne accepts this latest challenge, then he too, wishes to accompany him to Poland to fight on this mission with the Bracia."

The room exploded with cheers but Josip stood up and raised both arms to beg for calm.

"Ladi, although his gesture is much appreciated, please remind Flying Officer McClain not to lose sight of the big picture and the reason we went to such lengths to free him from Stalag 306. His repatriation to Britain will, in itself, deliver a massive body blow to the Third Reich's propaganda machine."

Josip then walked over to place a firm hand on Chez's shoulder.

"And as for you and I, the problems for our two

countries will not end with the defeat of Germany. Both Poland and Yugoslavia are about to find themselves in bed with the Devil. I fear greatly that the payback for the military support we're currently receiving from the Soviet Union will cost us more in future suffering than the Germans could ever inflict."

The door to the room opened and Milo limped in. Going straight to his brother, he whispered in Josip's ear, then handed him a telegram. Josip read it carefully, almost impassively, and then cleared his throat.

"This was received five minutes ago," he announced. "It has just been announced, that General Alexander's 15th Army Group landed on the south coast of Italy this morning. Mussolini has capitulated and his troops have laid down their arms. Both British and American forces are sweeping up 'The Boot' with only a demoralized German Army left to resist them."

A pregnant silence followed; a silence from men who, for the first time in five years, could now dare to believe that their children might grow up in a peaceful Yugoslavia.

Early the next morning, a distant drone announced the now-eagerly expected arrival in Semic of two Bristol Bombay troop transporters from the new BAF base at Bari.

In addition to their crews, ten elite troopers from the British Special Air Service jumped down onto the airfield grass. The officer in charge formally saluted Milo Tito.

"Major 'Paddy' McBride, sir," he announced in what the Partizani had now come to recognize as a Northern Ireland accent. "Brigadier Bryan Zumwalt sends his best regards, and requests that the POWs, including Flying Officer Malcolm McClain, be flown back to Bari for physical examination in Bari Army Hospital. They will then be repatriated for well-earned rest and recuperation.

"My men are instructed to stay here to train the Partizani and Mr. Chez Orlowski, should they choose to fly to Poland after I outline the parameters of a special mission. We would like to employ his very distinct talents to accomplish this mission."

"Kind of you, Major," replied Milo, noting that Major McBride was one of the largest men he'd ever seen. "However, I assure you, my Partizani already number amongst the best guerilla fighters in the world. They don't need any training from your SAS."

"Fully understood, sir," McBride responded smoothly. "But these planes also contain parachutes— useful when you jump from two thousand feet—as well as the latest Allied weaponry and explosives. My chaps will merely instruct yours in their use. As an aside, my lads do have their own mission to accomplish. That's why we brought the extra aircraft."

He hesitated, eyeing Milo speculatively. "I understand you have been made aware of the invasion of Italy? Well, consequently, the Allied Command now fears reprisals on POWs all over Europe as the rats leave their sinking ship. Those prisoners still held in Maribor's Stalag 306 are particularly vulnerable, thanks to the bruising the Nazi propaganda machine suffered as a result of your raid. In a nutshell, sir, my boys are primarily here to free the rest of them.

"We've made radio contact with the camp's senior officer, Wing Commander Fagan, who reports the timing could be perfect. Apparently, leadership at the camp is in disarray. It seems its kommandant, Afonso Kappel, is considered hopelessly inadequate, even by his own army's standards. Once we liberate the rest of our men, we will focus on the mission to night-drop Mr. Orlowski and his friends into Poland. In the meantime, should they feel a nostalgic hankering to revisit Maribor—strictly on a training mission with us—they will be more than welcome. No offense taken if they prefer to stay here and prepare for the Carpathians."

Milo turned mischievously and indicated one of two men standing behind him. "You might care to ask him yourself, Major. Let me introduce Chez Orlowski, otherwise known as the Spider."

The giant SAS officer shook Chez's hand respectfully and cracked a quizzical smile as he looked down at the surprisingly youthful legend.

"So you're the mythical Spider, yeah? According to what I've heard, you're supposed to be seven feet tall."

"Only in the minds of little children." Chez smiled back.

As the SAS officer turned to the figure standing beside Chez, he beamed a giant grin and wrapped his arms around the RAF man in an enormous bear hug. Not at all the kind of gesture his perplexed Yugoslav audience expected and certainly not one in keeping with traditional British reserve.

"Malky! Holy shit, is it yersel'! The last time I saw you, you'd scored twice for Blackpool against Everton at Goodison Park!" Then, he held McClain at arms' length and studied him closely. "But, the first time I ever set eyes on you, I was trying to catch your arse in the hundred yard final of the Belfast Sprint Championships. When was that—Nineteen twenty six?"

"I was a hair bigger than you then, Paddy—but you still offered to smash my face in if I didn't let you win," Malcolm laughed. "Ever since that day, I've been grateful you turned your talents towards Rugby rather than football."

He turned to explain. "My old friend, Paddy here, is from Ballymena, a small town north west of Belfast. We have known each other forever. I was lucky enough to earn a little fame and fortune playing football in England, sure, but if you ask anyone in Northern Ireland who their favorite athlete is, the answer will be Paddy McBride; world class rugby player and heavy-weight boxing champion."

"All inspired by you, Malcolm," the chiseled soldier, who was taller and broader than any other man in the group, responded modestly. "Brigadier Zumwalt thought it a good idea for me to 'volunteer' for this part of the mission because I know you personally—just in case the Nazis were trying to fob us off with a fake McClain."

"Wonderful to see you, Paddy. I hear you've been racking up quite a tally of medals. In fact, I know you well enough to suspect, the real reason you came to Yugoslavia was not to identify me but to knock a few more Teutonic heads together," Malcolm joked as he nodded at the rest of the SAS squad. "Mind you, there's only twenty or thirty guards left at the camp, and most of them Volksturm. I can't believe you had to bring back-up."

"My boys are just along to watch; maybe learn something," Paddy bantered back. "But, back to business. D'ya reckon Mr. Orlowski here's up for a little more adventure?"

"Paddy, let me assure you, hand on heart. The Spider is every inch of seven feet tall. You will be amazed at what this guy can do."

It was agreed that an inaugural International Football Match be played between Yugoslavia and 'The Rest of the World' while the planes were being unloaded. The grass airstrip would serve as a perfect pitch with four wooden chairs to improvise as goal posts.

The home crowd cheered enthusiastically for the eleven Partizani chosen to represent their country. However, with the Rest of the World composed of extraordinarily fit, elite Special Forces lead by the formidable Paddy McBride plus having a spider in goal, they won the match handily by eight goals to one. That Malcolm McClain scored seven of those goals might also have been a contributing factor.

"I guess that proves you're no fake Malcolm McClain," Paddy beamed as the game ended. "And so goes my first excuse for getting Zumwalt to send me. Ah well, I wouldn't have missed the opportunity to play on the same team as you, mate. Not for all the tea in China!"

Finally, it came time to depart. The POWs who had been spirited out of St. Lorenzen dispersed onto the two planes, with McClain the last to board. Chez, Ladislav, Paddy and Milo walked him to the ladder.

"If you get into trouble, Chez, I'll send a couple of lads from Belfast to bail your skinny ass out," Malcolm said. "Thanks for everything, my friend. I'll always love you like a brother. Go find your girl and give her a kiss for me"

"Love you too, old man," Chez said. "See you in Belfast after the war and you can buy me a...what do you call it...a pint of Guinness? Go find your girl too."

The Bristol lumbered down the runway and took off beneath a squadron of Hawker Hurricanes that mysteriously appeared from nowhere to ensure safe passage back to Bari.

With a heavy heart, Chez watched them disappear into the southern sky.

"We'll meet again, Malcolm McClain," he whispered to himself. *"We've been through a lot together: I'm going to survive this bloody war and afterwards—I'll find you."*

CHAPTER TWENTY-ONE

1943 – Return to Poland

Early the next morning the SAS Special Raiding Squadron began training Chez and the fourteen Partizani who had volunteered to fight with him in Poland. Major Paddy McBride had nicknamed them, Spider Force and the term was adopted.

On a stretch of dirt behind the houses, Major McBride wore combat fatigue pants tucked into his boots and a khaki tee-shirt that only emphasized the impression he had muscles on top of muscles. Paddy, of course, was aware of the effect as he stood in the center of the ring of determined-looking men. In fact, he deliberately crossed his arms as he studied each one of them in turn.

The tension was broken by laughter when someone in the circle said in Yugoslavian, "They look like bloody tree trunks!"

"The easiest and fastest way for me to assess your fitness and physical combat capabilities will be for you to divide into groups of three and four men," Paddy announced. "Each group in turn, will attack me simultaneously from whatever direction you choose. I will try not to hurt you." There was no humor in his voice to leave anyone in doubt of his resolve. "By the way, no knives or weapons of any kind."

This raised a groan of mock protest from the rest of the Brits.

"That's not fair, Paddy. Even the odds and at least let them use knives?" Staff Sergeant Mike Johnston called out, straight-faced.

"Mike," Paddy ordered. "You're not here to play silly buggers, just to help me assess the combat readiness of Spider Force. Are you ready?"

The first group of four included Chez. They circled the mammoth British major, making tentative darts aimed at revealing his potential defensive weakness. In a sudden blur of action, dust flying everywhere, all the 'attackers' found themselves sitting in a circle, clutching their bellies and gasping for breath. Paddy had struck like a cobra, hitting each opponent with a precise, second knuckle blow to the solar plexus. Chez definitely remembered having sent a solid punch to Paddy's own gut mainly because his wrist still hurt.

"Either I've lost my edge, or the man's made of friggin' steel!" he gloomed to himself.

"How long, Mike?" Paddy asked his staff sergeant.

"Twenty three seconds, Paddy," Johnston replied before adding, "You're getting slow, old man."

McBride just scowled. "Next group!" he snapped.

And so it continued. Each group had four chances, by the end of which they were all visibly exhausted. On the other hand, Major McBride looked as fresh as when the exercise had started. Even the slightest sign of sweat on his bulging khaki tee-shirt might have offered some encouragement—but there was none.

"That'll do it," he finally announced. "I'm very happy with what I have seen. All of you men are in excellent physical shape."

Still, Milo's *best guerrilla fighters in the world* realized they had a lot to learn.

For the rest of the day, the focus of training switched to the skills necessary for parachuting at extremely low altitude coupled with how to handle the new RDX explosives and operate the latest Lanchester sub-machine guns.

It was towards the end of the day that Paddy sequestered Chez for their private meeting. They went over details of the mission suggested by Brigadier Zumwalt. Both surprised and intrigued, the

Pole asked Paddy several searching questions before agreeing to participate without further hesitation.

"Then one last warning, for your own safety," McBride cautioned grimly. "It's paramount to the success of this mission that you keep the details completely hush-hush. Allied Intelligence has strong reason to suspect the Nazis have infiltrated many bands of the Polish resistance. Thousands of lives may be saved if you succeed; thousands may be lost if you fail. Trust no one 'til you're certain of the loyalty of each cell you encounter. And watch your back.

"For what it's worth, Spider, if anyone does decide to fuck with you, I *will* take it personally. I am startin' to like you, wee man and, Malcolm was right, you're much tougher than you look."

The Spider spent his next two days studying the landing zone. He managed to make coded contact with the local battalion of the Armia Krajowa through his old friend Vedran Bozic and learned Vedron had assumed the late Jan Kowalski's role as leader of the Bracia in Krakow until Chez's return.

The initially disparate group continued to develop stronger bonds of friendship and trust. They slept, ate and played cards as a tight-knit gang, waiting for the long range weather forecasts to become predictable enough to risk making the long flight to south-eastern Poland.

During this time, Chez confirmed to Paddy that Spider Force would indeed like to tag along as part of the main SAS mission to repatriate the remaining POWs from Stalag 306 in Maribor.

"After all, Paddy, I have been there fairly recently and might be able to prevent your lads from getting lost!"

"Glad to have you along, wee man," the giant Ulsterman retorted, unfazed by the good-natured jibe. "But then, I never anticipated you wouldn't. You and your hoodlums are already figured into my operational plan." Then his face relaxed into a smile. "Seriously, Spider Force is now as good a fighting unit as I've ever seen."

Chez watched the square-jawed Brit saunter off to bellow at his pressured colleagues and couldn't help but marvel at this machine of a man. He never tired, yet never seemed to sleep. Anyone who had come up against the major during training commented that his muscle mass felt as if it had been cast from metal.

It was only after he saw McBride changing a dirt-soiled shirt that Chez noted several vicious knife scars and two bullet wounds on the otherwise perfect, rippled torso.

"Well, son-of-a-bitch. You are made of flesh and blood after all. Just like the rest of us—to a point."

At dawn the following day, the group of twenty-five drove directly to the outskirts of Maribor in three trucks. En route, they maintained constant radio contact with the local Partizani, to determine whether there was enemy activity ahead of them. Somewhat surprisingly, there was none. Suspicious that they were walking into an ambush, Paddy demanded extreme caution be taken during the group's final approach to the camp.

Even more discomforting was the sight of the camp's main gate standing wide open with not a Wehrmacht guard in sight. Major McBride wasn't the only one feeling uneasy.

"Paddy," Mike Johnston whispered. "Why do I feel like a mouse looking at a piece of cheese?"

They abandoned the trucks in the center of the road, melting into shadows cast by the trees framing the entrance gates of Stalag 306. McBride gave silent hand signals that instructed the SAS and Spider Force to adopt the attack formation for which they had so assiduously trained.

But then, as Alice in Wonderland said, things got *'curiouser and curiouser.'*

For within the boundaries of the camp, British, Australian and American Officers appeared to be loafing around the parade ground area; some kicking a football, some playing cards. Through his sniper scope, Paddy scanned this scene of military idleness in disbelief for five full minutes, relieved he'd just sent Chez to reconnoiter the perimeter fence and perhaps get a better vantage point.

Then, the imperturbable major did a double-take. "What the hell…"

His scope picked up the unmistakable figure of Chez Orlowski on top of a guard tower at the far end of the compound, thumbs raised in the 'all clear' signal, a triumphant grin on his face.

"That young Pole is totally insane, though he does have balls of steel," McBride grunted. "How the hell did he get over there so damn fast?" Then he chuckled. "Oh, I forgot—he's the Spider!"

Turning his attention back to the POWs, he cupped his hands and shouted.

"Attention all Allied officers! This is Major Patrick McBride of His Majesty's Special Raiding Squadron. Wing Commander Fagan…? Please identify yourself and confirm by giving me your middle name."

There was a hum of incredulity from the POWs and all attention switched to the center of the parade ground, where a card game had gathered quite an audience. Without letting his eyes leave his cards, a rotund man with a magnificent set of whiskers called back loudly.

"That would be me and the answer is Wallace. Be right there, old boy—in just a tick."

A few seconds later, the senior British officer sprang up, threw his cards face up onto the makeshift table and yelled excitedly, "Gin!"

Paddy just shook his head, flicked on the safety of his 9mm Sten, and led a chevron of five SAS men from the obscurity of the trees into the camp. As incredible as it was, the Germans had apparently abandoned the place.

"Talk about leaving the insane to run the asylum," Paddy mused.

It took six hours to ferry the men in shifts from the abandoned camp back to Semic. During this entire jovial exodus, the SAS conducted a systematic check of Stalag 306's buildings, cataloguing files, maps—anything that might be remotely interesting to Allied Intelligence. When the trucks returned for the last time, the rescuers piled themselves and their treasure trove aboard and rolled out through the gates of the now-deserted camp.

Suddenly Chez remembered something very important and called out.

"Wait a minute! Stop! Paddy, when I played SS bully-boy during my brief meeting with Commandant Kappel, his clerk had the door to a floor safe open. Did anybody find it?"

Immediately, Paddy jumped from the truck and, motioning Chez to follow, went straight back to the commandant's office. Chez heaved aside the corporal's desk and sure enough, hidden under the carpet they found a large, steel safe bolted through the framed floor.

"Bingo! Step outside please, Chez," Paddy ordered quietly.

Reaching into his pack, he pulled out some C-2 explosives and a timing fuse. The grey plastique gave off the faint smell of almonds and resembled modeling clay. He rolled it into a long snaky tube, pressing it down onto the wooden floor about six inches away from the body of the safe. Thirty seconds later, he calmly sauntered from the office, motioning for Chez to join him. The two men's pace remained steady and the C-2 exploded less than five seconds after they turned behind the protection of the truck.

"Mike," he called to his staff sergeant. "Take a couple of men and retrieve a large black safe from the rubble in the crawl space under the building. Add it to our trophies for Brigadier Zumwalt." Then he added a casual afterthought, "Better get a move on, the rest of the C-2 blows in thirteen an' a half minutes."

They bolted the gates of the camp behind them as they departed, primarily to prevent any Maribor residents scavenging the buildings before the fireworks display started. At Major McBride's command, the convoy halted about a mile from the camp. He consulted his watch; held his hand up for a few seconds then slapped it down hard on his knee.

"Haul' onto yer knickers!"

A full three seconds followed that somewhat unorthodox military command before a merging series of explosions and a resultant plume of light brown smoke elicited a perceptible if distant cheer from the direction of Maribor.

"Make a note, Mike," the meticulous major complained irritably. "These timing fuses are runnin' 'bout three seconds late."

When everyone was safely quartered back in Semic, Wing Commander William Wallace Fagan sat down with his rescuers for a debrief.

"After the complete debacle of the work detail escape from St. Lorenzen, most of the Nazis' initial efforts were directed towards re-capturing our former jail-mate, Malcolm McClain."

At this point, another RAF officer interrupted. "G-squared, ask if there's any news about McClain. Love to know if he made it; damn poor show if he didn't. Rather a fine football player, don't you know."

"Malcolm's safely on his way back to Britain," Chez assured him. "But who or what the hell is G-squared?"

"G-squared? Just my nickname, old boy." Fagan's

splendid moustache curved up into a broad smile. "The G's stands for gin, my favorite tipple and gin rummy, my favorite card game. Anyway, let's press on. When the SS returned with von Keller's corpse instead of McClain, the guards' morale, already at rock bottom, plummeted even further. Within the hour, Fonzy Kappel—a supreme arsehole if you ask me—took his Luger and blew his brains out all over his damn office. Rather a surprising mess for someone who I seriously doubted had any brains." Fagan chortled at his own joke and his men sucked up with, "Ah yes. Nice one, sir!" before he continued.

"Knew he was finished; the SS was going to haul his arse back to Berlin for allowing McClain to escape. Of course, as soon as he did the dirty deed, the remaining Wehrmacht beetled out of camp in any vehicle they could find, most of them wearing civvies I might add."

The hirsute Wing commander appraised his liberators and then added a sincere afterthought. "Wonderful to hear the good news about McClain. We never figured out what the chap had done to deserve solitary. The betting was, he must have scored a couple against Stuttgart before the war and pissed them off!

"Anyway, on behalf of the chaps, I owe you all a tremendous debt of gratitude for coming to get us when you did."

"In my life, I've been grateful several times for the

cover of a friendly spitfire. Let's call it even. I'm sorry we couldn't get you out sooner," McBride responded modestly.

"Oh, we knew you were coming, Major," the irrepressible Fagan confirmed. "Didn't really start to panic until we were down Kappel's last case of port."

Over the next two days, the Balkan Air Force transported Billy Fagan's POWs to the port of Taranto, Italy where a Royal Naval destroyer was waiting to initiate the last leg of their repatriation. While the SAS soldiers boarded the last plane, Chez walked Paddy to the grass airstrip, not without a pang of emptiness.

"I must confess, Paddy, I've only met two men from Northern Ireland and, considering it's such a small country, they're both impressive as Hell! Is there something in the water over there?"

Paddy just shrugged and replied with a typical Ulster idiom.

"Ah well; there y'are now."

Then he vaulted up into the cargo bay of the plane and was gone.

Forty-eight hours later, a radio message from the fledgling Balkan Air Force base in Bari advised that a week of moonless nights with little or no wind was forecast for the Krakow area of Poland. That same evening, a brand-new Dakota III aircraft bearing the double blue roundels of the BAF, touched down on the grass strip at Semic. It carried all the necessary supplies for a late night departure on a dangerous mission.

After loading, it took off into a moderate easterly breeze. On board were the fifteen members of Spider Force plus four equipment canisters.

The Dakota III was the RAF's designation for the highly successful Douglas DC-3 so, compared to earlier troop transporters, the mission was commencing in relative luxury. They flew at 10,000 feet for fifty miles in an easterly direction towards Zagreb, before climbing to 14,000 feet for the next 520 miles to Kosice, a landmark town on the River Hornad in Western Slovakia. Once Kosice had been identified, they changed course onto a north-westerly heading for the final ninety miles over the mountains.

An English public-school voice, with the slightest trace of a South African accent, crackled throughout the aircraft audio.

"Spider Force, Spider Force. This is Baker Able Foxtrot, 352 Squadron—Flight Lieutenant Alastair

Collins, at your service. Brigadier Zumwalt sends his best regards in the form of my squadron of Hawker Hurricanes. You cannot see us but we will be above, below and astern of you until the High Tatras—*Over*."

"Thank you, Baker Able Foxtrot. We appreciate the insurance—*Over*." The Dakota's pilot responded.

Collins' voice clicked back through the intercom,

"Least we can do after you rescued our chaps. Good luck, Spider Force—*Over and out*."

Chez and his men huddled under blankets in the belly of the plane for what seemed an eternity, the combination of altitude and cold mountain air threatening to sap their initial vitality.

Eventually, the co-pilot left his right hand seat and came aft to check their chutes, readying the static line on which to clip the breakaway portion of each pack. As they crossed the border with Poland, passing over Rysy at the crest of the High Tatras, Captain Gary Trotter switched off all navigation lights and descended to 10,000 feet. The navigator, F.O. Bob Olsen was concentrating hard on identifying the villages of Krauszow to starboard and Dlugopole to port, hopefully helped by the glint from the Bialy River. The plane descended again, altering course to head due north on final approach.

"This is it," Chez thought as he peered at the grim faces lined in readiness down the fuselage. The drop signal would be given as they neared a triangular copse of trees south of the river. Previous reconnaissance had indicated flat farm country surrounded both villages, with a distinctive lake between the road and the river.

These trees represented their rendezvous point with the local Tatra Confederation, a battalion of the Armia Krajowa (AK). Commanded by Aleksy Krol, a resistance leader about whom Chez knew nothing. This group was charged with securing the landing area and helping Spider Force to make the next leg to Krakow.

McBride had specifically cautioned Chez, "On no account give Krol any hint of your final objective. His group does not need-to-know; they are just a stepping stone in the chain."

And then it was party time and there was no going back.

Trotter steadied his plane at 2,500 feet while the co-pilot yanked open the Dakota's side door. Adrenaline-fueled apprehension was tangible within the confined space; none of Spider Force had ever jumped before.

"Three white signal flashes at twelve o'clock," Olsen snapped, immediately followed by, "green light. GO–GO–GO."

All fifteen took deep breaths, several crossed themselves and then they leapt blindly into the night sky without hesitation. The equipment containers, pushed out of the plane by Olsen after a count of five, followed the men. Had a main chute tangled, the men still had their reserve chute option from this altitude—if they remembered to use it.

By the grace of God, the drop went smoothly. The cluster of dark olive parachutes drifted north over the road before landing just short of the trees, no one broke anything and each man shed his chute successfully. Seven men had been designated to bundle and hide the chutes while the other eight ran ahead to retrieve the four containers. Last out of the plane, they had fallen neatly between the men and the trees.

Within minutes, these tasks were all completed in efficient silence and Spider Force dissolved into the tree cover.

The AK had been instructed to secure the road between Krauszow and Dlugopole for the entire landing window, so Chez and his men were not surprised when greeted in Polish by six local freedom fighters. After warm handshakes, they were directed into three, canvas-topped Polski Fiat trucks with engines running and promptly headed towards Krauszow.

The sound from the Dakota's twin, Pratt and

Whitney engines quickly receded as they used all of their 2,400 horse power to regain altitude. But first, instead of banking to starboard and disappearing back over the High Tatras, Captain Trotter circled at 5,000 feet to drop 50,000 leaflets.

Each leaflet bore the Armia Krajowa flag, top and bottom and their message was simple:

FEAR NOT BRAVE POLISH PEOPLE
THE SPIDER HAS RETURNED

The Fiats continued for three kilometers beyond Krauszow, crossing the River Bialy at Ludzmiertz before entering the dense forest that concealed the Tatra Confederation's main camp. Aleksy Krol was waiting to greet Chez and his Yugoslavian friends, extending one of the leaflets with a grin.

"So it is true, huh? But not only has Pająk returned, he has brought an army with him!"

"We're at your service and the service of Poland," Chez responded formally. "I'm pleased to report only two twisted ankles amongst us while, in addition, we've brought enough weaponry to chase the Nazi bastards all the way back to Berlin!"

"Changing times," Kroll announced to everyone.

"Six months ago, we were engaged daily in pitched battles against the Wehrmacht garrison at Nowy Targ. Now, they're too scared to venture out after dark. Perhaps before you join your new command in Krakow, you can help us get rid of the pigs once and for all?"

"Delighted to," Chez rejoined straight-faced. "But let's eat first. None of us had the stomach for food before the flight. Now, we're bloody starving."

CHAPTER TWENTY-TWO

1943 – Spider Force

The Armia Krajowa was an attempt to band together previously separate underground groups of Polish Freedom Fighters into one cohesive resistance movement. The AK unit operating in this area of southern Poland was known as the Tatra Confederation and Commander Aleksy Kroll had over one hundred members secreted within the wooded camp.

Similar to the Bracia, these men were never able to contact their loved ones for fear that the Gestapo would imprison and torture them until they betrayed the organization. Nevertheless, Chez was equally aware that such a situation meant each and every one of them was susceptible to pressure. The Gestapo had many ways to make a father put family before country.

"Watch your back, Chez," Paddy McBride had cautioned and the Spider had learned to pay heed to the warnings of an Ulsterman.

The following morning dawned crisp and cold. Plumes of snow swirled upwards from the jagged Tatra Mountains to join the high, wispy clouds already painted across the pale blue Polish sky. These clouds seemed to mimic the breath of the men as they moved restlessly, stamping their frozen feet to bring back the circulation.

Chez grasped a mug of steaming coffee. The stimulating aroma reminded him of his barge ride through Gyor. He sensed a movement as Kroll approached from behind and sat down beside him. Chez shifted uncomfortably; there was something about this local guy that bothered him. When Aleksy put his arm around Chez's shoulder, it only made him more defensive. The man's patronizing attitude set the tone for their initial conversation.

"Pająk, you and your men appear surprisingly well trained and equipped for a Partizani group. Other than taking over command in Krakow, might you have an additional mission to accomplish while you're in Poland?"

An innocent enough remark but nevertheless one that triggered Chez to be on guard.

"Our only plan is to return to the Krakow Bracia and continue the good work started by Jan Kowalski," Chez replied guardedly. "Obviously, in return for you assisting us towards our next waypoint, we can try to help solve your local problem before we leave…. if that's what you're asking."

The Spider took a long sip of coffee from the white enameled mug, mottled with chips that revealed the metal beneath. Would Kroll's eyes reveal anything?

"Call me Aleksy," Kroll said. "I was just wondering why you have Yugoslav guerillas with you? You certain there isn't some Nazi target you have in mind to hit en route? I ask only because we may be able to assist you."

"I promise you, Aleksy," Chez lied smoothly. "The simple truth is, those Partizani and I have been through quite a few adventures together and they've run out of Nazis to harass in Yugoslavia. I didn't ask them to join me in Krakow but the SS killed a good friend of theirs and I couldn't stop them if I wanted to. … Now, let's hear your plan to deal with the local Boche, yeah?"

While Kroll laid out his plans to attack the Wehrmacht garrison at Nowy Targ, Chez was becoming increasingly distrustful of the man. Something was out of place, too pat by far. Perhaps it had been too easy to get back into Poland; the drop zone suspiciously free from German patrols. Perhaps it was something minor. Kroll's fingernails for instance were immaculately manicured, not dirty and chipped like his own. When did a guerilla get access to a manicure?

His mind a whirl of uncertainty, Chez finally rose to stretch his legs.

"Okay, Aleksy, it's a good plan. To recap: we create a diversion designed to entice the bulk of the Wehrmacht to leave their fortified compound, baited by the real possibility of capturing the Spider,—me. Our combined forces will subsequently take out whatever skeleton crew remains in the garrison. My men will be responsible for disabling their vehicles and communications while your men hunt down the surviving troops. We'll also leave some surprises for the main force when they return." Then, he smiled wryly. "Hopefully, without finding me! As a bonus, the entire event should also create enough mayhem to ensure our safe journey north."

He paused. "Now, if you'd be so kind, I need to borrow your radio to contact the Krakow Bracia before briefing my own men on your strategy."

Chez did not disclose that he had a powerful radio included within his supply containers, choosing instead to follow Kroll to the outskirts of the camp. They entered a small building bearing an aerial that extended to just below the tree line.

One of Kroll's men turned on the radio and the three waited for the Baumuster PQK1 transmitter to warm up. When all valves were glowing consistently and the 'Ready' light flickered on, Kroll left the building, ostensibly to allow Chez privacy.

Chez passed the radio operator a small piece of paper that had a frequency penciled on it. After the third try contact was made, the large black Bakelite dial was switched to Transmit and Chez was handed the microphone.

"Bracia one; this is the Spider. Our ETA at the *'Cathedral'* is noon on Thursday. I have *'the baby'* with me. I say again, I have *'the baby'* with me— *Over and out.*"

The radio operator then swiftly shut down the transmitter and Chez left the building to talk to his men, knowing that his message would already be in the hands of Bracia One's Vedran Bozic.

Chez frowned grimly, certain that Aleksy Kroll would also be scanning the import of his message. It was why he'd deliberately inserted the key word, *Cathedral*; code to warn Vedran that all was not completely secure and to expect a follow up signal from their own set later.

He also put some bait on the hook for Commander Aleksy Kroll by obtusely referring to *the baby*. This was pure nonsense Chez had made up on the spur of the moment to fan the flames of the commandant's curiosity.

But then, misinformation can be as much a weapon of war as a field gun.

Among the fourteen Partizani who had come with Chez, roughly half spoke passable German. Chez's Yugoslavian had improved to the point that he was able to switch between both languages as he later briefed Spider Force on Kroll's plan to attack the German garrison the following morning. When the briefing broke up, Chez pulled Triain and Nili, his two most trusted men, aside.

"There's something about Aleksy Kroll that makes me very nervous," Chez whispered. "This whole mission has gone far too smoothly. That Dakota made a helluva noise when it dropped us, yet no patrol arrived from Nowy Targ to check it out?

"Kroll's also been pumping me for information a little too much. All in all, guys, I don't like this situation one bit."

"I've picked up the same danger signals," Nili agreed. "Not from Kroll, but from his men. So much so, I've kept it quiet that my mother is Polish and I speak the lingo myself. It's amazing what people say in front of you if they think you can't understand."

"Okay then, I need for you and Triain to get a little rowdy around the camp fire in about 10 minutes. I am going to need the diversion to call Vedran in Krakow and explain our proper situation."

As Chez sneaked away to crank up his own high-powered transmitter from a supply bundle, he heard Nili and Triain leading the Partizani in a boisterous argument about the best goal ever scored. On his first attempt, he got a loud and clear connection.

"This is Czeslaw. Have Vedran at the receiver in 10 minutes; I'll call back—*Over*."

"Wait, Czeslaw," said the voice. "Vedran is standing right here—*Over*."

"Put him on. *Over*." Chez waited less than 10 seconds before he heard Vedran's familiar voice.

"Czeslaw! What the Hell's going on, old friend? *Over*."

"Vedran, we are safe and at a Tatra Confederation camp. Very quickly, what do you know about Aleksy Kroll, the local Tatra AK commander here in Nowy Targ?—*Over*."

"Tread carefully. We've never been able to find any hard evidence proving he's on the Nazi payroll, but he always seems to be in the right place rather than the wrong place. For a resistance man, he stays pretty high profile; his lifestyle borders on the lavish...And another thing to bear in mind, Czeslaw, for him to be a collaborator, all or most of his group would have to be in on the act as well. Need a little help?—*Over*."

"Thanks, Vedran, I can handle it. Be in touch—*Over and out*."

Chez shut down the transmitter and stowed it

away before wandering nonchalantly outside to join in the argument.

"The best goal ever was by Malcolm McClain and responsible for the win by Blackpool against Liverpool in 1937," he said. "A left foot rocket from twenty meters cannoned off the back of a defender's head and into the top corner. Trust me, I have that straight from the horse's mouth."

The next morning, Chez and Aleksy Kroll strolled boldly into Nowy Targ and surveyed the distant Nazi compound from the clock tower above the town hall.

Kroll's plan involved creating a disturbance at a restaurant on the north side of the Bialy River. This restaurant was popular with the local German garrison and strong rumors would be fed to them by the waiters about the Tatra Confederation believing that the infamous Spider was in the vicinity and would be dropping by for dinner late that afternoon. When the Wehrmacht returned in force to investigate, Chez and five of Krol's local militia would lead them on a wild goose chase through the countryside as darkness fell. The Spider would then be secreted in a safe house while the AK and Spider Force decimated the virtually undefended garrison.

While they were in the clock tower, Chez suddenly

informed Kroll about a last minute change he wanted to make to the plan.

"I have been thinking, Aleksy. I want the time of the disruption at the restaurant moved forward two hours. Let's make it noon."

"W-Why w-would you want to d-d-do that, Spider?" stammered Kroll, with a reluctance bordering on panic.

"Because it'll be lunch time. More Wehrmacht in the restaurant and when I do a job I like to do it under optimum circumstances," Chez responded, smoothly adamant. "If you need my help, then there's no argument, right? Better get moving, we only have an hour to get our teams together."

Chez left Kroll, ostensibly to reconnoiter the restaurant but the moment they parted, Aleksy Kroll hurried furtively across the square and into a small tobacconist's shop. There, under covert observation by Triain, he urgently slipped a note to a youth who, in turn, jumped on his bicycle and headed in the direction of the garrison. Triain signaled to a couple of Spider Force heavies at the end of Waksmun-dzka Street, whereupon they intercepted the young messenger and bundled him unceremoniously into a nearby alley. The youth was bound and gagged; the note recovered and returned to Chez.

Even a brief glance at the note revealed the content to be damning. Now Vedran could be supplied with indisputable evidence against Kroll. Chez shook his head, knowing that traitors were top of Vedran's list of 'most hated occupations'.

"Nili, go back to the Tatra camp with a couple of lads and load our supply containers into the three trucks we used yesterday. Using your best Polish, tell the Tatra Confederation that our supplies are needed in Nowy Targ. Drive to the outskirts of town, beyond the river bridge. We'll meet you there…Triain, take some Partizani and snatch that sleazy bastard Kroll and whoever's with him at the time. Then rendezvous with us at the trucks."

"Are we still intending to create Kroll's diversion at the restaurant?" Triain asked uncertainly.

"No, Trian," the Spider responded grimly. "In fact, Hell no. We've a much more satisfying task to complete."

CHAPTER TWENTY-THREE

1943 – The Quisling Visits Krakow

S ome ninety minutes later, Nazi collaborator Aleksy Kroll recovered consciousness when a pail of ice-cold water was emptied over his head. His mental fog lifted to the realization he'd been drugged, gagged and was now lying prone, apparently in the back of a parked truck.

"Ah, Aleksy, so you're back with us at last," Chez greeted him, with ominous pleasantry. "Welcome to Bracia Headquarters in Krakow and please, allow me to introduce my good friend, Vedran Bozic."

The bearded Yugoslavian beside Chez was not pleasant at all. He scowled at Kroll through hooded eyes, black with menace. *"Dear God,"* the bound man thought to himself. *"Bozic looks even more fearsome in the flesh than his reputation suggests."*

"No doubt you are wondering what brings you to visit us in this beautiful city?" Chez continued. Then he stopped smiling and his voice took on a sharp, menacing edge. "Well, I'll tell you why, you bastard. You were setting us up to be ambushed, that's why.

"You—and probably all of your local Tatra Confederation members—have been collaborating with the Nazi scum for some time. When I tested you by changing the schedule for your so-called disturbance, you realized your Nazi masters wouldn't be in place to ambush us—and you panicked. I only went along with your scheme to confirm your treachery for Vedran's benefit. Although, to give you your due, Kroll, you're smart as a gypsy's monkey. You were right to suspect we were here on a secret mission so, just to satisfy your treacherous curiosity, Herr Kroll, I will now tell you exactly what our mission is."

The Spider leaned forward, positioning his lips beside the shivering Kroll's right ear, and whispered very quietly for several seconds. At that moment Alexy Kroll completely lost control of his bodily functions. He realized that the information the Spider had whispered to him secured his death sentence. He could not possibly be allowed to live, privy to such sensitive material. Chez left the truck without another word.

Under Bozic's deliberate and emotionless stare, Aleksy Kroll began to convulse in fear. Anxious he be denied his vengeance by a heart attack, Vedran impassively advanced on Kroll while caressing his signature weapon of choice. The garrote, a seemingly innocuous loop of cheese wire, ending in two well-worn wooden handles, glinted softly in the light filtering through the truck.

Just over an hour earlier, before the execution, Nili and two of his friends were in the Tatra Confederation camp preparing the three trucks for a discreet evacuation, when a couple of Kroll's henchmen approached them.

Nili called to them in Polish. "Hey, you two; we'd appreciate a little help loading these supply containers? Maybe you can ride with us as guides to the north side of town, so we can meet up with our boss in time to pursue this crazy plan of yours, yeah?"

The three trucks left the camp and as soon as they were parked at the rendezvous, the Partizani overpowered the two locals and tied them up, leaving them unconscious in the rear of the truck. The rest of Spider Force emerged from hiding and loaded a limp body onto the back of the truck. It took only minutes for the caravan to leave Nowy Targ behind them on the road to Krakow.

The trucks raced north for only seven kilometers before they crossed the River Obidowiec into

Klikuszowa, stopping as a small grey car coming towards them flashed its headlights. The bearded man behind the wheel was Vedran Bozic.

"Well done, gentlemen! Do any of you speak Yugoslavian?" Bozic laughed. "I understand that the SAS has taught you how to make a bridge disappear. If you can spare a little C-2 from your supply containers, we can make sure that bridge you just crossed does not allow any pissed off Nazis from the Nowy Targ garrison to follow us."

Although the captured AK henchmen were not present at Kroll's execution, they were left in no doubt as to what had happened. While they feared that every moment might be their last, blindfolds, gags and bindings were suddenly removed and they were instructed to return the body of their former commander to the main square in Nowy Targ. They were to drive through Dlugopole from the west, thereby avoiding the damaged bridge and park the truck outside the tobacconist's shop.

Six men met in the relative safety of the Bracia's Krakow headquarters. This group comprised the upper echelon of the Bracia—Vedran Bozic, Brunon and Filip—plus the new arrivals, Chez Orlowski and his lieutenants, Triain and Nili.

Chez hadn't realized how much he'd missed his homeland and he savored every moment. The Bracia headquarters were warm and, above all, smelled of Poland. They snacked on Baltic herring in cream and several varieties of pierogi, washed down with the unique Grodziskie beer from Poznan.

However, there was little time for nostalgia and after a few bites, Chez shook off his memories and got down to business.

"Believe me, my friends, I am trying not to sound melodramatic but what I am about to tell you will affect the outcome of the war. It must remain top secret and never leave this room. All will become apparent soon enough!" He took a deep breath, noticing that the other five were glancing nervously at him.

"I decided to return to Krakow the moment I learned of Jan's death. Anticipating what I intended, Brigadier Bryan Zumwalt of the Balkan Air Force, approached me with the following suggestion. Before I take over command of the Bracia from Vedran, he asked me to lead a top-secret mission that could save millions of lives and shorten Hitler's so-called Thousand Year Reich to a matter of months. Triain, Nili and the Partizani who came with me, know nothing more than that, yet were prepared to take the risk regardless. In fact this is the first time I've breathed a word of it since I was briefed by Major McBride."

He hesitated and smiled a very cold smile. "No, I

tell a lie, gentlemen. I did take one Pole into my confidence—but Aleksy Krol had less than thirty seconds to digest the secret before meeting his Maker."

Triain grinned. "Before meeting the Devil," he corrected, while Chez poured himself another Grodziskie and his listeners leaned closer.

"You may have heard reports on the BBC about a German weapon called the V-1—*The Doodlebug*. It's an un-manned flying bomb that has caused all sorts of damage, mainly to London and Britain's south coast. However, that's not the Allies' main concern. Intelligence reports now indicate that the Germans are testing a colossal, even more powerful successor to the V-1."

"What could be worse than a flying bomb?" Bozic growled uneasily.

"A weapon against which the Allies have no defense; a weapon so powerful, that even at this late stage, it could turn the tide of the war against us," Chez answered grimly. "In brief, a group of German scientists, led by an SS boffin called Wernher von Braun, have been developing a second generation rocket called the V-2; sometimes referred to as the A4 by its designers. By either name, it represents the world's first operational long-range liquid-fueled rocket: a terror weapon that makes their V-1 look like a firecracker."

"Holy Christ," someone muttered as Chez continued.

"Originally, the research labs were in Peenemunde, Germany, until the Allies sent 600 heavy bombers over and gave it a pasting about six months ago. With Peenemunde compromised, Hitler has been forced to move the research out of bombing range."

"Where to, Spinne?" Nili asked with the look of a man who'd already guessed the answer.

"Here in Poland," Chez growled resentfully. "Aerial reconnaissance has linked the new location of the V-2 laboratory to an SS Division that commandeered the village of Blizna, about 120 kilometers due east of us. Blizna used to have less than 250 residents and held no strategic importance whatsoever. Now, all of a sudden, it's heaving with forced labor, heavily fortified and surrounded by ack-ack emplacements. No unauthorized personnel are permitted to approach within a five kilometer killing zone."

"It sounds as if you're going to need your trucks again, Spinne," Vedran interrupted. "We can put you in touch with Bogdan Dobrowolski, our local AK Commander in Radomysl. It's the safe area nearest to Blizna. Bogdan is someone you can trust and I'm embarrassed to admit that he has sent me several memos about SS activity around Blizna and I never followed up. So what do you hope to achieve when you get there?"

"In essence, I have to try and confirm the new research labs are located in Blizna. If I can send

Brigadier Zumwalt some solid evidence, even better. Accomplish that, and we can return to Krakow. It will be up to the RAF to handle it from there. Sounds like Bogdan Dobrowolski and his guerrillas might be very useful to us. Any questions at this time?"

"How big are these V-2 rockets?" Vedran's second-in-command, Brunon Mazur asked. "I mean, can they really make such a difference?"

"Bloody big and bloody terrifying. All the major players in this horrendous war are now involved in a frantic contest to build a *'super weapon.'* Just as we are about to annihilate the silly bugger once and for all, Adolph Hitler is on the verge of controlling a sub-orbital rocket that flies at five-times the speed of sound to drop 900 kg. of explosives on top of any city he chooses. That big enough for you?"

In the shocked silence that followed, Chez selected a last Pierogi and savored it to the full. Courageous as he was, Chez wondered whether after the Blizna assignment, he would ever see his home-land again.

CHAPTER TWENTY-FOUR

1944 – The Last Mission

A bitterly reluctant Vedran Bozic had to remain with the Bracia in Krakow but Brunon and Filip enthusiastically lobbied to be conscripted into Spider Force for the mission to Blizna. Chez welcomed them gratefully. Had General Patton offered his entire Army Group he'd have taken them too and not felt over-prepared. Most likely, this would be Chez's most dangerous mission and he knew he could use all the help he could get. Now, he had seventeen men he could rely on; seventeen of the toughest, most committed guerrilla fighters Yugoslavia and Poland could produce.

They planned to travel in small, unobtrusive groups, using varied routes and means of transportation before reconvening in the relative safety of Radomysl Wielki, a small village carved into farmland east of Krakow.

Easily defended, this village had become a famous stronghold of Polish Resistance. During their occupation, the Germans had mounted many assaults to eradicate the thorn in their side that was Radomysl Wielki but the AK always caused them more pain than the steadily depleting Nazi resources were prepared to endure.

Without the availability of Luftwaffe air cover, the Wehrmacht were now limited to two possible approaches to the village: from Mielec, fifteen kilometers to the north, and Tarno, 30 kilometers to the south. In either case, the surrounding terrain favored the Armia Krajowa, always affording them time to melt into the landscape when a battalion was sent against them, or defend aggressively against minor patrols.

Radomysl was one hundred kilometers from Krakow but only about twenty kilometers west of the recently fortified village of Blizna, the site where British Intelligence suspected the Peenemunde research facilities for the V-2 rocket had been relocated.

They were about to find out if MI6 was right.

Despite the extreme measures taken by the SS to maintain secrecy around the site, the East European section of Britain's MI6 had long been receiving remarkably detailed information about rocket testing from Bogdan Dobrowolski. His regular radio transmissions, relayed by the Armia Krajowa to London, contained news of test launches and, most crucially, eye witness accounts that pinpointed debris locations when it fell into local fields.

A critical piece of evidence had surfaced a few weeks before when several independent eyewitnesses reported seeing a heavily guarded, rocket-shaped object loaded on a freight train headed to Blizna.

Over the course of two days, numerous bands of Polish sentries challenged Chez and his men as they converged on Radomysl. For the anticipated short duration of the mission, many extra guards had been posted at strategic locations on the hills surrounding the village. As they arrived, each group was bedded down in a large hay barn just outside the village center. When all of Spider Force was present and accounted for, Bogdan extended his considerable hospitality with an evening feast featuring bottomless pots of Bigos, the Polish national dish.

The strangest, yet most wonderful thing about Bigos, is that the recipe changes from village to village. The Radomysl version of the famous stew added fresh lamb and goat meat to the sauerkraut and kielbasa. Slow cooked for the last thirty six hours, the Bigos approached perfection, and then exceeded it when

Bogdan's men brought out mounds of fresh rye bread and some cases of Tyskie beer to help wash it all down.

The following morning, the mood reverted to pure business as the briefings began. The group, numbering close to thirty with the inclusion of the local AK, sat around trestle tables in the barn as Dobrowolski clambered onto a chair and clapped his hands to gain attention.

"Pająk," Bogdan declared. "It is indeed an honor to finally meet you. We've heard so many versions of your Yugoslavian exploits that I hope you take time to write a book after the war so's we can find out how much of the legend is truth."

Amid fairly raucous whooping and fist pumping, Chez rose to acknowledge their applause. Then, Bogdan continued in deadly serious vein.

"Blizna is only fifteen minutes from where we sit. It's a very small village, with no resources to speak of except a strategic railway spur.

"Towards the end of last summer, a battalion of the Fuhrer's elite Liebstandart SS took over the village without warning and evacuated most of its inhabitants to Mielec. They set up fortifications and roadblocks to prevent anybody getting within five klicks of Blizna. Even food supplies cannot be delivered without intense scrutiny. However, we have learned from drivers that the guards keep warning them to keep well clear of a Top Secret area to the west of the village. They refer to it as the *'The Heidelager.'* The more they tried to keep it quiet, the more curious we became."

Bogdan drew a ripple of laughter when he continued, "Twisted psychology, yeah? I know the Germans consider us dumb Polaks but even a dumb Polak can tell they're trying to conceal something sensitive...such as the rocket debris which fall into our fields following their numerous failed launches."

He grinned broadly. "Plus the fact that the bastards reinforced our suspicions by...no, wait: I can do better. Take a look at this photograph taken by Ziggy over there." Dobrowolski indicated a young Pole who sheepishly waved his hand so the visitors would recognize him. "It's of one of the many signs, written in Polish and posted along the Bug River Valley, warning locals to keep their distance."

Chez studied the grainy photograph before passing it round his men.

WARNING!
Dangerous fuel tanks may be found.
Do not touch, but report location immediately
to your nearest German Military Detachment.
Failure to do so will be severely punished.

"Which pretty much advertises where their test flight path is aimed," Chez grunted.

"Exactly. The missiles follow a corridor defined by the Bug River Valley. After each launch, the Schutz-staffel recover the parts and ship them back to Blizna for analysis. Fortunately, we are often able to annex quite a few souvenirs for ourselves before the Boche arrive. Look, I'll show you."

Bogdan made a gesture and one of his men moved to the rear of the barn to haul aside several bales of hay. Behind the hay and against the wall were twisted pieces of metal, including what appeared to be parts of missiles and some form of combustion chamber.

"Although we think this is what you're looking for, I must point out that we've found A4 stamped everywhere rather than V-2." This remark came from an apologetic older man who stood beside Bogdan and was aimed at the hunched-over backs of Spider Force as they intently examined the debris. "I hope you didn't waste your journey."

"As a matter of fact, the A4 designation for the V-2 is something very few people know about," Chez said. "We would have had to worry about being set up by the Germans with fake debris if it had V-2 stamped all over it. This looks like the real thing to me."

Fot almost an hour, the Spider and his men continued their examination of every single item at close range, discovering that the souvenirs also included propellant tanks, fragments of a rocket body, graphite rudders and two sections of twisted pipeline.

"You've done well, all of you," Chez finally acknowledged. "This was a lot easier than I thought. We have the Brigadier's evidence, met some very brave Poles and had a great meal last night. Technically, we can go back to Krakow—mission accomplished…but it feels kinda anti-climactic!"

"Well, seeing as how you came all this way, we have a little bonus gift for you." Bogdan Dobrowoloski looked rather pleased with himself and his men, obviously in on the surprise, were all grinning broadly. "In addition to this collection of small parts, how would you like to take a whole rocket back to the Brigadier?

"Less than a week ago, a virtually intact V-2 fell into soft mud on the banks of the Bug, near the village of Sarnaki. My men were there a full thirty minutes before the first Waffen SS scout car. They'd managed to manhandle the entire rocket into mid-river, where it remains submerged, out of sight. As my men watched, the SS troops searched for over two hours before returning to Blizna without finding a damn thing. They were pissed and blamed the launch crew for miscalculating the crash position."

"Holy shit," Chez breathed. "Are you certain you can find it again?"

"Dead certain," Bogdan affirmed.

"Hopefully, without the emphasis on 'dead,'" Chez thought to himself.

With fresh coffee, Chez formulated the bones of a plan with Bogdan.

"Spider Force will create a diversion at the Blizna facility to allow your men time to retrieve the rocket from the river and get it back to this barn. Once safely here, I'll have Jerzy Sawicki and a team of Polish aeronautical engineers from Krakow dismantle it into sections that will fit into a plane.

"I'll coordinate with BAF transportation but we'll have to get the parts out of this valley to a suitable landing zone. Zumwalt will figure out the details; he's very good at that."

Then, the Spider changed his tone, the snap of resolve evident to everyone in the barn as he stood to make an announcement.

"My brothers from Radomysl and Semic, you've made our primary task much easier. The goal of our mission will have been handsomely exceeded if—and when—we deliver your rocket to Brindisi.

"However, my head and my heart both continue to

tell me that there is unfinished business here. Personally, I cannot leave Blizna without doing everything I can to destroy the research facility. I am only speaking for myself…"

He paused to grin, the kind of calculating yet reckless piratical grin that defined the essence of 'The Spider' persona.

"…but I would be damn grateful, if any of you men wish to volunteer to fight alongside me."

It was impossible to say whether a Polish or Yugoslavian hand went up first; in the blink of an eye, the barn was filled with a sea of raised arms.

Chez spent the rest of his morning making radio contact with Brigadier Zumwalt at the BAF base in Brindisi and coordinating his plans with Vedran in Krakow.

"Swear to God, sir, we were ready to exfiltrate after verifying the barn full of twisted parts. Then Bogdan asks me if I'd like to have a whole bloody rocket! From the way he describes its condition, we could damn near fly the bloody thing to Brindisi."

"Chez, fine job. Please convey our thanks to Dobrowolski and the Radomysl chaps," the Brigadier responded enthusiastically. "But I don't quite understand why you want to confront an entire division of the Waffen SS with your men. Not even Paddy McBride would do that. Well, let me take that back—on second thought, maybe he would.

How about an alternative? Next week, I shall send five hundred bombers over to turn Blizna into a gigantic crater. As a result, we annihilate the place and eventually, Poland will have a nice deep lake to fish in!"

"Sir, I would rather not do that for three important reasons. Number one, my homeland has been bombed enough and I don't want any Poles killed as collateral damage. Secondly, I believe I may be able to seize plans and technical data–anything marked TOP SECRET—that will cause the Nazis more damage and confusion than your bombers could ever inflict. Remember, last time you bombed them at Peenemunde, they picked up and relocated the facility.

"But lastly, Brigadier, what have you got to lose? If I cannot report success in the next few days, I will be dead and you can send the bombers over anyway."

For a full half-minute, the silence was palpable.

"You are a very special man, Chez Orlowski. Take extraordinary good care of yourself on this little jaunt of yours. I fully intend to buy you a drink after the War...And that's an order!"

After lunch, the men split into several groups, each led by a resistance fighter familiar with local conditions. They studied every square meter of Blizna and its environs from various maps, some dating back to the previous century. Chez's group was led by Bogdan.

"So, Bogdan," Chez said. "Precisely where do you reckon laboratories and the launch pads are?"

"We've not been able to tell for sure, Pająk." Bogdan shrugged. "Obviously, we must suspect the west of the village in this so-called Heidelager area, it has extremely dense tree cover. If I were in charge, I'd build anything sensitive right there to minimize the threat from reconnaissance planes."

Chez rubbed his chin for a moment. "Can you get me to this side of the forest tonight without being seen?"

Bogdan frowned. "How many men?"

"Just me, I work better alone."

The AK commander's jaw dropped. "I am not sure that this is a good idea, Pająk. You're proposing to go alone, overnight into a strange forest, guarded by a crack contingent of the Waffen SS? Your chances of survival will be slim at best!"

However, not everyone in the barn agreed. While Chez's plan generated evident consternation amongst the local AK, it clearly didn't overly concern the members of Spider Force.

"Nobody can figure out how he does it but the SS cannot boast a very good record against the Spider." Filip grinned, as he tossed a thinly veiled challenge to the men. "If any of you are interested in a little action, I'd like to wager on the exact time he returns to this barn tomorrow—and I don't mean *IF* he returns. Put me down for 100 zlotys. My personal bet is 10 o'clock in the morning."

"I'll go for, say… 09:50," Brunon followed. This created quite an uproar as the men put their bets into the pool.

Bogdan had instructed one of his guerillas, a tall blond-haired country boy named Roman, to drive Chez to the edge of the forest on the west side of Blizna and, just as night closed around them, Roman's truck lurched off the road to halt in a small clearing.

"Okay, my friend," Roman said as Chez got down from his truck. "Tomorrow morning at six o'clock, my truck will 'break down' right here. I'll wait for you until noon. After that, you must ask for God's help! Good luck Pająk."

"I'll be here," Chez guaranteed flatly. He was wearing black trousers, a black turtleneck, black shoes and gloves, topped off with a black woolen balaclava. He paused to touch up the shoe polish on his face. Although he stood less than a meter from Roman, when Chez closed his eyes, he became invisible.

"Holy shit, that is truly scary," Roman muttered softly. Then the Spider disappeared silently into the trees.

The next morning, as the barn stirred with the sounds of waking men, word spread that Roman had left for the forest in his old truck well before sunrise. As time progressed, so mounted the conspicuous tension in the barn. Bogdan, the most restless of all, was visibly upset that he had let the legend talk him into such a harebrained scheme.

"Damn it," he muttered to himself. "After everything I have tried to do for my country, the name Bogdan Dobrowolski will be synonymous with the stupidity of sending our greatest hero to certain death."

As the minutes dragged by, the aroma of strong coffee became overpowered by air, thick with cigarette smoke. There was very little talk and it all served to amplify the growing pressure.

And then, the tension peaked as the big door suddenly cracked open enough to allow one of the village sentries to squeeze through.

"Roman's truck is approaching the village," he announced breathlessly. "Can't see if he has a passenger though."

The men, led by Bogdan, rushed out to watch the

old truck sputter into view and roll to a halt outside the barn.

After what seemed like an eternity, Roman got out—followed by the Spider.

"Oh my God!" Bogdan bellowed in relief, rushing over to Chez and embracing him a crushing bear hug. "Come inside and tell us what happened."

"First,—what time is it?" Chez asked with a mischievous smile.

"Er, twenty five past eight." Bogdan frowned, puzzled.

"Anybody put their zlotys on eight twenty-five?" Chez enquired, looking cherubically at Filip and the men.

"No," Filip said, as he scanned the betting pool. "But you have eight-thirty, you sly bastard."

"I should've got Roman to slow down a little," he grumbled, soon replaced with a radiant smile aimed at Bogdan. "Please accept my winnings as a donation to our good friends, the proud freedom fighters of Radomysl Wielki." Swinging his arm theatrically, he gave the local leader a low bow.

With everyone other than the on-duty sentries crammed inside the barn, Chez spent a further 10 minutes in private conversation with Bogdan before calling for the group's attention. He jumped, cat-like onto the table and the hubbub died away.

"Last night, I was able to refine the plans we discussed yesterday. You're already aware that we need to transport the undamaged rocket from the river near Sarnaki into this barn. It is essential we do this before the engineers get here so's they can start dismantling it immediately. We'll then load the separated sections into three trucks and cover them with tarps. The trucks must look as if they're carrying worthless scrap. Bogdan will organize teams to scavenge for hubcaps, exhaust pipes—any car parts they can find. We'll pile this scrap on top of the rocket parts as subterfuge.

"The Bracia controls a salvage yard in Zabno, forty kilometers from here. Once there, the trucks will blend in until we're ready to make the final run to the landing zone. I've not yet been given the precise location but the BAF plans to land within 15 kilometers of Zabno itself."

"Coffee, Pająk?" Triain asked, never one to be unduly fazed by the intensity of a situation.

"Biggest mug you can find. Treacle-thick, three spoons of sugar," Chez responded placidly, before returning to his briefing.

"So all this can occur, Spider Force will create unholy havoc in Blizna. We'll make a diversion big enough to give you a full day without interruption so you salvage the rocket. We will not return here for obvious reasons, but will meet you later in Zabno. Any questions?" Chez paused.

"You're deliberately keeping us all on tenter-hooks," Brunon chided fondly. "What did you learn from your visit last night?"

"Thought you'd never ask," Chez said with a gentle laugh, knowing that the details he was about to reveal were the root cause of all the curiosity that blazed from every set of eyes before him.

"Bogdan guessed correctly. The launch pads, workshops and, most importantly, the research labs, are deep in the thickest part of the forest, within a supplemental, heavily fortified area the Germans call the Heidelager. It is only 300 meters from where the actual village is located but extremely well hidden from aerial recce. The rail spur backs right into this area and facilitates direct transportation to and from Germany.

"As you might expect, the Heidelager is extremely well guarded—twenty-four hours a day—by a platoon of crack SS guards. I had to wait until after midnight before climbing onto the roof of the main research lab. Even a Waffen SS Leibstandart sentry loses his edge after several months of boredom." Chez shrugged modestly. "Anyway, from that viewpoint, I was able to produce this rough layout of the place."

There were whistles of amazement from all corners of the barn, as Chez's sketch was passed around. It was highly detailed and he waited almost ten minutes for the men to review it before he continued. "You'll notice there is a potential blind spot between two of the eastern guard towers." The Spider smiled coldly. "This blind spot will increase significantly when we detonate the C-2 plastique I've placed at their bases.

"Our diversion will be an attack from the east, the opposite side from Radomysl, with the express aim of blowing up those guard towers. We will retreat to the southeast, hoping to draw as much attention as we can before we double back to meet up with you in Zabno."

"Pająk," one of the Radomysl men called out. "What if the SS chases you but the scientists proceed with test launches? Won't they be landing in the Bug River Valley right where we are trying to spirit our rocket from? Half the Germans might be chasing you but the other half will be on top of us, trying to get their rocket back."

"Don't see how blowing up a couple of guard towers will cause more confusion than the BAF idea of bombing the shit out of the place," a second voice chipped in.

"There won't be any successful launches for several weeks, my friends." Chez's tone hushed the men as he elaborated. "I had several hours to kill before my morning appointment with Roman, so I visited the assembly workshop. There were about twenty V-2 rockets in various stages of assembly so I screwed open the instrument panels and left a small magnet behind every gyroscope I found. I had about fifty in my pocket, having been told by Jerzy Sawicki, the Polish engineer you'll be meeting, that this'll have the same effect on a rocket guidance system as if each of you drank five bottles of vodka. The rockets will not be able to complete their launch sequence but even if they do, they will crash almost immediately. With any luck, it'll take von Braun's eggheads weeks, maybe even months to figure out the problem."

"I don't understand, Czeslaw," Bogdan said. "How the hell were you able to walk around a high security compound—apparently quite freely—without getting detected and shot?" The rest of the men obviously had the same question and leaned forward to catch the reply.

The Spider smiled as he replied softly. "Bogdan; to quote two very special friends of mine from Northern Ireland: *Ah well, there y'are now!*"

CHAPTER TWENTY-FIVE

1944 – On the Offensive

C hez had just turned twenty-three years old but already the legend surrounding the Spider's many exploits were being recounted as bedtime stories all over occupied Europe, a continent that craved for hope and heroes. Children, especially in Poland, were going to sleep dreaming that 'Pająk' could single-handedly take care of Hitler and the bad guys, just like Superman would. After all, wasn't the Spider three meters tall and made of steel?

The truth was, Czeslaw Orlowski stood five feet eight inches tall, very much human but gifted with astonishing gymnastic abilities, enhanced by an extraordinary power/weight ratio. However, if he had tried to explain this to Bogdan, or anyone whose miserable wartime existence was only made bearable by a belief in legends, they would not have wanted to accept such a mundane truth.

The morning of the mission dawned soon enough and with it an awareness that some of the men might not see each other again or worse, they themselves might be looking at their own last sunrise.

Then, as Chez called quietly, "All right lads, move out!" the apprehension dissipated within a mounting surge of adrenaline.

Riding in a battered, dirty-red Zawrat migrant workers' bus, Roman drove Spider Force on a circuitous route for almost 80 kilometers to ensure they completely evaded the village of Blizna. Eventually, they stopped just north of Sedziszow. Roman made the journey twice for security reasons, transporting seven to eight men on each trip. It was one o'clock in the afternoon before the group reunited.

From there, it was a straight run north to Blizna with an SS control point expected approximately halfway along the route. Predictably, the black-uniformed troopers had positioned their checkpoint just over a river bridge, affording themselves a long vista to preview any approaching traffic. But this tactic also worked in reverse, as it allowed Spider Force plenty of time to assess the situation and be assessed as 'non-threatening' by the guards as they trundled slowly towards them.

Seven guards were identified and two well-concealed Partizani were assigned to each, guns to be used as a last resort. The migrant bus slowly rolled up to the barrier, Roman looking lost and befuddled as he rolled down his window to ask for directions. As one of the guards was about to order him to turn around, the concealed Partizani sprang from the back door of the bus, weapons raised. One of the guards bolted towards the radio but received a hunting knife between the ribs for his trouble after only two paces. The others raised their hands in surrender, weapons discarded at their feet: Their throats were slit regardless and the bodies hauled off the road to be unceremoniously dumped under the bridge.

Parked to the side of the checkpoint, were two Waffen SS motorcycles equipped with sidecars. Two Partizani, Haris and Karol, selected for their marksmanship, joined Chez and Triain on the next, most dangerous part of the mission. While they kick-started the bikes and headed towards the Heidelager, the remainder of the group set about rigging the bridge with timed charges set for quarter past the hour.

"Okay, you lot. Make damn sure we've left no trace of any Partizani being here, then get back onto the bus." Nili had a last look around and then said a small prayer to himself as he stared, narrow-eyed in the general direction of the village. Everything was still quiet but the fact that the Spider was about to kick open a hornets' nest did not escape anybody.

"Roman, start her up and head back towards Sedziszow 'til we find a good place to wait for the bikes."

The bus stopped after three kilometers at a bend in the road they had noticed on the way in. There was still no unusual activity from the direction of Blizna, so it seemed certain the checkpoint had not been able to warn the garrison before the Spider mayhem would begin.

Chez and Triain steered the motorcycles off the road and into the woods well before they came within sight and sound of the village. They parked, shouldering their rifles prior to stalking through the trees at the edge of the forest. About a hundred meters from the Heidelager, Chez re-identified the guard towers and gestured to his three companions to stop.

"Bottom left column of each tower. Each detonator is hidden under a pile of leaves with a pinecone on top. Confirm?" Chez whispered, tapping each man on the shoulder as he pointed towards his assigned target. The four men focused on their designated objective through a No. 32 Sniper scope attached to each Lee Enfield 4T rifle—courtesy of the SAS. The other three men gave Chez a thumbs up. They were ready.

He carefully checked his watch. It was two o'clock. "On my command... Fire!"

Four bolt-action rifles each barked off 10 rounds within the next thirty seconds. Both guard towers blew up almost simultaneously but it was the resultant conflagration that entirely confused the guards. Hastily, the four men crawled backwards, retreating to the motorcycles.

That marked the point when it all started to go horribly wrong!

Either Chez miscalculated the dead spot in the cone of fire or a supplemental machine gun had been activated. Within just a few seconds, the four guerrillas found themselves pinned under a random hail of machine gun bullets directed from within the compound, a rate of fire that increased in intensity by the second.

Haris Pacic, Triain's Croatian friend and sidecar passenger, slipped on wet leaves as he rose to run for the protection of a tree.

"Stay *DOWN*, Haris!" Triain screamed but too late. Pacic was dead before he hit the ground, the hail of bullets continuing to buffet his body for several more seconds. An ashen-faced Triain hesitated and made to rise but Chez urgently waved him off, knowing that they did not have the luxury of time.

"Take Karol and get back to the motorcycles. Give me no more than one minute, then leave without me."

The Spider hid motionless behind a tree, watching Haris' inert body for a full five seconds, just in case there was a chance of life, but it had been carved into several pieces by the vicious curtains of lead. Although it was unpleasant to an extreme, he wormed back to the body to repossess the Lee Enfield and remove any identification before retreating after the other two.

Karol had taken Haris's place in Triain's sidecar and they were revving impatiently as they waited for the Spider. After almost three minutes, it was just as well they stayed. When Chez leapt astride his motorcycle and stamped down on the kick-starter—nothing—no sign of life!

"SHIT!"

After another four frantic yet futile attempts, he abandoned it, jumping instead onto the rear seat of Triain's bike. The extra weight slowed them down and made the bike quite unstable but the three men were racing against certain death anyway and could not afford to lose.

"Go!" Chez bellowed, sick to his stomach that his miscalculation had caused Haris Pacic's death. "Get the hell over the bridge before it blows."

It took only minutes for the SS to mobilize and figure out that their attackers were no longer shooting. Their commander radioed each of his outer three checkpoints. There was no response from the sentries on the southern bridge; only the crackle of an unmanned radio. The extremely well-trained troops did not hesitate to choose this direction for their primary pursuit.

Shouts of *"Schnell, schnell, SCHNELL!"* could be heard above the gunning engines and spinning wheels, as half the garrison roared out of the compound in chase. At ten minutes after two , the unstable, swerving motorcycle driven by Triain, hurtled back across the mined bridge at a perilous 120 kph, both driver and passengers hanging on for dear life.

The first of the pursuing SS troop carriers crossed the bridge almost five minutes later but then, the C-2 exploded right on time and the second troop carrier was tossed five meters into the air, destroying it along with the bridge. All trailing vehicles had to skid to a halt to avoid crashing into the river.

The driver of the lone pursuing KFZ 69 Krupp Boxer raced resolutely after the over-laden motorcycle he had locked in his sights as a cloud of dust. But, as he caromed round a blind bend, he was suddenly forced to stand on the brakes, swerving into a sideways spin to avoid a recently felled tree blocking the middle of the road. With black rubber painting the asphalt and smoke billowing from the wheel wells, the Boxer was barely upright, its right side supported by branches. The troops were jumping out frenetically to clear the obstacle when eight Partizani, concealed behind the hedgerows, stood up and cut all but one of them to shreds within a merciless triangulated barrage from their new Lanchesters leaving the road strewn with a bloody mélange of tree limbs and black-uniformed bodies. As the remainder of the men righted the vehicle, Nili checked the carnage and noted with satisfaction that one guard was breathing the quiet breaths of a scared man praying that he would escape execution.

Nili smiled and jumped into the bullet-scarred Krupp.

With great haste, the ambushers backed away from the tree and then roared off to catch up with the lone motorcycle, now parked beside the red bus. Roman started the engine of the Zawrat as he watched Spider Force set fire to the German vehicles in the center of the road behind him. After the Partizani had all piled onto his bus, he accelerated back towards Sedziszow.

An uncharacteristically downcast Chez waited until their adrenaline levels had subsided before breaking the sad news about Haris to everyone.

Meanwhile, back at the tree barricade massacre, the surviving German soldier, 'lucky' to go down with non-life threatening injuries, was able to witness the terrorists steal the Krupp. Way in the distance, he could just see it rendezvous with another vehicle. There were explosions of fire, and the now identifiable red bus drove off towards Sedziszow. Twelve minutes later, the survivor was able to feed an excellent eyewitness accounting of the getaway to his comrades.

"*Gotte mitte Uns...*" The SS-Hauptsturmführer had an expression of triumphant revenge on his face, as he reached for his radio to deploy yet more search parties. "The Polish peasants have screwed up. One of my men saw them drive towards Sedziszow in a red bus. I am going to execute every fucking one of them personally."

Roman drove the red bus noisily through the center of Sedziszow, attracting as much attention as he could by sounding his horn several times before making the turn east on the road to Rzeszow, the next main town. Then, after only two kilometers, he slowed to take another left, this time onto an unkempt gravel side road and brought the bus to a halt in a shower of small stones beside three waiting trucks.

Spider Force disembarked rapidly, taking all their equipment with them before piling into the parked vehicles. One of the waiting truck drivers, an elderly man with a pronounced limp, gave his keys to Roman and took over the driver's seat of the overheated red Zawrat bus that had served them so well.

Within minutes, the empty bus was back on the road to Rzeszow. The driver, Stanislaw Pawlac, was happy to do his small part for the resistance, especially if it was this easy.

The three trucks now transporting Spider Force reversed direction and headed back slowly through Sedziszow, en route west to the large regional city of Debica. Several German troop carriers passed them going the opposite way as, for the second time in fifteen minutes, they crossed the junction that went north to Blizna.

With furious urgency, the SS were questioning the locals about a red, migrant worker bus. Considering the hubbub, they could not deny remembering and responded grudgingly by pointing in the direction of Rzeszow.

At exactly two o'clock that same afternoon, Bogdan and a large group of the local AK were just outside Sarnaki on the Bug River, ostensibly changing a tire on Roman's old truck. Coupled to this truck was a battered logging trailer.

Bogdan checked his watch and with a nod of his head, the men formed sentry groups to the north and south to allow the rest of the men to wade, unobserved, into the water to locate the submerged V-2 rocket.

With ropes, muscle power and not-inconsiderable help from the powerful truck, the rocket reluctantly slid from its hiding place in the river and was eventually winched onto the trailer. Within the hour, a large 'tree,' covered with tarpaulins but with convincing branches protruding from both ends, was moving slowly back towards the barn in Radomysl Wielki.

The recovery had gone well. Only a couple of local farmers had tried innocently to bypass the sentries but had been convinced that a large tree would be blocking the road for the next couple of hours until it could be chopped up and moved. They both accepted the explanation without argument and silently turned to find an alternate route.

Jerzy Sawicki had studied advanced engineering at the University of Warsaw; his doctoral thesis focused upon sub-orbital rocket propulsion. Conrad Nowicki, a member of the Bracia, drove him and two of his former research students from Krakow to Radomysl. The four men arrived at the barn some twenty hours after the rocket.

Jerzy could not believe what he saw when Bogdan Dobrowolski pulled the covering tarpaulins aside. He laughed aloud as he walked around and around, patting and caressing the skin of the only V-2 rocket he had ever seen outside a textbook.

"Absolutely unbelievable!" he said. "Look at the

fuel reservoir. I never dreamed that this configuration would work. Von Braun is a genius."

The scientists started dismantling the rocket, cataloging each part as it was loaded carefully into the waiting pickup trucks. As soon as Jerzy determined enough was enough, Bogdan's men covered the sensitive equipment with innocent looking tarps and then randomly tossed automobile parts on top, securing each completed load with old ropes. As soon as the first truck was ready to make the forty-kilometer journey to Zabno, there was a pause to check its authenticity as a scrap truck. Then, the barn door opened and Bogdan gave the order to roll.

They had hoped to use three trucks to transport the rocket parts to the scrap yard but in the end, they had to scramble to find a fourth before they dismantled it.

The last truck, which also carried Jerzy Sawicki and his colleagues, left the barn in Radomysl less than eight hours behind the first.

CHAPTER TWENTY-SIX

1944 – Hide and Seek

S tanislaw Pawlac was not an active member of the local Polish resistance. He was fifty-six years old, a meek and kindly man with advancing arthritis in both knees. But, when one of his neighbors asked him if he would mind lending his old truck to help transport some AK contraband through Sedziszow, he agreed without much thought.

Happy to play his part, the next day he followed his neighbor to the remote rendezvous. A third man, whom he did not know, joined them and together, they waited patiently on the gravel road for almost an hour before the red migrant workers' bus skidded to a halt before them in a cloud of dust.

Understandably, he was alarmed when a gang of fierce looking foreigners, armed to the teeth and speaking a strange language, poured out of the bus and jumped into the three waiting trucks, one of which was his. However, the tall blond driver of the bus was a local man he vaguely recognized, so his fears calmed somewhat after the young Pole politely asked the three truck donors for a volunteer to drive the empty bus and 'lose' it somewhere in the general direction of Rzeszow.

"I'll do it," said Stanislaw, caught up in the moment. "When do I get my truck back?"

"Thanks," Roman replied to all of them. "We need your trucks for less than a week. Somebody will contact you and arrange for the return handover. Now we must hurry.

"Mr. Pawlac, take the bus and park it somewhere it won't be found for a while, then leave the keys inside and walk away. Believe me, what you are doing is of vital importance to Poland."

The last to leave, Roman started Stanislaw's truck, now weighed down with six large Partizani. He ground the gears through a three-point turn that made Stanislaw wince, before heading back towards Sedziszow after his friends.

"It would be really nice to have a transmission in my truck when I get it back but, from the way that young lad drives, I don't think I'll be that lucky." Pawlac gloomed ruefully, as he slowly limped over to the old red Zawrat. It vaguely crossed his mind that he still had no idea what was going on but, what the hell, if it screwed with the Nazis, it was the least he could do for the war effort. His contributions to date seemed inadequate and the mood in Poland sensed an end in sight.

Stanislaw Pawlac did not have room to turn the lengthy bus on the side road so he backed it on gravel all the way to the main road, before driving leisurely towards Rzeszow. Although specifically told to hide the bus in a remote place, that didn't appeal to his arthritis, so in his mind, he was planning to park it in Kleczany, where he could perhaps get his cousin to drive him ho…?

The flashing, imperious headlights were impossible to ignore, as were the jagged Waffen SS decals painted on the vehicles that filled his rear view mirror. Within minutes, a dozen Schutzstaffel vehicles containing too many troops to count overtook Stanislaw. They forced him over onto the grass verge and ordered him out of the driver's seat under the deadly gaze of several Schmeisser machine pistols.

"What the fuck have I done to deserve this?" He thought, his heart racing.

"Hands above your head, peasant!" SS-Hauptsturmführer Bernhard Stitt barked, while several armed troops pounded aboard the bus. "Where are the rest of the murderers?"

"Herr Captain," a very nervous Stanislaw improvised. "I have no idea what murderers you are talking about. I am just driving this bus to pick up some workers from the fields around Rzeszow."

"Which fields? How many men? Where are your papers for the bus?" The SS captain shrieked his questions in rapid succession, which only served to disorientate his prey further and, when a corporal emerged from the bus carrying an overlooked empty ammunition pouch, Pawlac's previously secure world completely disintegrated.

He was brutally felled by a gun butt smashing into his kidneys and, as he lay in shock, Stitt grasped his jaw to force his mouth open.

The SS captain jammed his Mauser into Pawlac's mouth.

"I repeat only once. Where—are—the—MURDERING SWINE?"

Stanislaw blurted out everything he knew—which, thanks to Chez's need-to-know policy, was very little—but the harm was done. Even with such scant information, it did not take Stitt long to figure out they had been duped and were heading in the wrong direction. Now desperate to mollify his captors, Pawlac offered a description of the three trucks.

When it became apparent that the crippled old man had been telling the truth and was devoid of further useful information, Stanislaw Pawlac was accorded the benevolent Waffen SS's traditional reward for such unstinting cooperation—the double tap: Two bullets into the base of his skull.

While a couple of SS vehicles still continued to Rzeszow—just in case—the rest turned and sped back to Sedziszow, before continuing on the main road to Debica. SS Hauptsturmführer Bernhard Stitt used radio to call his headquarters. He knew they wouldn't be pleased by having to deploy still more troops, but in order to track the three trucks through Debica, the large town ahead to the west which controlled this region, he had to arrange for roadblocks. He had to prevent the terrorists escaping his net and roadblocks on the two possible routes west from Debica, at Jaslow and Tarnow, might just do that.

Coincidently, back in Radomysl Wielki, Bogdan Dobrowolski had been monitoring the situation through coded phone calls from friendly villagers. Debica was home to one of the better-organized branches of the AK so accordingly, Bogdan instructed them to create another ruse, in an attempt to buy more time for Spider Force—so Stitt and Dobrowolski were involved in a chess match—each unaware that the future of the free world was on the line.

Roman assumed lead of the three escape trucks as they entered the eastern environs of Debica. This was his country and these were his people. Bogdan would have already told them what was going down and he was keenly alert for any signs of help from the local Freedom Fighters.

"And there we go!" Roman exclaimed, spotting a vendor lounging idly at the side of the road. The Pole held a wooden sign that read:

"ROMAN pottery"

He pulled to a stop and identified himself, after which the vendor spat out rapid instructions.

"Continue to the center of town. Turn right in the main square and park in front of the Railway Station."

Roman was already accelerating back up to speed as the other two trucks tucked behind him. His left arm made broad circles out of the window to indicate that they should follow him as he entered the town square. On a side road to the north of the square, he easily identified the Railway Station. It was a handsome, large building, denoting Debica's importance on the busy main rail line from Lwow to Kraków.

When all three trucks had parked as instructed, a man Roman recognized from a previous mission, strolled up to him.

"Hi, Roman, remember me? I'm Jacques Weber. We worked together on the rail heist last year. Those parked trucks should help convince the SS you took a train. Follow me without undue haste and try hard not to look suspicious by gawking around." Nili and Chez quickly passed on a translation to the Partizani.

So, attempting to look casual, Spider Force unloaded the supply bags and entered the vaulted interior ticket hall through the main door of the Station. Once inside, Roman acknowledged several more AK brothers he recognized. It became evident to Chez that the entire station had been secured by the AK for their benefit. Even though the obligatory, field-gray uniformed watchers were present, they were all grouped at the far end of the ticket hall; amused by a fracas created by well-endowed Polish girl who had misplaced her papers.

"Keep your eyes on the tits, Krauts. For once, your lives depend upon it!" Chez mused, knowing that if the Germans passed up the entertainment in favor of searching the new arrivals, they would most likely never fondle a woman again.

Under cover of this diversion, Jacques redirected Spider Force to the outside, this time through a small service door that opened into the sheltered delivery yard.

Now completely out of view from the ticket hall or the town, Spider Force piled into a single, much bigger truck with a canvas top—another of the anonymous Polski Fiats that seemed to be everywhere. With Roman again at the wheel, the truck rumbled unnoticed from the station's side yard and back to the town square, where it turned right to resume the journey to Tarnow. Prying eyes could only report that the dark-bearded militia that arrived in the three abandoned trucks must have caught one of the many trains that passed through Debica every day.

Unavoidably, the next part of the journey would take over twenty minutes—more than enough time for SS-Hauptsturmführer Stitt's roadblock to be established across the fork that separated traffic to Tarnow from traffic turning north to Kielce.

They were still two hundred meters from the roadblock, when Roman was forewarned of the pending threat by a collection of army vehicles fronted by several Wehrmacht soldiers with Schmeissers. The troops were setting up behind a spiked chain that effectively blocked the road. As Roman began to ease off the accelerator, Chez cautioned him.

"Wehrmacht, Roman. Much easier to surprise than the SS. Chances are they're still on the lookout for three small trucks. Don't slow down too quickly."

Chez improvised a quick plan and turned to tell Triain and Nili to warn the Partizani in the back to prepare for a fierce fight.

"Brothers," Triain said as loudly as he dared to be heard over the rumble of the heavy truck. "There are about a dozen Germans manning a road block just ahead. We're going to stop the truck at a forty-five degree angle. When we hear Chez's pistol, four of you will remain in the truck and open fire to the left. The rest of you, dismount from the protected side. Half attack to the front, half attack by coming round the rear. Try to get into the roadside ditches for cover. Good luck, my friends."

The truck skewed to a clumsy halt in front of the chain, still several meters from the Germans. Roman killed the engine, a submissive gesture intended to imply they were not a threat—perhaps they were lost and prepared to turn around.

Casually, Chez leaned out of the passenger window, smiling as he waved a map.

"Ah, mein herren, perhaps you can help us, ja?" he appealed in his best Berliner German. This had a calming effect on the Wehrmacht and two of the guards looked at each other with a shrug before shouldering their weapons and walking towards the truck. The rest of their bored colleagues continued to talk amongst themselves as they smoked cigarettes.

"For Poland," Chez said quietly, before shooting both the guards between the eyes from a range of less than one meter. Then, both he and Roman ducked low in the cab to take protection from the engine block.

The canvas on the left side of the truck raised and automatic fire erupted towards the remaining guards as they frantically scrambled for the cover of their vehicles. Only four made it but this did not save them from the Partizani who had vaulted into the roadside ditch.

Within thirty seconds of Chez's initial request for help, all the Wehrmacht soldiers were down with two of the Partizani also wounded. Any Wehrmacht survivor was dispatched swiftly and without mercy, while the chain was hauled off the road, allowing Roman to advance the big truck onto the road to Kielce.

They then repositioned the roadblock as best they could, moving bodies and vehicles to imply that, whoever had killed the soldiers, had proceeded in the direction of Tarnow. It was all they could do but the devil is in the details and it might buy them a few extra precious minutes.

Several mercifully uneventful miles later, Spider Force arrived at the salvage yard in Zabno. The two wounded men were soaked in blood but the wounds were dressed and assessed as non-life threatening.

Although neither Bogdan nor Stitt knew the chess game had been played—Check Mate Dobrowolski!

Roman had to keep moving to put as much distance between the rendezvous and his truck as possible. He said his goodbyes with genuine regret as his comrades helped him remove the canvas off the truck and attach vendor advertising to the side panels to minimize its profile should it encounter an enemy patrol.

Spider Force was safely ensconced in the scrap

yard, several hours before the first truck, carrying rocket parts, drove up. It took another full day before all three trucks were accounted for, the last carrying Jerzy Sawicki and his associates.

The scene was now set to make radio contact with Brigadier Zumwalt in Bari.

As a fluent Polish ex-patriot familiar with the Zabno area, Flying Officer Mikolaj Duda had been assigned as co-pilot on the Dakota, tasked with flying from Taranto to Poland on the top-secret mission. The aircraft carried extra fuel tanks, installed in the fuselage to increase the safety margin—especially important when they would be returning with cargo of undetermined weight.

After crossing the Adriatic Sea, the Dakota eased north over Yugoslavia, Hungary and Czechoslovakia. For the past several weeks, a prime targeted landing site for any designated missions to southern Poland had been a flat, open meadow to the south of Opatowiec, a small town near Krakow. Its visual orientation point would be the outlet of the River Dunajec into the River Vistula. Last minute coordination between the Bracia, Spider Force and the BAF Command confirmed that the Opatowiec landing site was still viable.

It was already pitch black when the Dakota

went into a holding pattern after crossing the Polish border, circling before its final approach to conform to the estimated time of arrival. Then, at twenty knots out, F.O. Duda tuned the Dakota's transmitter to a pre-determined frequency and announced in Polish.

"Big Bird has six eggs in her nest—*Over.*" After sending Spider Force the coded message that they were six minutes from touchdown, Mikolaj clicked the Bakelite knob to receive. Ten seconds later, there was a crackle in response.

"Ready for Easter, Big Bird—*Over and out.*"

Courtesy of local Bracia members, as the Dakota gradually descended over the next five minutes, lights appeared dead ahead of the plane, positioned at each corner of the makeshift grass runway. The meadow was actually quite large but naturally concealed—as were the lights, by thick perimeter trees that enjoyed the waters of the adjacent rivers.

Maintaining as low an altitude as he dared, Dakota pilot, Captain James W. Kuhlmann, disregarded his altimeter and switched on customized under-wing lights, both positioned down and slightly towards each other. This was a phenomenally successful technique, developed by the Royal Air Force 617 Squadron for the famous dam buster raids over the Ruhr Valley. The specifically calculated angles of the wing lights were first visible to the navigator as two circles of light. As the plane descended, the circles gradually converged into one. At this point, the pilot knew his plane was exactly 50 feet above the ground. The landing was much bumpier than expected, but Captain Kuhlmann was of the old school who believed that any landing you can walk away from is a good landing!

"Mind you," he reflected wryly once they landed, *"getting her down is only half the battle."*

Once safely on the ground, he powered the Dakota through 180 degrees and waited for the reception party.

Several trucks converged on the stationary plane when the cargo door swung open and the Dakota's crew jumped down, scurrying to mark off a safety zone around propellors that continued to spin in anticipation of a very fast turnaround. All hands formed a well-organized daisy chain to load and position the rocket parts, securing them within the cargo bay by ropes to Copilot Mikolaj Duda's satisfaction. Only then did Duda signal permission for his passengers to board.

Led by Chez, Vedran Bozic and Jerzy Sawicki joined the thirteen returning Partizani, two of whom were badly wounded and strapped to make-shift stretchers.

"Brothers," Chez shouted above the roar of the engines. "My old friend, Vedran, is finally returning home to *Yugoslavia* with you. What he has contributed to *the Polish* cause will never be forgotten. Professor Sawicki is accompanying his rocket to show the Brits how to put it back together! As you know, I'll not be making the journey with you, as I'm taking over the leadership of the Bracia.

On behalf of Poland, I owe you all an immense debt of gratitude. After we've kicked the Nazis out of my country, as you have done out of yours, there is a lovely girl in Zagan that I would very much like to see again. But, until then…

"…Veliko sreče; Varno potovanje!—Good luck and travel safely!"

CHAPTER TWENTY-SEVEN

1943 – Back to England

I n stark contrast to the long, bitterly-cold night flight to Poland that Chez had endured, Malcolm and the Maribor POWs enjoyed a most pleasant, almost touristic, two hour journey—flying over the azure Adriatic Sea most of the way from Semic to Bari.

The Bari airport was several kilometers north of the ancient Italian city and after the four planes touched down in the warm sunshine, the escapees were escorted immediately to a nearby field hospital to be medically checked before repatriation. The cluster of tents struck Malcolm McClain as odd, but he was informed that the main hospital adjacent to the ancient port had been quarantined within the past week due to a freak accident.

It would be many years after the war before

McClain discovered the history behind that 'accident' and precisely what horrors it had unleashed.

The Allied Forces had commandeered the Port of Bari as a first priority in bringing supplies to the Italian mainland and vital in support of Field Marshall Sir Harold Alexander's 15th Army, as it continued to battle its way north to Rome. In a futile attempt to disrupt these supplies, a small flight of Luftwaffe Junkers 88's bombed the harbor in a daring night raid. One of several ships sunk was the US Liberty Ship John Harvey, a fleet supply vessel caught square in their bombsights while unloading her top-secret cargo.

That cargo included hundreds of tons of mustard gas, one of the most lethal, barbaric chemical weapons ever devised by man. After the carnage it caused in the First World War, it was considered illegal by the mutual consensus of all civilized nations...Nazi Germany was not on that list.

The reason an Allied ship would be carrying mustard gas can only be attributed to paranoia. The Big Three, Roosevelt, Churchill and Stalin, were united in that the only surrender they would accept from Hitler and his cronies would be unconditional. That widely quoted dictum led some backroom boys in the Pentagon to suggest a scenario in which the Third Reich, given no hope of an honorable surrender, would have to defend their homeland with all available means. These, most likely, would include chemical weapons.

So, as fate would have it, during that desperate raid by Luftflotte 2, the Liberty ship John Harvey was covertly unloading containers of mustard gas to be used as swift retaliation against the Germans, should that ugly scenario unfurl.

The resulting deaths and injuries inflicted on Bari's resident and transient population that terrible night would prove numerous and horrific. When US records relating to the John Harvey's destruction were finally declassified in 1959, it was estimated that as many as two thousand Allied service men and Italian civilians died because of what would become known as the 'European Pearl Harbor.'

To further compound the catastrophe, many of those deaths might have been avoided had the security hawks not had their way. The international opprobrium that would have been directed at the Allied side was considered dangerous for morale and a massive security clampdown was implemented. Even while the disaster unfurled, the attending physicians were not informed of the nature of the vessel's deadly cargo, thus putting them at a lethal disadvantage when speedy diagnosis could have proved crucial.

Unknown to McClain and his fellow former prisoners, the aftermath from the toxins was still being cleaned up when they landed at the Bari airport and the clandestine reason they were being processed in the tents of a field hospital.

A young doctor with the ubiquitous stethoscope around his neck examined Malcolm thoroughly. "Flight Officer McClain, you've been through quite a lot in the past few months, haven't you?" His nametag read Captain D. M. Collins and in his hand, he held the clipboard that secured McClain's laboratory results.

"It had its moments," Malcolm conceded modestly. "Can I go home—please?"

"Not immediately," Doctor Collins replied as he peered over the top of his spectacles. "Despite you being a quite remarkable physical specimen, you seem to have picked up a mild kidney infection, coupled with the final throws of a severe case of dysentery. I'm going to put you on medication and will continue to monitor you for about a week. After that, you should be good to go."

Malcolm smiled gratefully. "Your middle initial doesn't happen to stand for Michael, by any chance?"

"It does indeed," the captain replied with a long-suffering smile. The question was asked by every Irish patient he had ever had. "But not Michael Collins, the Irish revolutionary you would be thinking of. I was named after my dad, also a doctor, but everyone calls me Don.

"Malcolm, don't worry about a thing. You're going to be back terrorizing Arsenal and Manchester United before you know it."

"I can't tell you how worried I was about the stomach pains I've been having. I think I can prove conclusively that it is possible to actually shit three times the volume of what you have physically eaten over the course of a week!" Malcolm was laughing in relief as he shook Dr. Collins's hand.

One night during his convalescence, a strong southeasterly wind blew remnants of the mustard gas towards the hospital tents on the periphery of the airport. By the time he awoke the next morning, Malcolm had developed a distinctive cough that, though not life threatening, followed him for the rest of his years, taking a toll on his stamina when he did make his return to professional football.

Captain Collins treated the cough and kept McClain under observation for a further week before finally discharging him as 'Fit for Service.'

In the interim and despite Doctor Don's cautions, Malcolm stubbornly insisted on jogging several miles a day to rebuild his fitness. Early one morning, as he was about to begin his regime, a motorcycle messenger pulled up to the administrative tent and shouted out his name.

"Over here, Corporal. I'm McClain," Malcolm called out, whereupon he was handed a very official-looking manila envelope containing orders to report immediately to Command Headquarters.

Thirty minutes later, showered, shaved and wearing a full dress uniform procured from the barracks by Captain Collins, he was collected by an army staff car and driven 75 kilometers southwest to Taranto, for an audience with none other than, Field Marshall Sir Harold Alexander.

The journey took over an hour, which allowed Malcolm to reflect on how much the course of the war had changed during his unintended sojourn in Yugoslavia. When his ill-fated Wellington had taken off from Alexandria, the upcoming counter punch from the Allies was by no means certain of success. Now, the skies above him were full of Allied aircraft, flying north against a clear blue sky with none of the grey puffs of *'FLAK'* he remembered so vividly from the past.

He was jerked back to reality when the driver halted the staff car outside Sir Harold Alexander's Taranto Headquarters. After negotiating the stone steps of what must have been a local Italian government building before the war, he walked into the reception hall to find himself face to face with a tall, highly decorated Brigadier who greeted him knowingly.

"Flying Officer Malcolm McClain, I presume?" The impressive officer had a very slight Canadian accent and beamed warmly as he extended his hand. "An honor to meet you, young man. I'm Bryan Zumwalt."

"Well, sir, the feeling is mutual, I can assure you." Malcolm responded, his eyebrows rising in surprise. "I understand I owe you a great deal, quite possibly my life!"

The door behind them opened and an orderly announced, "The field marshall will see you gentlemen now."

At six feet four, Brigadier Zumwalt towered above the other men as he summarized Malcolm's recent adventures to Field Marshall Alexander. At the conclusion, Alexander smiled broadly.

"Jolly well done, both of you!" Then he directed his gaze at Malcolm. "You were a hero on the football field to millions of Brits before this war started. Now you've become a genuine hero on the battlefield. I trust you were well looked after in Bari? Captain Collins is an excellent physician; he has kept me informed about your condition. I am deeply sorry that you had to endure that damn lung infection on top of the kidney problem and I hope you'll have a complete recovery."

Malcolm's eyes widened, surprised that the field marshall, in charge of hundreds of thousands of troops, had taken time to monitor a lowly aviator's health.

Alexander registered the reaction, acknowledging it with a fleeting smile before he continued. "Mrs. Hitler's little boy hatched a bloody cunning plan to exploit your celebrity status in an attempt to demoralize Britain. That plan has been successfully thwarted and your escape has left lots of egg on his face. You and I can both take enormous satisfaction in that.

"With your permission, a press release will be written to inform the people of Britain that you are safe and returning home. The war is over for you, McClain. You have certainly done your part and I thank you on behalf of His Majesty King George."

Then he turned, straightened the jacket of his tunic and nodded to Brigadier Zumwalt who, in turn, snapped to attention as he announced.

"Flying Officer Malcolm Partridge McClain, I hereby take great pleasure in granting you a field promotion to the rank of flight lieutenant, Royal Air Force and awarding you the Distinguished Flying Cross for saving the lives of your crewmen during the crash." Dropping the formalities, he confided in a lower voice, "In case you are wondering, both Stewart and Dunlop filed unsolicited accounts of your bravery with HQ as soon as they escaped."

"Thank you, sir," Malcolm braced to a smart salute. After a hesitation, he added, "Permission to speak, sir?"

"Of course, Flight Lieutenant."

"I must stress that none of the subsequent adventures would have been remotely possible without the assistance of a quite remarkable Polish Freedom Fighter named Chez Orlowski. He's one of the bravest men I've ever met and has since returned to Poland to continue the fight for his homeland. If he is still alive at the end of the war, can strings be pulled to get him safely to Britain?"

"Ah-ha, you are referring to the legendary Spider, are you not?" smiled Sir Harold, as he shared a knowing glance with Bryan Zumwalt. "Well, you will be relieved to learn that he has in fact survived so far, McClain. He continues to contribute to the war effort in ways that are totally classified and beyond the scope of this discussion. Believe it or not, the Spider might be just as famous amongst the youth of Europe as you are and he is most definitely not finished with his exploits! I will open discussion with Mr. Churchill and you will be kept informed. Good afternoon and thank you again for your service."

With that, Brigadier Zumwalt and Flight Lieutenant McClain stood to attention, saluted smartly and withdrew to the Brigadier's offices. As they walked the long corridors of HQ, Zumwalt confided to Malcolm in a low voice, "Malcolm, I am not in a position to amplify but, as Field Marshall Alexander implied, Great Britain is acutely aware of the special talents Mr. Orlowski has contributed to the war effort. Hopefully, what I am referring to can be revealed to the world someday."

An adjutant then handed Brigadier Zumwalt a sheet of paper, which he scanned quickly before handing to Malcolm:

Noted International Footballer
Flight Lieutenant Malcolm Partridge McClain, DFC;
Shot down over Yugoslavia
and previously reported Missing in Action;
has made his way
to the safety of Allied Lines in Italy

This announcement was time-released to all the major European newspapers. However, Margery Singleton, back living with her parents in the Fleece Hotel, Blackpool, had received her version by telegram the day before.

CHAPTER TWENTY-EIGHT

1944 – Mission Accomplished

" V *eliko sreče; Varno potovanje!"*

Chez leapt to the ground and the loadmaster hauled the cargo door shut behind him. Captain James Kuhlmann pushed forward on his throttles without realizing the increased payload was causing the plane's wheels to dig deep into the soft loam prevalent between the two rivers. The soil quickly whisked into mud, burying the wheels up to their hubs. From his vantage point on the ground, Chez witnessed the unfurling disaster and sprinted to the front of the plane, waving his arms frantically to warn Kuhlmann who responded immediately by easing back on the power. He left the props idling under the control of Mikolaj Duda and joined Chez on the ground to assess their options. The whole mission had suddenly been catapulted into unexpected jeopardy; the Germans could arrive at any minute.

After tense discussion, a daring and desperate plan was hatched in lieu of any other real alternatives. Using 15 meters of the strongest rope they could find, a powerful truck was hastily hitched to the top strut of the Dakota's port wheel mechanism with both ends secured, at least in theory, by slipknots. The truck eased forward to take up the slack after Kuhlmann returned to the cockpit and tentatively re-applied the throttles.

The rope began to thrum and then squeal audibly as its fibers elongated under the strain until, ever so slowly, the big plane moved forward onto sacking that had been placed within hastily dug trenches in front of both wheels.

Chez positioned himself precariously above the port wheel, ready to release the slipknot in a towrope that was now vibrating violently—ready to part at any moment and cut him to shreds. Finally, the plane shuddered forward, the wheels began slowly rolling and briefly, the situation began to look good—at least for the plane—until Chez pulled, pulled and then tugged frantically to release the rope. However, under an impossible load, the slipknot had morphed into solid block of fiber.

Alfred Wolczac, the AK Freedom Fighter assigned

to the back of the towing truck, took in Chez's fraught situation. Risking immolation under the spinning props accelerating towards him, he delivered two chops with his machete. As he screamed a warning to his driver, the truck, now released from its restraint, hurtled forward and swerved violently to the left. Alfred was thrown out onto the meadow and hugged the grass as the port propeller, followed by the port wheel, missed his prone body by inches.

Jim Kuhlmann, unaware that Chez was still wrestling with the rope on the wheel assembly, continued to apply power in his attempt to rotate the aircraft. Meanwhile, under the plane, Chez was now attacking the concrete ball of twine with his trusted knife, tossing it to the ground as the rope fell free. Then, he squandered an extra couple of precious seconds to make sure that no debris would impede the wheel's retraction mechanism before pushing himself away in an astonishingly graceful forward tuck, hitting the ground at close to 30 kilometers per hour. His body a ball, he rolled several times across the meadow, staying on axis with the Dakota as the plane hurtled past him.

He laughed aloud and continued to lie on his back, as beautiful stars twinkling peacefully against the infinite black of the Universe, replaced the huge dark shape of the aircraft.

"You've done it again Pająk," he thought numbly.

"You've bloody survived again! Your luck has to run out one day."

The diminishing Dakota trundled into the air and headed back over the Tatra Mountains on its three-hour flight back to safety. Frustratingly, Vedran Bozic and the Partizani heroes had to fly over their beloved homeland, eventually landing in Brindisi. They had to stay there for a full week before Brigadier Zumwalt was able to commandeer a Bristol Bombay for their well-deserved and triumphant return to Semic.

Truth be known, this strange flight plan had been pre-designed by the Brigadier. He had to prioritize getting Professor Sawicki and the V-2 rocket to Taranto but he was also cognizant of what the Partizani had been through; he wanted to reward them personally with well-deserved R & R, supplemented liberally with the hospitality and gratitude of His Majesty's Armed Forces.

The Royal Air Force had flown eight of Britain's top rocket scientists to rendezvous with Jerzy Sawicki and the priceless rocket in Brindisi. The rocket parts and scientists left Taranto harbor loaded aboard the carrier HMS Indefatigable, escorted by a full task group of warships. A course was set for Portsmouth.

During the long voyage and under Sawicki's guidance, the scientists worked as a team to rebuild the V-2 rocket in the Indefatigable's hanger. Every evening before dinner, a report of the progress was radioed back to London so by the time she docked in the Naval Yards, Britain's High Command knew almost as much about the previously secret German V-2 rocket as Werner von Braun's boffins in Blizna.

Perhaps even more important to the war effort, was the Spider's unsolicited gift to the Nazis of the mini-magnets. Those he placed behind the gyroscopes were never discovered and caused critical delays to the German rocket program.

When the SS guards found the remains of Haris Pacic, they concluded that the raid on the Heidelager had been nothing more than an act of isolated terrorism by local freedom fighters. They never suspected that the Spider had been roaming freely around their assembly plant on the night prior to the raid.

When the next 20 successive test launches went hopelessly out of control, the cause was never associated with the demolition of the guard towers. Nor was the loss of the top-secret plans stolen by Chez. After several laboratory workers suffered under brutal Gestapo interrogation—courtesy of the paranoia by then rife in the Third Reich—the loss was attributed to fire damage caused by the terrorists' attack.

Von Braun suspected the launch setbacks were due to a weakness in the metal used to fabricate the alcohol tank. To determine the cause, five V-2's were ignited with their engines continuously running, until all of the alcohol was depleted. The tank was then examined microscopically for signs of failure—to no avail.

By complete coincidence and dumb luck, after the entire stock of Spider-sabotaged rockets had been depleted, the next three launched rockets also spiraled out of control, even though Chez had never even touched them. The scientific German minds were baffled but, as coincidence was never considered an option, when they eventually got around to testing the gyroscopes, the guidance systems were found to be working perfectly.

Von Braun's team was completely mystified but the scientists continued to test and re-test, methodically attempting to pin down the cause of the failures. Every change resulting from this research meant that the production line at the underground facility in Mittelwerk was stopped to allow retrofitting on undelivered missiles.

On July 13, 1944, with substantial knowledge about the V-2 rocket program in his possession, British Prime Minister Winston Churchill contacted Joseph Stalin. The Soviet Army was already surrounding Debica, so Stalin redirected them to find the village of Blizna and preserve any hardware found at the site. Churchill also asked Stalin to permit British scientists to visit Blizna after it was captured but Stalin was not exactly a team player in this regard and he declined.

Testing of the V-2 rocket had already been relocated to Mittelwerk and the Waffen Schutzstaffel were attempting to decamp when the Soviet Army arrived at the entrance of the Heidelager facility. The very brief, token resistance by the German soldiers ceased the moment that SS-Hauptsturmführer Bernhard Stitt was shot in the head for a perceived lack of respect to a junior Russian captain.

The Soviets took a fearsome revenge on the German Army as they rolled through Poland, Hungary, Czechoslovakia and Yugoslavia. Hitler had tried to stab them in the back with Operation Barbarossa and the Soviets repaid that betrayal with abject cruelty and no mercy. Their vicious tactics were not limited to uniformed troops; the Russians eliminated anyone they encountered carrying a weapon and this specifically included the Armia Krajowa.

As leader of the Bracia, Chez called an emergency meeting of the Polish residents of Krakow. The Wehrmacht had fled the city the day before and the triumphant gathering was held in the beautiful, thirteenth century Market Square.

Between the magnificent architecture of the Sukiennice and St. Mary's Basilica is a famous statue, erected to honor the beloved Polish poet Adam Mickiewicz. Therefore, to the thousands of Krakow residents who knew today that they had survived the Nazi tyranny, there was an overwhelming symbolism when Pająk climbed onto Mickiewicz's Monument to address the crowd. Front and center were over three hundred current and past members of The Bracia.

"My brothers," Chez announced as he held up both arms to quiet the crowd. "We have been taught since we were children that our beloved poet, Adam Mickiewicz, died in 1855 in Constantinople. His remains travelled across Europe through many cities before he was finally interred here, in Wawal Cathedral, forty-five years *after* his death in 1900. This only goes to illustrate that sometimes it takes a long time for the Polish people to get what we want. But somehow, with patience and national fortitude, we always do."

The crowd thronged eagerly around the monument to catch every word, their pent-up patriotism welling into a tremendous roar that took several minutes to subside before Chez was able to continue.

"Another great Pole, my dear friend Jan Kowalski, died while trying to protect his beloved country." At this remembrance, heavy silence blanketed the crowd. Chez waited a full ten seconds before he continued. "Many citizens of Krakow would not be alive today, while conversely, many Nazis would not be dead today, were it not for Jan's fearless leadership of the Bracia within the Armia Krajowa. Someday, I hope to see him interred in Wawal Cathedral alongside Adam Mickiewicz. Perhaps in time, this Market Square can spare a little room for another monument?"

The happy assemblage reverted to their rousing, patriotic chanting, so Chez smiled and waited again. He was enjoying his control of the crowd and pondered how much he might owe to the Tito brothers for his improved oratory skills.

"We have accomplished our mission for now. The Third Reich is thrashing through its final death throes in Berlin. We have driven the enemy into a full-scale retreat across our borders and I wish I could say that finally, Poland belongs to the Polish people.

"However, you must all be painfully aware of another menace that now threatens our freedom. We can only pray that the Soviet Bear will blow through like a strong wind but, for the next few months, we must all hide our weapons and become ordinary, Polish civilians in order to survive.

"The Armia Krajowa—and myself—must disappear for a while. Poland thanks you all for your fortitude and I thank you personally for the privilege of serving you."

In closing he added, "Tell your children and your grandchildren that Pająk will always be there when they need him—I guarantee it."

With those words, he jumped down from the monument and melted into the crowd as they began chanting, at the top of their lungs,

"POLSKA, POLSKA, POLSKA!"

CHAPTER TWENTY-NINE

1944 – Return to Zagan

F or his journey into anonymity, Czeslaw took great care in selecting clothes that were worn, patched and typical of a Polish farm worker. Brunon and Filip walked around him for several minutes, their critical eyes looking for anything that might trigger suspicion with a Russian patrol. But, once a Pole, always a Pole and the Spider had become invisible yet again.

Later that same afternoon, the two local men took him to a disused warehouse outside Krakow and gave Czeslaw carte blanche in choosing from an amazing collection of vehicles, all commandeered by the Bracia during the war. His eyes were instantly drawn to a 1937 Wul-Gum, a Polish bike made in Poznan from German parts, with a well-earned reputation for reliability. This particular Wul-Gum was far from ostentatious, sporting tired and faded dark green paint but it roared into life with his first kick and was exactly what he wanted.

After fond farewells to his Krakow compatriots, the Spider disappeared on the journey north-west to Zagan, intent on re-emerging as Czeslaw Orlowski, a simple Pole interested only in farming his fields.

Technically, Germany still occupied this western part of Poland but the only evidence he saw of the retreating Wehrmacht Army was the randomly abandoned military vehicles lying at the side of the road, rusting steel carcasses that occasionally provided a useful source of fuel.

The Germans were entrenched in their garrisons, preparing to return to Germany to take part in the defense of their Fatherland or, in the case of the Waffen-SS, to try frantically to eliminate any traces of concentration camps—anything that could be used as evidence against Heinrich Himmler in the increasingly likely event of War Trials being conducted.

So, tempered with caution, Chez travelled openly on the main road from Krakow, passing through the towns of Gliwice, Wroklow and Lubin, before making a familiar turn northwest towards

Zagan. The entire journey covered only 360 kilometers but to avoid suspicion in his new persona as a regular Polish peasant, he took his time, stopping to gather intelligence from locals as he ate his meals along the way.

Forty-eight hours after kick starting the motorcycle in Krakow, Czeslaw prepared to make the final short leg of his journey from Przemcow. Before departing, he struck up a conversation over an early breakfast of coffee, hard rolls and cheese with the aging owner of the small grocery store.

"Mr. Majewski, everything seems remarkably quiet around here since I left to visit my relatives in Rekle?"

"Czeslaw, is it?" the old Majewski reconfirmed. "To be honest, I really can't explain why. For years, we were inundated—Germans coming into my store two or three times a day. Now there are none. Anyway, I'm not complaining—rude bastards, every one of 'em! Mostly guards from a POW camp near here in one of the valleys. Rumors say it used to be a concentration camp in the early days of the war. Anyway, it's been about a month since I've seen any damn Germans: good riddance to the swine!"

"I'm seeing that everywhere," Chez prompted conversationally. "Most of us think they're running away from the advancing Russians. We can only hope they don't decide to stay in Poland once the war is finally over."

"Bigger bastards than the Germans if you ask me," interjected the crusty shopkeeper.

Chez subtly switched the conversation to his prime purpose. "Good sir, I've been sleeping at the side of the road most nights, but plan on seeing my sweetheart as soon as I reach Zagan. Is there a chance I could use your facilities; maybe grab a shower and a shave before I set off? I've a few zlotys left after that delicious breakfast and I can't think of a better investment."

"There'll be no charge, Czeslaw. From what I'm smelling, this is as much to my advantage as yours." Majewski chuckled. "There's a bathroom of sorts in my yard, behind the store. The water will be cold but the towel rags are clean.

"You look to be the same size as my son. He disappeared six months ago and I suspect he is dead. Pick out whatever clothes you want. I don't think Waclaw will mind."

Feeling emotionally and physically refreshed after cleaning up, he shook hands with kindly old Sawicki outside the store in Przemcow, jumped on the Wul-Gum and rode away.

When Chez saw the familiar Zagan railway station appear in front of him, he started to laugh to himself in an uncharacteristic release of nervous energy.

"Wait a minute, am I not Pająk, the legendary Spider; a three-meter tall superman who's killed a thousand Nazis? Why then, is my heart starting to race and my head starting to spin?"

He did not have long to wait before answering his own question. After he'd cruised to a halt, dismounted and lowered the kickstand, he turned around... and there she was—exactly as he remembered! Her lustrous black hair framing a face that glowed with the sheer joy of seeing him.

Jadwiga Brzozowska had been alerted by the sound of his motorcycle and was concerned at first that the Wehrmacht might still be in town but she recognized the unmistakable broad shoulders from one hundred meters away and quickly retreated into the bathroom to freshen up.

That moment, combining ecstasy and disbelief, lasted several seconds before they rushed into each other's arms. Somehow, the two were managing to laugh and cry at the same time. They talked excitedly like teenagers, Jadwiga studying the handsome, strong adult who had been driven to leave her as a youth, Czeslaw mesmerized by her deep, chocolate-brown eyes. After a while, Jadwiga eased from the embrace but her hands remained clasped around his neck.

"Czeslaw, if you would be so kind as to drive me home to the farm, I can promise you the best meal of your life." Then, with an impish giggle that curled

Czeslaw's toes, she added. "I've waited a long, long time for the dessert I'm planning!"

Czeslaw started the Wul-Gum and rolled it off its stand. Swinging his muscular right leg over the saddle, he gestured for Jadwiga to climb onto the back. This particular model had not been designed to accommodate two people but even if it had been, Jadwiga snuggled so close to Czeslaw's back that they rode as one.

They followed the same short route that Bernice and her family had walked on that early morning when they first arrived in Zagan, turning left onto the lane beside the river. When they arrived at the large red barn that signified the Brzozowski farm, Jadwiga led Czeslaw into the kitchen. A middle-aged woman was standing with her back to them as she prepared vegetables in a large ceramic sink. She turned, conscious of a presence in her kitchen and saw the couple, sheepishly holding hands and giggling like children.

Looking at her daughter, she said in a soft voice, "This must be Czeslaw!" Then, wiping her hands on her pinafore, she hugged him as if he was her own.

And within a few months—he was. Czeslaw and Jadwiga got married in March. Zagan's small Catholic Church had seen much heartache but few weddings over the past six years. However, that day brimmed with laughter, Bernice giving away her daughter and the four sisters, Wanda, Helena, Teresa and Zofia, serving as maids of honor.

There was no honeymoon and Czeslaw and Jadwiga moved into the Brzozowski farm to begin their married life as free Poles. It was all they asked for and all they wanted.

As the spoils of war, Joseph Stalin had always planned to occupy Poland along with the rest of Eastern Europe but, even with this looming Soviet threat, many of the Armia Krajowa chose not to take the Spider's advice to disappear into civilian life. With this in mind, the evil genius had halted the Soviet Army short of Warsaw. There, the previous October, they simply sat back and watched the remains of the Armia Krajowa fight the German garrison to the death. Uncle Joe allowed his sworn enemy to kill over 55,000 supposedly Polish allies, annihilating the AK without the Soviets having to fire a single bullet. With this strategy, Stalin, the most calculating of cold-blooded dictators, put Poland into his portfolio with confidence there would be little or no insurrection from the locals.

As the Russians marched through Zagan and the other western towns of Poland on their way to Berlin, their standing orders were to find and arrest any remaining members of the Polish underground and ship them to Siberia.

It was only a few weeks before a routine Soviet patrol arrived at the Brzozowski farm to find a powerfully built young man tending his pigs.

"You there!" a Russian corporal barked in halting Polish on behalf of his sergeant. "Are you the man of the house?"

Grabbing a towel to wipe himself down, Czeslaw smiled broadly and, to the astonishment of the troops, replied in excellent Russian.

"That I am, Corporal. So how can I help you fine soldiers today?"

Disarmed by such evident charm rather than the Polish truculence they had come to expect, the Soviet patrol relaxed visibly while the sergeant took over the conversation.

"We're interested in contacting local members

of the Armia Krajowa. If you know of any—perhaps even yourself—we're authorized to offer a commission in the Soviet Army and an immediate cash payment of 500 zlotys,"

Czeslaw sensed the trap immediately and continued —his charming smile undiminished.

"I do not know, nor do I wish to know, any of those lazy bastards," he lied smoothly. "I've not left this farm since we came here and I work my ass off, eighteen hours a day, to scrape an existence for my mother-in-law and her five daughters in this God-forbidden country. Meanwhile, those AK glamour boys are off playing freedom fighter because they are afraid of hard work, not because they know how to fight.

"Apart from that, I have little contact or loyalty to the local peasantry. Our family came here to Zagan from Molodeczno, near the Russian border a few years ago."

Then noticing Jadwiga standing beside him, he politely introduced her to the Russians.

"And you, young lady," the sergeant asked, somewhat impressed. "Presumably you will vouch for your husband's story? We, of course, consider Molodeczno to be in Russia. That would make you as Russian as I am. Da?"

"Yes, it would, Sergeant," Jadwiga agreed in equally fluent Russian. "Now, if you and your soldiers would like a cup of tea, you will be most welcome. Otherwise, please continue your hunt for Polish conscripts elsewhere."

The sergeant and his patrol touched their caps out of newly acquired respect but then, the sergeant paused and asked, "How about the Polish freedom fighter known as *'The Spider'*? Ever heard of him?"

"Oh, who hasn't heard of the amazing Spider?" Czeslaw dismissed scornfully. "If he does exist, he's supposed to be over three meters tall so he shouldn't be too hard to find. Be careful though, Sergeant, I heard of one story where he juggled five Germans in the air at once!"

The Russian patrol was grinning broadly as they returned to their vehicles, waving to the nice 'Russian' farmers as they started back towards Zagan.

"Jadzie, my love," Czeslaw gently mused, as they watched the Russian vehicles disappear back down the lane towards the river. "Times are not going to get any easier in Poland for quite a while. All it will take is for one of my old comrades to identify me to the Soviets for bounty and we're finished."

"They would never do that, would they?" Jadwiga's brow furrowed with concern.

"I heard of a brave Yugoslav Partizani selling his soul when a Nazi major cut out his daughter's eyes right in front of him. And I know of no man who blamed him for an instant."

Ever so tenderly, Czeslaw put his arm around her shoulder.

"For the safety of our family, Jadzie, I'm going to play my ace card before it is too late."

CHAPTER THIRTY

1944 – Calling a Favor

After the Germans had been pushed back into their Fatherland, the Soviet Union controlled Poland with an iron fist. The People's Commissariat for Internal Affairs—the infamous NKVD—enforced Stalin's authority over the Poles with a cruelty that rivaled the German tyranny of the past six years. Skeletal pockets of resistance, mostly stubborn remnants of the Armia Krajowa, were still attempting to stem the Soviet juggernaut but they were mercilessly hounded down and arrested as traitors. Many of the AK leaders were shipped to Siberian Gulags, never to be seen again.

Czeslaw, Jadwiga and the womenfolk of the Brzozowski family at least had the advantage of being able to speak fluent Russian. They were able to hide under the guise of a Russian family when questioned by the Soviets. However, the recent visit by the Soviet patrol indicated that the writing was already on the wall.

As Czeslaw correctly predicted, the NKVD mission to snuff out the legend of 'The Spider' became synonymous with snuffing out all Polish resistance. The bounty for his capture increased on a weekly basis and the newly wed Orlowskis came to the crushing conclusion that their luck would soon run out.

In desperation, Czeslaw crafted a letter to Malcolm that succinctly stated their plight. His biggest problem was the daunting task of getting his appeal out of Zagan. The Polish mail service had collapsed now that Soviet censorship had become the norm and a barrier of mutual suspicion guarded every European national border.

One evening during a family dinner, an equally worried Bernice suggested a possible solution. "I hear there's an international deputation visiting that old labor camp you escaped from, Czeslaw. Maybe some official in that group can take your letter out of Poland?"

"Ma Brzozowska, you might just have hit upon something," Czeslaw said. "Actually, I escaped from Stalag Luft Three, by then a prisoner of war camp but, you're quite correct in stating that it was previously a hard labor camp of dubious distinction before it was disinfected. If an international deputation is digging for evidence against the Nazis, I might well be the only person left alive who could testify to the death lines and the barbaric ways they exterminated our fellow Poles before they sanitized the place. If I can convince someone that I've got reliable information, perhaps I can barter for the delivery of my letter."

Early the next morning, Czeslaw left the farm on the familiar route back to Stalag Luft Three. Russian guards patrolled the gates and fence line but, from a position concealed by trees, he could make out several buses adorned with large red crosses painted within white circles. For a few bitter moments he found himself reliving his nightmares, as memories of the months he'd spent in that accursed place came flooding back.

"Not in my wildest dreams did I think I'd go back inside *that* frickin' place!"

Then the nightmares gave way to the Spider's

clinical ability to analyze and respond to his immediate mission—that of saving his new family.

In the open compound of the abandoned camp, a Red Cross official, Captain Laura Moore, was in animated conversation with her colleague.

"Total waste of bloody time, Kevin. Rumors about genocide in this camp before it became Stalag Luft Three are impossible to prove. No indication of any mass graves anywhere and the bastards left no witnesses. It's completely futile. I say we wrap up here and take the delegates to the next camp."

A calm voice from behind caused them both to spin around in surprise. The voice spoke fluent English and incongruously came from a smiling young Pole not two meters away.

"If you will please excuse me, Captain, my name is Czeslaw Orlowski. I survived the original hard labor camp and went on to escape from the POW camp several months later."

"How on earth did you get in here—through all the Ruskis?" the stupefied Captain Moore asked the young man. "More important, your claim to have been imprisoned here sounds ridiculous—there are no documented survivors—but, can you prove it?"

The young man shrugged. "I was first brought here at the beginning of the war, when it was full of young Poles rounded up to provide slave labor for the Nazis. Only a couple of dozen of us survived and we were the *'fortunate ones'* who converted the place into a POW camp. Several months later, I escaped with three USAF captains, at least one of whom lives in Eugene, Oregon. You can be certain they will vouch for me. In any event, I can reveal all sorts of things about this camp, all the dirty secrets, backed by solid evidence for your delegation."

His expression then hardened. "Can you both assure me, if I cooperate to your satisfaction, that you will consider returning one small favor to me?"

Czeslaw spent the remainder of that day with the grim-faced Red Cross officials. He related horror stories about the two daily lines of life and death and then took them to a grove of young saplings where he was certain the mass graves had been dug. As they waited for an excavation team to prove out his claims, Czeslaw sat down with Captain Moore and named several in the German hierarchy who had administered the camps, names quickly confirmed as authentic by the Red Cross from their own existing documentation.

After only a few hours, the excavation team returned to the camp with undisputable, horrific proof of the legitimacy of Czeslaw's information.

Captain Moore was good to her word and accepted Czeslaw's precious letter in return for a promise to get it out of Poland. The brown manila envelope was simply addressed:

Mr. Malcolm McClain
Blackpool Football Club
England

Though they never admitted it to each other, Czeslaw and Jadwiga refused to cherish any hope that the letter would ever be delivered, let alone achieve its purpose.

As the following days turned into weeks, they and the rest of the Brzozowski family resigned themselves to fate, all the while living in terror that a thunderous knock on their door would signal the last moments before Czeslaw disappeared forever.

Hope slowly drained from their lives and was replaced by despair.

However, His Majesty's Royal Mail eventually took over the baton for the last leg of the letter's journey and the travel-worn missive arrived at Bloomfield Road three months after Czeslaw penned it. Malcolm had never seen Czeslaw's handwriting which was why, when the Club Secretary passed it to him, he opened it in the assumption it was yet another appeal from a young fan eager to get his autograph.

His expression immediately changed to shock when he saw the signature. The letter itself was devastating in its impact, causing Malcolm to fear desperately for the life of his friend. With letter in hand, he knocked on the door of Joe Smith's office. The two old friends caucused in private and quickly came up with a plan of action.

With generous assistance from the Board of Directors at Blackpool FC, by the end of the day the wheels were in motion. Contact had been established with Sir Barrie Todd, president of the Football Association—the sport's ruling body in London. Todd, in turn, arranged for a high-level meeting between McClain and Lord Acheson at the War Office—scheduled for the next mutually convenient occasion. When word filters from the top down, bureaucrats can move with uncharacteristic speed and by the following weekend, after Blackpool played away to Chelsea, McClain was granted permission to remain in London, the Club granting him a week's leave to attend the special meeting at Whitehall.

The British armed forces have many quirks, one of which is to recognize those select few who had their lives saved by parachute in combat. These extremely fortunate individuals are granted membership in the Caterpillar Club, its motto being *'Life depends on a silken thread.'* The Irvin Airchute Company sponsors this club and presents every member with a small gold pin depicting a caterpillar with ruby eyes.

On the Monday morning following the Chelsea game, Malcolm pinned his golden caterpillar onto the left lapel of his new dapper suit. It was a pleasant day in the nation's capital so he walked from his hotel in Knightsbridge down Whitehall, where it was not hard to locate the massive War Office building.

At the ornate entrance, two Military Policemen snapped to attention as he mounted the steps.

"Good morning. I'm former Flight Lieutenant Malcolm McClain, with at 10 o'clock appointment to see Lord Acheson." Malcolm announced as he reached inside his jacket for identification.

"You are expected, sir. Once inside the foyer, you will be accompanied to his Lordship's reception area on the sixth floor."

The MP then winked at his companion and, as McClain passed between them to enter the building, both guards looked straight ahead, saluted again and barked in unison, "Nice goal against Chelsea—SIR!"

Malcolm just shook his head and laughed as he entered the foyer. Once inside, a kilted Black Watch corporal approached him and requested the identification. The Scot escorted McClain to the lift and, after the slow mechanical ascent, smartly announced his arrival to the attractive female sergeant who oversaw the sixth floor reception. When she spoke, Malcolm noted with surprised approval that she still accorded him his courtesy military title.

"Flight Lieutenant McClain, Lord Acheson is waiting to see you, sir."

Behind her desk loomed a pair of massive, mahogany-paneled doors, embellished with gleaming brass hardware. She knocked on the door and a voice from within bade them enter. Malcolm followed her into a very elegantly appointed office with windows overlooking the famous Horse Guards Parade and St. James' Park.

Seated in rich, maroon-leather armchairs, separated from a roaring fireplace by a low Georgian table, two men huddled deep in conversation. Both heads turned as they arose to the knock and the shorter of the two stepped around the low table.

"Thank you, Sergeant Staples. Please have an orderly bring in tea." Then, extending his hand, he smiled, "I am Acheson. Sir Barrie relayed your message."

He indicated to the other, taller gentleman who gave Malcolm a fleeting nod of recognition. "I believe you have already met Earl Alexander? We are privileged; he has made a special point of popping into see you… Busy chap, y'know? About to be appointed

Governor General of Canada and all that. … Well, take a seat, dear boy, take a seat."

"Malcolm," Lord Alexander began. "It is wonderful to see you here in London. I can only re-iterate what I said when we last met in Italy. The boost to this nation's morale, once our people realized you were safe, cannot be overstated. His Majesty's government is acutely aware that your deliverance could not have occurred without the considerable assistance of your Polish colleague, Chez Orlowski, perhaps better known as the famous Spider." The field marshall allowed a bleak smile as he deliberated, "…more likely the *Infamous Spider*' should you happen to be a Nazi."

"As if this alone were not enough," Acheson interjected neatly, "Mr. Orlowski went on to successfully complete a classified covert mission behind enemy lines which, were I able to make you privy, you might consider as I do, to have been one of the pivotal operations of the entire war."

"Indeed, the United Kingdom does not hesitate to recognize an enormous debt of gratitude to you both," Alexander added. "Furthermore, I have not forgotten the promise I made to you in Taranto. Accordingly, having been apprised of Mr. Orlowski's current situation, I spoke to the Prime Minister yesterday, and Winnie pulled a few strings—with remarkable speed I might add, even by WSC standards.

"Consequently, McClain, I am pleased to inform you that Chez Orlowski, his wife Jadwiga and their immediate Brzozowski family have forthwith been granted citizenship of the United Kingdom of Great Britain and Northern Ireland, by order of His Majesty, King George VI."

"Wow! Thank you, sir," Malcolm mumbled softly in amazement. His voice was cracking and there were tears of emotion rolling down his cheeks. "I'm most grateful to you both for what you've done."

"Don't be too hasty with the congrats, dear chap. That was the easy part," Lord Acheson cautioned. "We have yet to devise a way to extricate our new British citizens out of Poland without rocking Uncle Joe's boat too much!"

"As you are aware from his letter, a full-scale manhunt has been launched throughout Poland, aimed at capturing the Spider. He is being hunted down by the Soviets as a major propaganda target." Earl Alexander smoothly relayed his assessment of the tactical considerations. "Fortunately, the Ruskis don't have a clue what he looks like, so we still have a chance but, tempus fugit.

"We'll handle the details from here but you might be interested to know, your friend, Major Paddy Blair and the SAS are taking this extraction very personally. In fact, I suspect the cheeky buggers would have gone in to get him whether I authorized it or not. Needless to say, Major Blair has been given full authority to do what he does best."

"From what I've heard of the SAS, I would be willing to wager my money on the Spider and Paddy Blair," Acheson laughed.

Malcolm McClain nodded to both men as he prepared to leave, and then turned back with a broad grin. "Gentlemen, knowing both characters as well as I do, there is absolutely no way I would wager against that bet!"

As he passed the sergeant's desk, he was walking on a cloud. She noticed, smiled and called after his retreating back, "Great goal last Saturday, Malcolm… Oh, please don't forget to take Corporal Kersey with you."

The disgruntled Black Watch corporal would have readily stayed on the sixth floor and admitted to Malcolm on the way down to reception, "Ah laddie, I could look a' her al' dey an' ne'er git teer'd!"

Malcolm caught the train back to Blackpool, where an excited Margery flung her arms around him at the station. After over three years of separation, they were more in love than ever and planning their wedding for the following June. As they walked back to the Fleece Hotel in Market Street, Malcolm recounted his remarkable meeting with the *'Lords of London'*.

Although McClain tried to focus on his return to football and the upcoming nuptials, his concern about Czeslaw's welfare and whereabouts increased by the day. Despite his bravado regarding Lord Acheson's wager, he couldn't help but fear the worst.

'Was no news supposed to be good news...or bad news?'

CHAPTER THIRTY-ONE

1945 – After the War

The McClain wedding was a high society affair; St. John's Church filled to capacity with celebrities. Twelve months earlier, Margery's sister-in-law, Peggy, had tailored her own beautiful lace dress; today, with a few minor alterations, it transformed Margery into the most stunning woman in the church.

The groom's friends were a veritable *'Who's Who'* of international football stars and other national sporting personalities, many wearing military uniforms festooned with medals and ribbons that told of incredible acts of courage. Like McClain, they too had risen to the occasion, unselfishly protecting their countries when called upon.

After the ceremony, Arthur Singleton, the father of the bride, hosted a lavish reception at *The Savoy*

Hotel. Throughout the rehearsals, his only daughter suspected that he was hiding a secret but she could not get it out of him, no matter how hard she tried.

The newlyweds were greeting their guests in a traditional reception line when, just as Malcolm was enjoying a little champagne with Stanley and Betty Matthews, he did a double take, as he caught sight of a tall, elegant brunette standing near the bar. His bride elbowed him playfully in the ribs and giggled.

"Malcolm, don't tell me your eyes are roving already! We have only been married for one hour and I catch you staring at that attractive young lady over there."

"Sorry, Luv, but I am certain I've seen that girl somewhere before and I cannot for the life of me, think where. Is she from your side of the family?"

"No, I don't think so. But, she and her boyfriend seem to be having a joke with Daddy, so he can probably explain who she is."

"I've got it!" Malcolm realized with a start. "The hair is different but now that I see her boyfriend wearing the Black Watch tartan, I'm pretty sure I bumped into both of them when I visited the War Office in London. Last time I saw those two, they were both in uniform. I never expected to see them at our wedding!"

Arthur Singleton had been sharing a joke with Billy and Annie McClain before he made his way over to give his daughter a peck on the cheek. Malcolm was just about to ask his father-in-law about the couple from Whitehall when he stopped dead in his tracks, as the next couple in their reception line confronted him. This man, elegantly resplendent in the uniform of a general in the Royal Horse Guards, stepped forward with a broad smile. Malcolm was stunned, not really believing who was now standing in front of him.

He struggled to hide his surprise. "Margery, it gives me enormous pleasure to present Lord Acheson. If you recall, he and Earl Alexander were kind enough to meet with me in Whitehall."

"Mr. and Mrs. McClain, it is a delight for me to be invited to this wonderful, if long-postponed occasion. Permit me to introduce my wife, Lady Elizabeth. Arthur and I go back a very long way and he granted me the privilege of bringing an additional couple of special guests with me on this doubly joyous day."

"Doubly, sir?" Malcolm asked uncertainly.

While Arthur Singleton hovered in the background, wearing a smile that would have done credit to a Cheshire cat, Lord Acheson stepped to the side in an unashamedly theatrical manner as he announced, "Flight Lieutenant and Mrs. McClain. Please allow me to introduce you to our newest British citizens......Mr. and Mrs. Chez Orlowski!"

Simultaneously, both old friends shouted, causing the rest of the guests to wonder what was going on. Then the two held each other in a long bear hug. Margery and Jadwiga looked at their men, looked at each other, shrugged—then hugged each other too.

Finally, Chez broke away and grinned broadly. "Enough of us, my friend. This is your special day. We have some great tales to tell, but they must wait until after your honeymoon. To your health! *Na zdrowie,* to you both!"

Chez and Jadwiga enjoyed two weeks in Blackpool as honored guests of the War Department, then extended their stay by a further week to meet up with Malcolm and Margery McClain after the happy couple returned from their honeymoon.

The four piled into Malcolm's brand new, 1946 Armstrong Siddley Lancaster to tour Poulton-Le-Fylde, a picturesque region of England just north of Blackpool, where narrow country roads meander through the beautiful Wyre Valley. It was a blustery day, so they decided to sacrifice views across the

Wyre, in favor of warmth and a Lancashire pub lunch. The Black Bull, a popular three-story country pub in Preesall, fitted the bill perfectly.

Margery opened the conversation, as the four sat down around the fireplace.

"Chez, while we've been away in Scotland, Malcolm has told me so much about your adventures, I feel I've known you and Jadwiga forever."

Jadwiga was still not comfortable with her English but her beautiful smile and Chez's quick translations melted any awkwardness. As the food and drinks arrived, she held up her glass of sherry and everyone in the bar hushed as she sang 'Sto Lat,' the traditional Polish toast that wished everyone present good health for one hundred years. Her voice was so pure and soulful, spontaneous applause broke out among the other patrons. She blushed in embarrassment and quickly sat down.

Margery held Jadwiga's hands in hers and whispered softly, "That was so beautiful, Jadwiga. Malcolm has told me the story of how Chez fell in love when he heard your voice for the first time. Now I can understand why."

Malcolm clinked glasses with everyone. "Don't worry, I'm not going to sing but I wanted to remind my friend that the last thing we said to each other as we parted company in Semic was..."

Chez continued the thought. "...Go find your

girl–and both of them are even more beautiful than we remembered!"

"Okay Chez, give us the real inside story. How in God's name did you get yourself and Jadwiga's entire family out of Poland to show up with Lord Acheson at our wedding?"

"To tell the whole story will take many hours and several pints of this wonderful Guinness but, as I don't want our first British fish and chips to get cold, I will tease you with this nugget. Quite a few Russians in Zagan wish they had never met our mutual friend Major Paddy McBride!"

CHAPTER THIRTY-TWO

1955 – The Next Generations

B y the late 1950s, Chez's Spider Gymnastic Academy had earned recognition as the leading fitness training establishment, not only in Belfast, but most of Europe. Over the years, a disproportionate number of Northern Irish youngsters made their mark on the Olympic stage, with Chez, shamelessly exploiting his heavy Polish accent to great effect, becoming a legend, not as a freedom fighter, but as the National Olympic coach.

Meanwhile, Spider Academy co-founder, Malcolm McClain, was appointed Special Consultant to the Northern Ireland International Football Association. His keen eye for talent allowed the cream of Belfast's sixteen year-old soccer players to have the same opportunities he had been given. A few even crossed the pond to make their mark in the First Division. However, it was through his soccer camps that he enhanced his already solid reputation.

By the 1970s, the two friends established themselves as pillars of Belfast society; philanthropic to a fault, both men embraced the community with love and gratitude. As a natural consequence, the families settled down in adjoining houses, sharing an enormous backyard. The location they chose was in Jordanstown, a small village between Belfast and the old Norman town of Carrickfergus.

Their families grew up as one but the astute eyes of both men came to accept that no Olympic gold medals were going to materialize from either brood.

Those halcyon days of inseparability were not to last. During the 1980s, the Orlowskis decided to cross the Atlantic to visit Jadwiga's sisters, by then living in Chicago. A trip scheduled to last ten days became twenty years when Chez was offered—and simply had to accept—the lucrative appointment as coach of the United States Olympic Gymnastics team.

However, it was not until the occasion of the eldest Orlowski son, Jan's wedding that the opportunity arose for the McClains to make the trip to Chicago for the celebrations and a fabulous reunion.

What a reunion it turned out to be. It was almost as if they had never been apart. Of course, the young children, close friends of yesterday, had all matured into adulthood and now hardly recognized each other.

On the first evening, as Chez, Jadwiga, Malcolm and Margery went downtown to explore Michigan Avenue, the offspring decided to go out as a group to Salerno's in Berwyn.

Salerno's baked the best pizza on the planet and served it with frosty pitchers of Pilsner Urquell. That night the laughter and genuine love flowing from the young people at the large center table allowed the strong childhood friendships to skip fluidly over the years as if they had not been apart for more than a month.

To the Salerno management's relief, their other patrons appeared to enjoy the impromptu entertainment, even joining in some of the bawdy Polish and Irish songs. This could have been because Jan and his brother Bogdan had donated several extra pitchers of Pilsner to the surrounding tables but, equally likely, the other patrons were Chicagoans, a people who love a good time like no other.

Uncharacteristically, Guy McClain was the quiet one that evening, finding himself mesmerized by the eldest Orlowski daughter, Tereska. Apparently oblivious of the effect she had on him, she was laughing with abandon on the opposite side of the table. Seven years younger than Guy, he vaguely remembered her as a skinny five year old in Jordanstown but now she had morphed into the most beautiful woman he had ever seen. Occasionally, their eyes would meet during the meal but most likely that was a reflex due to Guy unabashedly staring at her. Tereska was certainly used to the attention her extraordinary beauty caused and was most gracious in not embarrassing the Irishman, even though the rest of the group, Jan being the ringleader, made increasingly ribald comments and observations as the celebration progressed. Guy's younger sister, Janna, just shook her head at all the nonsense.

The evening had been fabulous, full of happiness and reminiscences of their youthful adventures in Belfast. Well after midnight, the friends headed for their cars to go home, each passing out concerned warnings for everyone to drive home very carefully.

The four McClains were staying as guests of Chez and Jadwiga in their massive, eight-bedroom house on Euclid Avenue in Berwyn. It was on their way home that Fate decided to intervene in Guy's favor. Tereska, an undergraduate at Northern Illinois University, had been first to leave Salerno's parking lot, driving alone in her dark blue VW Beetle, with

Guy and Janna following her in a rental Buick. After less than a mile, one of Chicago's finest slipped in behind Tereska's Bug and began following her. It was the end of the month and police officers were eager to fill their quota of traffic tickets. So, when the Beetle did not signal a lane change, the flashing lights and siren snapped on immediately. Guy, following behind, accelerated spontaneously to overtake the cop car and the Beetle at speed.

"Are you bloody crazy? What the hell are you trying to do?" Janna yelled at her brother.

"You'll see."

The police car immediately lost interest in Tereska's Beetle and sped after the Buick. Guy stopped within a block and got a stern warning but no ticket. It could have been much worse but both Guy and Janna had Northern Irish drivers' licenses supplemented by thick Belfast brogues, so the police just shook their heads in weary acceptance.

"Damn stupid foreigners need to be more careful!"

Tereska watched the whole incident from down the street and could not help thinking to herself, *"That lunatic is really different from what I usually get stuck with. This one might be a keeper!"*

They were inseparable from that moment until the McClains had to return home to Belfast.

It was inevitable that Tereska would invite Guy to visit Chicago again, ostensibly to attend the occasion of her graduation. He waited patiently for just the right moment and when the McClain family all gathered around the family dinner table, he broached the subject of what in effect had become a courtship-at-distance relationship.

"So how long are you planning to stay in Chicago, Guy?" Margery asked innocently, at the same time struggling to mask the amusement she was sharing with Malcolm.

"Oh for God's sake, why don't you just marry her?" Janna, a forceful, willowy blonde interjected pragmatically. And, giving Guy no opportunity to answer. "Even if we all go, the wedding will be a damn site cheaper than all the money you've been spending on long-distance bloody phone calls!"

So it came as no surprise to anyone when, following Graduation Day, Guy McClain decided to stay on in Chicago. He and Tereska married six months later, providing yet another excuse for a massive family get-together.

Subsequently, the couple moved to Florida where

within four years, they bore a daughter, Margery Jadwiga—beautiful and academically gifted. A decade later—as a complete surprise—Remington Malcolm Chez McClain was born.

Malcolm McClain and Chez Orlowski had shared many adventures together, oftentimes staring death in the face and always knowing that each would sacrifice himself for the other. Neither man believed that anything could supersede that bond...until they were blessed with the opportunity to pass all their knowledge through to this child.

EPILOGUE

Return to Belfast

A breezy Thursday morning in April found Remy McClain practicing one-touch passing with his teammates at Carrington United. As one of the most lucrative sports franchises on the planet, CUFC protects its super stars to an extreme; one aspiring journalist recording that he'd felt he was trying to break into some top secret nuclear plant once he had found the entrance to the training grounds. Security guards denied him further access.

Young McClain had had a brilliant first season with the Club but the older players in the drill were still quick to banter him if he missed a touch.

A fledgling apprentice in a gray and red tracksuit emblazoned with the large white letters, 'CUFC', ran over.

"Remy, the boss needs to talk to you. Immediately."

"Shit, what've I done wrong?" was McClain's first reaction as he ducked out of the circle.

"I heard the Old Man sold you to a team in the Mongolian second division," a Welsh voice lilted above the good-natured laughter following him as he hurried off to find the legendary manager.

He had left Orlando at the tender age of 15 to complete his schooling at the Carrington Academy, four hours a day of academics, six of intense football training. Sunday was listed as a day of rest and the young class of apprentices needed it; the rest of the week's schedule was brutal.

His parents had been determined to ensure that, should he not make it in the sport, he would not lose ground academically. Their decision was made easy when backed by the reputation of one of the greatest managers the sport had ever seen and, since the day Remy arrived. Sir Mark Dillon proved as good as his word, treating the American boy like his own son.

"Mr. and Mrs. McClain," he'd concluded at the end of his third scouting trip to Florida. "From what I've seen of your lad—and I've been following young Remy since he was twelve—the boy has the temperament and skills to carve out a very successful career as part of the Carrington family."

Sir Mark then laughed. "Apart from all that, if he's inherited only ten percent of the athletic blue blood that runs in his family's veins, I'm certainly getting the better part of this deal!"

Then he became serious again. "You're both aware that I owe a considerable amount of my professional and personal success to your two fathers but, in all honesty, I have seldom seen a prospect more attractive to us than your son. Can I ask why you chose Carrington United in preference to my good friends at Barcelona, Ajax or Arsenal?"

"There are two reasons, actually," smiled Tereska McClain, "…and the two of them jointly made the decision for us—about five years ago!"

Remy was puzzled by this urgent interruption to his training but eventually he caught sight of a famous profile headed into the management complex, so he followed. Thirty seconds later, he was knocking on the Boss's door.

"Come," a soft voice with a Glaswegian accent called from within.

"You wanted to see me, Boss?" Remy then smiled with relief, as he noticed his mentor's wide grin.

"Close the door, son, and take a seat. What I'm about to tell you must remain confidential for a wee while but I just received a call from the Northern Ireland Football Association. They're callin' you up as reserve to the squad for next month's home game against Wales. Now, I know you're torn between playin' for the United States and your grand-da's country—and it says a lot that you want tay' honour both o' them for all they've done for you. But quite frankly, and to bring you back tay' earth, this is the first and only offer you're likely to get at this stage of your career, so I strongly recommend ya' take it."

He walked around the table and laid a reassuring hand on his protégé's shoulder before leaning back against his desk.

"Ciaran McArdle of Carlisle United is still recovering from a back injury but they're going to keep him listed as first choice for the right wing. If he is noo declared fully fit by match day, there's a real chance you'll get your first cap next month."

"Sir, I don't know what to say!" The youngster choked and the manager grinned at his delightful innocence.

"Congratulations, son. After last season, it's well deserved.

"The other news is that Northern Ireland is planning tay' honour yer two famous grandfathers in a ceremony before the game. Knowing how Belfast feels about their two heroes, it's recognition long overdue and I'm noo surprised. Make whatever arrangements you need to; CUFC fully supports this and releases you for the game.

"Whether you actually play or noo, it's going to be a very special and well deserved occasion for your family."

"Thanks, Boss." Remy said when he found his voice. "Can I phone my parents and my sister?"

"Be my guest, son. Give Guy and Tereska my regards."

With that, the great man gestured towards his phone before leaving Remy alone in his office.

His heart pounding, Remy picked up the receiver and punched in 001 followed by the Washington area code and his sister's seven-digit, private number.

M-J McClain was only 10 years older than Remy but already a partner in one of the most powerful law firms in the world and heading a special division of their Washington office. She did not recognize the incoming number from the United Kingdom but guessed it had to be her brother; hardly a routine call as Remy had never been much of a communicator.

She picked up immediately with concern in her voice.

"Rem, is everything okay? Mum and Dad all right?"

Remy and his sister were close. She had graduated

from Vanderbilt University and Georgetown Law School, therefore quite vociferous in her objections to their parents' decision to let her brother leave private school in Florida to play professional soccer half way across the world but, deep down, there was nobody more proud of his special talents.

Remy explained what he had just learned from Sir Mark and M-J squealed with delight. Her secretary, Catherine Reeves, stuck her head through the door, just in time to hear, "Let me handle this end, Rem. It will be my treat. Love ya!"

She turned to a puzzled Catherine. "Cancel everything on my calendar for the weeks either side of May 13. I'm going to need your help in making some arrangements."

M-J McClain requisitioned the firm's Gulfstream G650 for a flight that originated from Reagan National Airport and flew south to Orlando Executive. Guy and Tereska McClain were waiting in the lounge of Showalter Flying Services when M-J breezed through the airside door in her typically confident show-stopping manner. Beautiful like her mother and with the same blonde hair that she and Remy could both trace back to Albrecht Wah, M-J was used to men spilling coffee, dropping their newspapers, even walking into columns when she floated through their space.

"Mom, Dad, this is so exciting. Let's go; I have

lunch for us on the plane." As the McClain parents picked up their bags and followed M-J out to the Gulfstream, one of the pilots in the lounge was heard to remark,

"Who the hell was that? And, why am *I* not flying *her* plane?" causing the whole lounge to erupt in laughter.

The plane returned north, this time landing at Chicago's Midway. The same rapid transit was repeated, only this time, the two additional passengers joining the plane were Chez and Jadwiga Orlowski.

The G650 was cleared again to take-off and rapidly climbed to a cruising altitude of 48,000 feet before accelerating to its 0.85 Mach cruising speed on the polar route to Belfast.

"M-J, this is a helluva way to travel." Chez sighed with contentment. "We were just about to book our tickets on United when you called. I can't wait to see your Nana and Poppa again even though I just talked to him last night. Will they be at George Best Airport to meet us?"

"Are you kiddin' me?" M-J responded. "I couldn't keep them away."

Relative to most countries in the world, Northern Ireland is very small. The National Stadium, Windsor

Park, was built before the Second World War and can only jam 20,000 fans in if they all hold their breath but those fans always turn out in force when called upon to support 'The Lads.' They generate an enthusiasm so Stentorian that any team opposing Northern Ireland might think they were deep in the cauldron of Maracana Stadium; playing against Brazil with 200,000 fanatics cheering against them.

Although the game would be between Northern Ireland and Wales, an always eagerly anticipated adversarial clash, the special event that preceded it caused the 20,000 faithful to get there early.

Under a typical grey Belfast sky, deafening applause too loud for thunder engulfed Windsor Park as soon as two men entered the field from the center line. Not one fan remained seated, out of respect for the two much-admired heroes, Malcolm McClain and Chez Orlowski, both now well into their twilight years.

Nevertheless, every person in the stadium listened in respect, as the announcer recounted their legendary exploits as athletes, war veterans, educators and philanthropists. True, many of the stories had been embellished over the years—as legends tend to be—but the cacophony rising from Windsor Park today clearly proved they had cemented a place in every Belfast heart.

The brave announcer risked telling the crowd what they already knew; that many years before, Malcolm McClain, synonymous with the number three on the back of his green jersey, had played an epic game in this very stadium against that day's opponent, Wales.

Most of those present had been touched personally or knew someone, who through exposure to Chez Orlowski and the Spider's Gymnastic Academy, had avoided the perils of adolescence to become stronger parents for their own children.

At least two individuals who could claim an even closer relationship, stood at the very back of the stands in almost complete anonymity. Coach Gary Russell paid for his own trip from Orlando, proud as punch that the confidence the grandfathers imbued in him by allowing him to coach their twelve-year-old grandson, would now be rewarded with a green jersey. The second man, quite elderly but still carrying majestic size and bearing—was retired Special Air Service Colonel, Paddy McBride, MC and Bar.

So, when Malcolm and Chez turned and saluted the fans by grasping each other's upraised hands, the crowd erupted to completely drown out the commentary from the speakers. As one side of Windsor Park began to chant 'Malcolm, Malcolm, Malcolm,' the other side gave it back with 'Spider, Spider, Spider.'

The announcer had to wait a full minute before he was able to regain control and, as he nervously flicked the microphone with his finger, he boomed back over the speakers with his best, albeit pathetic attempt at emulating a cool BBC voice, "Is this mike even workin' fer Chrissakes?…" Click, click, click. "…Ah well, there y'are now! Ahem: Here's today's startin' line-up for the Nor'n Irelan' team."

This of course, brought an eager hush to the stadium, punctuated only by the occasional murmur of approval and polite applause that rumbled around the stands when the name of each regular international player announced over the Tannoy. Then, as if scripted, an electrically charged stillness blanketed the crowd. Over the past few days, there had been hopeful rumors all over Northern Ireland. Could they be true?

"…and at right wing—recently voted Premiership Rookie of the Year—an' makin' his International debut for Nor'n Irelan' at age seventeen…REMY McCLAIN.

"McClain'll not be wearin' the traditional winger's number seven. Both teams voted that today, he should wear the number three."

AND THE CROWD WENT ABSOLUTELY WILD!

The End

ABOUT THE AUTHOR

G uy Butler grew up in Belfast, Northern Ireland, where he spent his youth playing soccer all day and bass guitar in 'Johnny and the Teenbeats' all night.

Despite the resultant horrific grades, he managed to get accepted into Queens University's College of Architecture, where he played soccer for the Northern Ireland national colleges team against Wales, Scotland and England.

Guy currently owns a boutique architectural firm that specializes in golf resort design all over the world. This novel was mainly written at 35,000 feet en route to China, Nigeria and the Far East.

The Butler family lives in Orlando, Florida.

Made in the USA
Lexington, KY
20 May 2012